Praise for

"Price creates a brilliant and unique world that you won't want to leave, filled with achingly real characters and heart-wrenching decisions. An unforgettable and adrenaline-filled ride from start to finish."　　　　　　　　—Alexandra Overy, author of
These Feathered Flames

"In this standout fantasy, Price has created an enthralling world that keeps readers engaged from the first page. . . . A wonderful read recommended for all fantasy fans, especially those who enjoy the works of Julie Kagawa, Leigh Bardugo, and Cassandra Clare."　　　　　　　　—*School Library Journal*

"Full of thrilling action, adventure, secrets, and a few surprising twists . . . The writing evokes a constant feeling of desperate last hope, which adds to the suspense. . . . A thrilling and fast-paced adventure."　　　　　　　　—*Kirkus Reviews*

"A gripping adventure filled with surprising twists and heart, *The Endless Skies* captivated from beginning to end."
—KayLynn Flanders, author of *Shielded*

"*The Endless Skies* deftly combines all the hallmarks of classic YA with the best of epic fantasy. The result is a perfect blend of sweetly tangled romance and realistic friendship dynamics in an action-packed story, with a magical world rich in myth and legend. Fans of fantastical creatures and fast-paced adventures will fly though this."　　　—Nicki Pau Preto, author of
the Crown of Feathers trilogy

"With themes of friendship, family, and loyalty at its core, *The Endless Skies* is a heartfelt adventure story that looks at the way learned hatred can fester in people, and the strength to be found in community, all against the backdrop of a harrowing race against time. This soaring fantasy is perfect for fans of *Sky in the Deep* and *Wonder Woman*."

—Kalyn Josephson, author of *The Storm Crow*

"Unique world-building, a fast-paced plot, and lionhearted warrior characters combine to make *The Endless Skies* a fresh twist in the classic epic fantasy genre. You'll fly right through it."

—Sarah Henning, author of
The Princess Will Save You and *Sea Witch*

ALSO BY SHANNON PRICE

A Thousand Fires

THE
ENDLESS
SKIES

SHANNON PRICE

TOR
TEEN

A TOM DOHERTY ASSOCIATES BOOK
NEW YORK

THE ENDLESS SKIES

Copyright © 2021 by Shannon Price

Map by Jennifer Hanover

A Tor Teen Book
Published by Tom Doherty Associates
120 Broadway
New York, NY 10271

www.tor-forge.com

Tor® is a registered trademark of Macmillan Publishing Group, LLC.

The Library of Congress has cataloged the hardcover edition as follows:

Names: Price, Shannon, author.
Title: The endless skies / Shannon Price.
Description: First edition. | New York : Tor Teen, 2021. | "A Tom Doherty Associates book"
Identifiers: LCCN 2021009114 (print) | LCCN 2021009115 (ebook) | ISBN 9781250302014 (hardcover) | ISBN 9781250302007 (ebook)
Subjects: CYAC: Fantasy. | Soldiers—Fiction. | Shapeshifting—Fiction.
Classification: LCC PZ7.1.P7529 En 2021 (print) | LCC PZ7.1.P7529 (ebook) | DDC [Fic]—dc23
LC record available at https://lccn.loc.gov/2021009114
LC ebook record available at https://lccn.loc.gov/2021009115

ISBN 978-1-250-21943-5 (trade paperback)

Our books may be purchased in bulk for promotional, educational, or business use. Please contact your local bookseller or the Macmillan Corporate and Premium Sales Department at 1-800-221-7945, extension 5442, or by email at MacmillanSpecialMarkets@macmillan.com.

First Tor Teen Paperback Edition: 2022

Printed in the United States of America

0 9 8 7 6 5 4 3 2 1

To Gaston, my brightest light

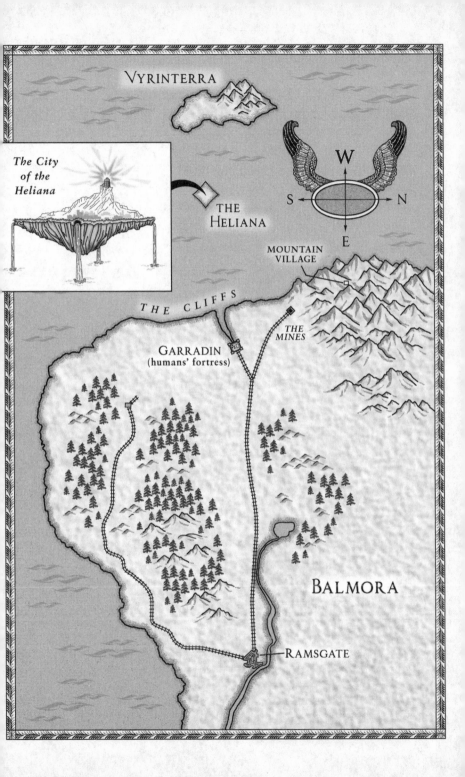

PROLOGUE

SHIRENE

"How many are dead?"

The healer kneeling before the king sways. "Two, Your Grace. With a dozen more in beds already. It all starts the same. A fever, then a cough that steals the breath."

No one in the Glass Tower dares breathe, let alone move. The Tower's high archways and polished windows that were usually let open wide are sealed shut. No one could know of this meeting, except for the ambassadors of the other kingdoms who would be briefed on it later this morning. Their fate is tied closer to ours than any of them would want to admit.

King Kharo frowns. "And how many know of it?"

"Just my team here, my king," replies the Chief Healer, indicating toward the group of healers behind her. "And one more, keeping watch over the sick right now."

The sky outside is dotted with stars just beginning to yield to the sun's light. I fix my gaze on the red line of the horizon. Today will be the longest day of the year.

Here and there, a winged lion flits from one end of the city to the next, bundles of flowers clutched in their arms as the last preparations for the High Summer festival are made. I'd often imagined what it would be like to celebrate my first High Summer as a sentinel—greeting the citizens, complimenting merchants on their wares, and awarding prizes at the various competitions scheduled from dawn to dusk.

Instead, I sit with the other sentinels in my sleeping clothes, having barely had time to secure a shawl around my shoulders

before making it to the emergency council meeting. A shiver
snakes its way down my spine as the cool stone beneath my
shoes pulls the warmth from my limbs. As Ninth Sentinel, my
chair is closest to the east, giving me a view of Balmora, miles
across the sea. I will be the first to see the messenger.

The king lifts his hand, indicating that the healer can rise.
"I trust you will be able to continue to keep this quiet," says
the king. "I ask for total silence from you and anyone else
tending to the sick. We cannot risk sending the citizens into a
panic."

The healer bows low. She knows the grave reason as well as I.
"Yes, Your Grace."

The king dismisses the healers back to their duties, thanking
them again for their discretion. Before she leaves, the Chief Healer's gaze goes to a figure huddling in the corner, clinging to the
shadows as if they provide some protection. *Ah,* I think. *She's
seen him.*

I wonder if she remembers him. The deserter's name was on
everybody's lips when he abandoned his duties a little over a
year ago. But no one knows his name more surely than I. He
had been the Ninth Sentinel before me.

Now I am sitting in his former seat, having taken his place as
part of the King's Council.

No one gathered here would address him with a title anymore. He is only Noam, a deserter at best and a traitor at worst.

I desperately want to ask him what caused him to leave the
proud city of the Heliana for Balmora—the continent that our
people sometimes call the "lost land"—but I set my selfish curiosity aside for now. Such conversations can wait until after we
receive the humans' reply.

With the king's permission, Sentinels Hammond and Renna
flew to Balmora's mountains last week in desperation, seeking
Noam's advice about the horrible illness spreading like a fire

among the Leonodai children, some just a few years old. The healers were unable to treat it, and the scholars were baffled. Noam listened to the symptoms with a growing dread in his eyes, and Renna told me later that he asked right away if we'd found dead birds in our city. We had.

"The birds carry the disease wherever they go," he had warned us. "If what you say is true, you have days to act. You must ask for aid from the human capital city, Ramsgate."

Though he was technically exiled for desertion, ironically, we couldn't have made an offer of peace without Noam. In the year since he'd left, Noam had learned much of the human language. While the king and council of sentinels had discussed our options, he alerted the humans in his village to what was happening. In a blur of days, each of the Four Kingdoms had agreed to offer peace, and the human leaders had agreed to meet our messenger at the Cliffs.

Back in the present, a flash of gold on the horizon stops time. I stifle a gasp, but not well enough. Other eyes follow where mine linger.

"My king—" starts Sentinel Renna when she sees.

"I see her," the king replies. "Skies keep us. The humans have given their answer."

Some agonizing minutes later, and the messenger lands. She drops the white flag in her jaws to the ground before taking her human form. In a rush of gold magic, her bronze lioness fur changes to cloud-white robes and gold armor as her body shifts to that of a woman with olive skin. The messenger's chest rises and falls as she catches her breath, but she wastes no time. Brushing back sweat from her brow, she kneels before the king.

"Your Grace," she says. She reaches into the bag at her side and pulls out a charred stack of parchment. "I delivered your message to the human leader. An offer of peace and permanent trade with the Four Kingdoms in exchange for the disease's cure."

The king leans forward. A lock of graying hair comes loose from beneath his crown as he does. "And? Where is their reply?"

The messenger's breath hitches. "They did not give one. They placed our offer in a fire and left."

"Skies keep us," the king says as I think the same. Why would the humans turn down our offer? The king covers his eyes, his fingertips rubbing his temples. "Did they give an explanation?"

"No, Your Grace," she replies. "I waited for one until they were out of sight before flying back."

They must not have understood, I think. We'd spent so much time convincing the ambassadors from the other kingdoms to agree to a permanent trade route. It took days of bickering, all while sick children continued to fill the healers' beds in the palace levels below us.

Fear twists like a knife in my gut. The disease would keep killing if left unchecked, but there was nothing we could do.

"Noam, step forward, please," says the king.

The deserter does so obediently. I know well enough now that he hasn't forgotten the sense of duty that he shirked when he left. Seeing Noam before the king now, I don't doubt his loyalty in this moment.

"Noam," the king says. "You say the cure for this disease is a wild plant, one that grows on the far side of Balmora."

"That is what my human friends have told me," he replies. "I have no reason to doubt them."

If the king has any misgivings about taking information from a deserter, he does not show it. "Then we will send teams," the king says. "To find the cure the humans have chosen to keep from us."

"They will know we're coming," the Second Sentinel, Hammond, says gravely from several chairs to my right. His gray beard reaches halfway down his chest, betraying his age, but his eyes are sharp and clear.

"I know," the king responds. "But I will not sentence a generation of Leonodai to death because of my own inaction."

"What of the High Summer festival?" asks another of my colleagues. "The citizens will be celebrating soon. Should we call off the festivities?"

The king considers this. "No. Let the people have their golden hours. We will need the time to consult the other ambassadors. If we are going to throw more fuel on the embers of war, we must get their blessing. Sentinel Renna, you oversee the warriors' training. I trust you are willing to choose the teams."

"Yes, Your Grace," the Fourth Sentinel says.

"Good," he replies. "There is one more matter we need to discuss before we leave here. When word gets out, the citizens will look to all sentinels for assurance. It would be prudent to speak as one voice, through one person. Sentinel Faera, as you all know, had for years served as the King's Voice, bringing the kingdoms together. Given her absence, I wonder if you would elect someone to serve in her place."

My peers and I exchange looks of surprise. Faera stepped down two months ago to start her own family as well as to care for her elderly father. Her successor had not yet been named. Per tradition, a search was being conducted for her replacement, and anyone on the Heliana could volunteer himself or herself, as I had a year ago when Noam deserted. The numbers of our ranks were only echoes of a past hierarchy. Every sentinel was chosen the same way, and any Leonodai could ask to be considered.

Hammond should be the King's Voice, I think. Older than the king himself, Hammond is a veteran soldier and always keeps the city's best interests at heart.

The sentinel in question clears his throat. "Your Grace," Hammond says. "I am a welder's son, not a politician. You know I am not one for diplomatic dances."

Beside me, my friend Sentinel Lyreina exhales a small laugh, and I share it. Wordsmith or not, I bet Lyreina feels as I do.

Then Hammond says, "I would elect the Ninth Sentinel,

Lady Shirene." *What?* I am too new and too young. My mouth opens to protest, but he keeps going. "A capable warrior, Sentinel Shirene has wisdom beyond her years and a depth of patience that the scholars could study." My heart swells out of my chest. Hammond isn't one to give compliments unless he truly means it.

And yet here he is, speaking my name before the king.

"I second the nomination," says Lyreina. "The citizens adore Shirene and trust her as well."

King Kharo turns his attention to me. "Sentinel Shirene," he says. "Would you serve as the King's Voice?"

My heart races. I am a sentinel, the same as everyone else gathered here. I can't hide behind the newness of my station forever. At some point, I will have to face the sun and rise into her light. This is that moment. I take a deep breath.

"I would be honored, Your Grace."

"Then it's done," he replies. "I'll leave you to gather the ambassadors. I will consult with Noam and the scholars to decide the route the teams will take."

Sunlight breaks over the horizon in the east as the king continues assigning duties. I take the moment to breathe. Beside me, Lyreina grabs my hand and squeezes it tightly.

"Congratulations," she says. "What an honor."

Serving as the King's Voice *is* an honor, and one that I had not thought to dream of, at least for a few more years. *Sethran will not believe it,* I think, reveling in that small excitement. Rowan will probably scream with joy. My younger sister isn't one to keep her emotions in check.

When the king stands to go, so do we all. The rising sun sends light directly into my eyes. I have never been in the Glass Tower at first light. Used for ceremonies and council meetings like this, the hallowed room lives up to its name. The twelve sides of the Tower alternate between arched mirrors and open windows. At all times of the day, it catches light and reflects it wildly into the skies. It is the best place in the city to see Vyrin-terra and the continent Balmora at the same time.

Our city, the Heliana, is a paladin in the skies between them. We Leonodai are one part of the Four Kingdoms: two on Vyrin-terra itself, one in the depths of the sea, and one in the skies. As far as we know, we are the last of the magical races. We never forgot what happened to the fifth kingdom, the fox-kin, long lost to the humans' greed . . .

For decades, we Leonodai had kept the encroaching humans at bay to the gratitude of the other kingdoms. No matter how bad the battles get at the coast and sea, Leonodai can always retreat and recoup. Humans can't fly and follow us.

But as it turns out, they don't need to fly, for birds already did, and they brought the humans' disease with them. For as long as anyone could remember, the Heliana had been the safest place in the known world.

And now that safety is gone.

1

ROWAN

Blood and feathers litter the arena. I flare my wings, digging my claws into the ground and taking a defensive position while I decide my next move. Across the pit, my opponent lets out a snarl of annoyance. Blood drips from the jagged cut above her eye. My strike caught her as her helm had slipped sideways just enough for my claw to slice into the skin of her brow. She shakes her head, and droplets fly.

Still, she's a warrior-elect like me, and she doesn't let up. We may not be fighting to kill as we will when the king calls us to arms, but that doesn't mean either of us are going to show much mercy.

We rush each other, teeth and claws bared and searching for any inch of exposed skin. My shoulder stings from a bite I should have dodged, but the heat of the wound drives me forward like a new flame. Leaping up, I use the wall of the arena to launch with my hind legs and try to hit her with my helm, but the other lioness reads my thoughts and dodges. As I twist to meet her again, she bats her wings hard, sending dust and debris into my nose and eyes. A moment later, she slams into my back legs, and I'm knocked off-balance, tumbling into the sandy ground.

Around us, the audience cheers, flowers gripped tightly in their hands. The blossoms, blue as the uniform of warriors, will be thrown to the victor.

My opponent's angry snarl rings loudly in my ear, spurring me to action. I jump to the side, flaring my wing, hitting her in the eyes as I do. Feathers snap and splinter in a shower of gold, and I brace myself against the ground. I shove my body weight into hers, the interlocking plates of our armor scraping shrilly against each other. She catches a bit of my wing in her jaws, and I yowl in pain—but she's done exactly what I hoped she'd do.

Shifting my weight back onto my left side, I hook my right paw between her belly and her leg, knocking her off-balance.

The other combatant digs her teeth farther into my wing as she falls, batting her own wings so hard that we're both lurched sideways with the force. I tighten my frame and twist quickly until my paw meets a vulnerable place at her throat.

I hold there, lifting my head to the sun, and let out a victorious roar.

A high trumpet sounds, followed by applause like rain. I back off my opponent. She shakes her head, blinking rapidly as blood continues dripping into her eye.

"Damn, I thought I had you," the other warrior-elect says.

"You fought well," I return, brushing my wing against hers. "I got lucky." It's not entirely true, but her expression brightens at my words. I've had more arena practice than she has, whereas she could best me in an archery tournament any day.

Across the arena, the royal pavilion is draped lavishly in gold cloth and weighty bundles of white blossoms, but neither the king nor queen are there. It had been empty all morning, so the previous fighters had told me. My heart sinks. I was hoping the king would make it in time. Instead, a warrior named Ezra—a swordsman in his early thirties who helped train the both of us—leads the formalities.

"Well done, warriors-elect," says Ezra. "And congratulations to you, Rowan."

"Thank you, warrior Ezra," I reply.

My forelegs tremble with excitement and strain as the wound in my shoulder throbs. The citizens toss their flowers, and the blooms start to pile up at my paws. Their excitement melts any momentary disappointment away. I keep my face proud and relaxed, but inside, I'm beaming.

This time tomorrow, the king will actually address me, but as a fully fledged warrior. After four years of brutal training, my very bones ache to take the oath and fulfill the dream I've been working toward since I was thirteen. Then again, maybe I shouldn't be so eager. Even though the human soldiers have not attempted an attack in months, once I am a warrior, I can be called at any moment to fight.

It is an honor, but am I ready?

As we exit the arena, I bat my wings idly, sending the flowers and loose petals into a flurry. The crowd responds with claps and cheers. A curtain sweeps closed behind us as the names of the next combatants are announced.

"Show-off," my opponent mutters good-naturedly.

Ahead of me, she takes her human form. The magic forged into her armor and clothes transforms with her, melting as easily as winter frost against the sun. The armor re-forms to her human head and arms as if it had never been anything but. As she lifts her helm, a healer comes over to her with a cloth soaked in something to halt the bleeding above her eye.

I summon my own magic. It only takes a thought, bright and brilliant as the sun. The rush of warmth flares at my chest, flowing outward like a cascade of warm winds, until I'm standing on two feet in my human form, my dark wavy hair flowing to my mid-back. Immediately, the throbbing of my shoulder intensifies. Even though I don't have wings in this form, the soreness will persist. A healer comes over and directs me to a chair.

"Be sure to stretch after bathing tonight," the healer says. She pushes the loose strands of sweaty hair off my forehead, then wipes my face with a damp cloth. "Your shoulder will be fine, but I'll put a salve on it to keep it from scarring."

"Thanks, Prena," I reply. After years of spars and mock battles, one gets to know the healers well. Prena is around my mother's age and just as sharp, making her one of my favorites.

"Your new uniform won't cover the cut," she says, her tone kind. "I guess you won't mind that, will you?"

"Not as long as that uniform is blue."

"You warriors-elect," she replies. "I swear on the skies it was just yesterday you were coming to me for something to ease your cycle pains. And now here you are, about to become a warrior at last."

"Prena!"

"They must be speeding up the bells so time goes faster, is all I'm saying."

The older woman gives me a smart nod as she discards one cloth and starts pressing ground herbs into a fresh one. Even though she was born without a right hand, Prena's skills as a healer are unmatched. "The skies had to keep something back," she told me once. "Otherwise, I would have been too good at my job and Leonodai would live forever, like the sea-folk."

Prena rubs a minty-smelling salve onto my shoulder. When she's done, I lean forward and swap out my armored boots for leather sandals that'll be better suited for the day's heat. The sounds of the next fight echo from the arena, while music plays from farther outside the palace grounds. I listen for the high-pitched bells that mark the hour, but I don't hear them. *I might not be too late.*

"You're all set," says Prena, wiping her hand on her olive-green uniform. The gold thread of the Leonodai crest sewn into the front catches the light as she does.

I leap up. "Thanks, Prena."

"Thank me by stretching that shoulder. Don't let my good work go to waste."

I smile and duck out of the room. In my chest, my heart flutters as if it's trying to fly from within me. An echo of cheers from the eastern side of the palace confirms that I'm not too late to watch the Race of the Four Gates. If I hurry, I can still catch the finish.

I take my lioness form, gliding above the palace and the massive crescent-shaped ridge beneath it. Toward the middle of the ridge, windows reveal the endless tunnels built into the stone. They're already illuminated with candlelight and lanterns made of colored glass. The same will be done to the other palace windows, from the lowest level to the Glass Tower at the very top, as per tradition. Only the hollow Keep deep inside the base of the ridge will remain dark, but no one ever goes in the Keep, anyway.

From this height, I can see all four rivers that mark the cardinal points of our diamond-shaped city. The waters pour from a magical spring far beneath the palace, rushing straight outward and off the edge of the island and into the sea below. Not many know of the grotto where the spring is hidden, but Callen, my oldest friend, and I had found it years ago in a game of hide-and-seek. My mother chastised the two of us when she found out, making us promise not to go back.

"That is sacred ground," she said. "Only the royal family should ever visit that place, to remember the magic of their ancestors."

Of course, immediately following our scolding, Callen and I made a pact to keep going there, but to keep it secret. As the years turned, we visited less and less. Now I can't remember that last time we were there.

I turn toward the city's center. Bundles of blue and white flowers, some from the hillsides beneath the palace and more from Vyrinterra across the sea, hang from windows let open wide to greet the summer air. More are strung through the soaring archways between homes and down the alleys toward the marketplace.

A dark blot of black in one of the garlands catches my eye. I swoop low to get a better look, but the sinking feeling in my stomach already tells me what it is.

The bird's glossy eye stares out blankly. Judging by the lack of smell, it can't have been dead for more than a few hours. Even though they don't possess the Knowledge that gives Leonodai our speech and magic, our people feel a kinship with birds. After all, we share the skies.

Ox told me that the warriors were reporting the dead birds' numbers to the sentinels. A day or two later, the sentinels asked warriors-elect to be on the lookout, too. I make a mental note to remember where I found this one so I can report it later.

Finding an open courtyard, I land and take my human form. I'm adjusting the sash at my waist when someone calls my name.

"Rowan!" a familiar voice calls.

I turn. Vera waves at me, shouldering her way through the crowd. Her pale blue skirt matches her shirt, which she's twisted up to keep her cool—and to show off her toned stomach, which some lucky artist has painted with a swirling sun. With her long, pale blond hair and shapely figure, my friend and former roommate of four years has had no short supply of people chasing after her since the day we met. And since her archery tournament isn't until later this afternoon, she can dress up all she wants for now. I hurry up to her, opening my arms for a hug.

"You look smug, so I take it you won," she says.

"I do not look smug," I reply. "But yes, I did."

"Called it."

I roll my eyes. "Did the Four Gates race start already? Who's in the lead?"

The High Summer festival brings hours of competitions between warriors—while I was competing in the arena, other warriors and warriors-elect were running footraces and weaving through obstacle courses while citizens made good-natured bets. It is not only a way for warriors to unwind but for the whole city to bask in the strength of its protectors. High Summer is when the sun hits its peak for the year, and the Leonodai do, too.

The Four Gates race—though antiquated and no longer considered the be all, end all of who the best warriors are—was the original event that the festival had grown from, and thus it is a city favorite. Elder Leonodai can still recount the winners from their youth. More than once, during late nights in the warriors' dining hall, someone has gotten into too much wine and droned on and on about how many members of their family had ever won it.

Vera loops her arm in mine and begins leading us down the street. "Last we saw them, Sethran was ahead with a bunch right at his tail, including Ox. He might still catch up."

I squeeze her arm back affectionately. "Where was Callen?"

"I didn't see him, actually."

"Oh. That's weird." Callen and I have been practicing the route all week, racing until we were out of breath and covered in sweat. He is a faster flyer, which I hate, but I beat him once after biting him in the wing. It was cheating, but I swear he'd let me do it just so I'd stop pouting.

"Anyway, don't worry. Your man's still got time to win."

I groan and look skyward as Ox's face flashes in my mind. "Ox is not my . . . anything." One look from the dark-haired, quick-witted warrior set my heart ablaze, but I was still getting to know him. I just couldn't hide that I loved what I was discovering.

But I won't gossip until I tell Callen. He's been my best friend for nearly ten years, from even before I met Vera on our first day of warrior training. If Callen is going to hear about me and Ox from anyone, he'll hear about it from me.

"Not your anything," Vera echoes. "And yet I recall hearing you sneak into your room pretty late last night."

I blush. "It's not what you think."

"Uh-huh," Vera says, her expression unconvinced, but she still has a playful glint in her eye. "Come on. Let's find a place to watch the finish."

I let her lead us to the pavilion draped in ivory cloth reserved for warriors-elect. A couple of our friends wave their greetings, but most keep their eyes trained on the skies, looking for the competitors. Vera, never one to not get what she sets her mind to, jostles our friend Bel, a broad-armed warrior-elect and adopted son of one of the city's finest ironworkers, to the side until we have a front-row seat.

"Thanks, Bel!" she says.

He rolls his eyes, flicking back his long, chestnut brown hair. "Not going to stand in your way, V."

"Such a gentleman."

"Thank me with a dance later?" he asks.

She grins. "You got it."

Vera turns back around, and I nudge her shoulder. "Don't break that one's heart, okay?"

"What?" she says, faking a shocked look.

"I *like* Bel. He's nice. So you be nice to him, okay?" Back in the early days of my training before I'd tamed my rebellious streak, the instructors made me do extra drills when I spoke out—which was often. More than once, Bel had gone out of his way to grab a plate for me before the dining hall closed up for the night so I'd have something to eat when I was done.

"Fine, fine," she says. "Not going to make you spar twice in one day."

"*True* friendship."

Vera starts chatting with the person on her other side as I lean forward. The white stone of the causeway pushes into my stomach, but I'm desperate for a glimpse of the racers. The Four Gates races takes competitors around each of the cardinal points of the city, as well as under. The Heliana floats high above the wide sapphire sea, an ever-present citadel sustained by the magic of old. Somewhere below us, a team of Leonodai hold colored pennants that they'll toss into the air for the racers to catch. Each racer will need five pennants—one from below and four from around the city—before they can circle back to the starting line.

A slight breeze sweeps over my skin, and I wipe the residual sweat from my match. I wish I'd had time to clean up, but time waits for no warrior.

"They're in the final turn," Vera says excitedly. "There!"

Six pairs of gold wings soar up from behind the Glass Tower to the west, followed closely by a second group of Leonodai, some of whom might be waiting for the last minute to make their break.

At the finish line, a single gold flag waves in the wind. To win, the warrior must fall from the sky as a lion, take their human form and grab the flag, then take to the skies once more in their proud lion form. It's not a difficult trick in and of itself, but to do so with the other competitors clawing at your heels takes skill and timing, unless you want to take a claw to the face.

Last year's winner, a warrior named Io, waves to the crowd from the victor's platform across from us. On a muscled arm, Io bears the sapphire-studded armlet that goes to the winner each year.

"Why aren't the sentinels up there?" I ask.

Vera shrugs. "Maybe they changed things this year."

"Yeah, maybe." I'll have to ask Shirene what held them up. I see less and less of my sister these days, but she'll be at my oath ceremony tomorrow.

First the king not at my match, and now the sentinels aren't at the finish line. I couldn't think of any matter of state that would keep them away on High Summer.

"Sethran's making a break!" Vera shouts, and my gaze snaps forward.

The competitors go into the final stretch. Feathers explode in the air as their wings collide, but neither slows . . .

Ox lets out a final roar, but with a flash of magic, warrior Sethran takes his human form early and falls faster. He grabs the flag, then transforms instantly and soars skyward once more. The others fall in a flurry of feathers and flashes of magic, then recover and fly off to the side. Triumphant horns sound, warm and rousing.

"Woo!" I shout as the city erupts into cheers. *Seth wins, and Ox got second!* It won't win Ox the iconic cuff, but I'm glad it went to Seth. He and my sister have been together for over ten years, having fallen for each other during their second year of training. At this point, I consider him an older brother.

"Come on," Vera says, leaning close so I can hear her over the din, "let's go walk around! We can find Ox after they wrap up the winner's ceremony."

The sound of Ox's name makes my stomach flip. I nod. "Yeah, let's go."

Vera and I leave the pavilion and head toward the marketplace. Around us, children huddle in groups, playing with the new toys they received this morning, per High Summer tradition. Dancers in dresses the color of sunsets walk in twos and threes, giggling and flirting with the warriors. Colorful tents of vendors sell hand-carved goods, sparkling jewelry, and every manner of beautiful new garments.

"The silversmith's got a long line, as usual," Vera says, frowning at a growing crowd ahead of us. "I was hoping to see if he's got a simple ring or something. I've always liked those earrings you've got." She pauses. "Well, earring."

I tuck my hair back behind my ear so the earring in question can show—a simple oval stud with a stone the color of a pale blue sky, and wrapped in silver. The set was my mother's, but I admired them so much as a little girl that one day I took them. I gave the other one to Callen, and like me, he never goes a day without it. I keep a simple pearl in the other ear, but Callen just wears the one.

Vera and I peer at the wares. Silver rings with blue stones are laid out neatly in front of the silversmith in rows as he barters with customer after customer. As Vera tries on rings, I look around at the festival, now in full swing. Swaying lines of pennants and bells stretch between rooftops. In the distance, I spot a stage that has been built for dancers and singers. A troupe of children dance in unison—or at least try to. A small girl toward the end gets stage fright and tries to leave the platform, her face in her hands.

Next to the stage is a collection of food stalls, each with meals more decadent than the last. Fruit from Vyrinterra is expertly cut into flowers and skewered onto wooden sticks in colorful patterns. Fish sizzles nearby, blackened with savory seasonings. Children dart about in pairs, collecting discarded plates that are color-coded for each vendor. It's a task I did myself when I was younger. They'll be rewarded with a special thank-you note signed by the queen, but more importantly, it's an early lesson on what it means to treat the city and your fellow Leonodai with respect. Here in the skies, we rely on one another.

A group of shadows passes overhead, and I look up. Ox and his friends swoop low and take their human forms off the side of the next street. Vera pays for her ring—a thin, silver band with a tiny triangle of blue—and catches my eye knowingly.

"Come on," she says.

Be calm, I tell myself, but my limbs are already light with excitement and nervousness. I've trained for battle. I can handle talking to a warrior.

Just a dark-eyed, handsome, intelligent warrior.

Ox's friend and one of Vera's archery mentors, Luca, nods his greeting when he sees us. "Happy almost ceremony day, warriors-elect," he says good-naturedly. "You feeling ready?"

"Ready to move out of the Underbelly," Vera says, referring to the lowest level of the Warriors' Hall. After tomorrow, we'll move rooms up a level to make space for the next cohort. Despite all of the Warriors' Hall being warm and well-lit, the nickname for the ground floor has stuck around for generations.

"Ah, I remember that feeling," Luca replies. "It's worth it, I promise."

"It'd better be," Vera quips. "I didn't spend all those hours firing arrows at your crazy targets for nothing."

"*Inventive*," he says. "Inventive targets. Everyone loves that one I built that sends your targets *at* you."

Vera groans, and as our friends keep talking, I give Ox a small, awkward wave. "Congrats on the race."

He shrugs. "Could have done better."

"You were second."

"Which, technically, means I could have done better," he replies.

"Skies, you're difficult. Fine. Next time, do better."

He laughs. "Will do, kind lady. It would have been nice to get a prize, though."

"How about a dance later tonight?" I ask.

"I'd love nothing more." He smiles, and a dimple on his right cheek makes my heart flip so wildly that I almost don't hear him ask, "So, Rowan An'Talla, are you going back to the Hall?"

I exhale a laugh. Ox has an annoyingly endearing habit of calling me by my full name. "Not yet," I say. "I want to go, you know, do festival things."

"Well, would you like an escort?" he says, gently pulling me away from our friends.

"Don't you want to go with Luca?"

Ox lets out an exaggerated sigh. "Actually, it's all been a charade, and I don't really like Luca. Archers, am I right?"

"First off, you're both archers. And he's your friend. Of course you like him."

"Not like I like you," he replies.

"Well, I . . . good." Heat sears my cheeks, but I mentally dig in my heels. I can't let him best me so easily. "But really, go with him. We already spend so much time together. If I recall, we were up until nearly second bell talking in your room."

He leans in closely so only I can hear. "And you could have been there all night, if you'd wanted."

My blush rises. I can fight with all manner of weapons, but Ox is relentless with words. The question about me staying the night—and all that it entailed—had come up, but something held me back. Ox didn't pressure me, but his eyes had ached for more.

"Come on," he says, taking my hand and bringing me back to the present. "Let's go do festival things."

Despite what he said, Ox of course invites Vera and Luca to join us. Music carries from one end of the marketplace to the next, mixed with the laughter between warriors and citizens alike as wine is poured from cask to cup. Wares of silver and bronze gleam in the sunlight.

I glance at the increasingly familiar lines of Ox's arms and chest beneath his cobalt-blue robes, the same robes that the sentinels will place in my hands tomorrow. For now, I'm stuck with the warrior-elect's uniform: a long ivory tunic with cobalt hems, banded at the waist with a matching blue sash. The tunic has slits on either side, and underneath, tight-fitting linen pants go down to my ankles. A set of throwing knives—my preferred weapon, at least when first engaging an opponent—is belted over my sash with the sheath resting at my hip.

For a dance or formal ceremony, I might wear a dress, but

I've worn this so often, it's practically a second skin. Still, after seeing Vera all dressed up, I wish I were wearing something else. Something . . . prettier.

"Congratulations, Warrior-Elect," a passerby says to me, placing her hand gently on my shoulder.

"Thank you," I reply cheerfully. "May the skies keep you."

"It's happening," Ox says, squeezing my hand as we move deeper into the crowd.

"One more day," I reply. "It doesn't feel real."

Victory in the arena or competing in a race: neither matters as much as the fact that in less than a day, I will be a true warrior. Every cut scarred over, every weapon mastered. Every sleepless night as our superiors pushed us to the limits so we'd be ready to face any enemy. It will all be worth it when I take the warrior's oath and accept my uniform.

I pause a moment to watch as a healer flies overhead, headed for the Glass Tower. Her shadow crosses over the two of us, and for a moment, I wonder why a healer would be flying straight to the king, during a festival of all days. I couldn't think of anything so urgent as to call him there.

"Oh, hey," I say. "I found a dead bird earlier, like the sentinels said to look out for."

"Sentinel Renna said to report any of them to her," Ox replies.

"I know," I say. "Even we lowly warriors-elect got the same orders." I resume walking. "I'll write up a report tonight. No need to do it now, right?"

A selfish fear rises in my stomach. I am *so* close. So close to becoming a warrior. Whatever is going on must be serious, but it won't change anything.

I've dreamed of taking the warrior oath for years: the king speaking the words, and a sentinel handing me robes the color of bravery and loyalty. I'll put them on immediately, and when there is a break in the celebrations, I'll go to my father's grave and tell him I did it, I became a warrior just like we'd always talked about.

Nothing under the skies can take that dream from me. Nothing.

SHIRENE

Sounds of revelry echo from far below us, just enough to remind me of all we are missing out on. I was supposed to have been judging a dance competition at the marketplace by now. The citizens will have already noticed us gone.

Sweat breaks at my brow despite the breeze. I know my role means I have to push away my fear, even more so than when I was a warrior. With the city's eyes on the sentinels for strength, calm is all I can allow myself to be.

Still.

We have been patient with the humans. We tried to do the right thing, and they closed off their hearts.

A palace attendant announces that the ambassadors have arrived. I sent the summons myself, and thankfully my first task as the King's Voice has gone smoothly. We sentinels start to take our normal places, and Hammond clears his throat when he sees me going to my chair.

"The King's Voice sits nearest the king and queen, Lady Shirene."

"Ah, thank you," I say. "Old habits." Sentinel Faera had been the King's Voice so long, it seemed to come naturally to her. I think of the older sentinel's posture and gestures, and hope I'll manage to live up to her legacy.

At least I remembered not to wear my hair in a warrior's style as I usually did. For this meeting, I left it completely down, save for twin pins on either side of my brow. The metal wings curl back and around my head, perched high enough to scrape the back of my chair if I lean too far back. I adjust my posture just as the ambassadors enter.

The embassy of the Sea Queen is first, the hush that they bring with their presence only emphasizing the silent grace with which they move.

Alys and Rhys are brother and sister, and identical in nearly every gesture. As children of the Sea Queen—as all the sea-folk refer to themselves, regardless of bloodlines—they are gifted with impossibly long lives, but they look like they are in their midtwenties like I am. Alys wears a long dress of pale blue silk, the fabric skimming the slight curves of her frame. Despite being ambassador for over two years, she forewent any trace of Leonodai culture. No earrings hang from her ears, no sash ties her waist. Her long silver hair is pulled back into a high ponytail, emphasizing her prominent cheekbones and soft eyes that give little trace of any emotion.

Her brother has the same look—an unreadable expression like ocean water trapped in glass. His hair is nearly as long as his sister's, and he wears it down and unadorned. His robes are secured with a large brooch on the left side bearing the emblem of the Sea Queen: two three-point crowns, one above and the other mirrored below, with a curved oval-shaped space between them. When we were kids, Rowan told me many times she thought it looked like an eyeball with pointed lashes, and despite all the years, that's still the first thing I think of when I see it.

The pair take their seats. Alys tucks her feet daintily beneath her dress, something I've noticed she does religiously, as if ashamed of their presence. Unlike Leonodai, the sea-folk do not transform at will. Their magic only comes to them when they are in the sea.

"Early, as always," Hammond notes with a nod of respect to

each of them. "I'm sure the king will appreciate your prudence in this matter."

"Our second abrupt summons in as many weeks. It's exciting," says Rhys.

"Quite exciting," his sister echoes.

I bristle at their lighthearted tone. This meeting is not a party—we are in a crisis. But who am I to judge what is interesting to beings whose lifetimes are measured in centuries and not years?

A sharp laugh breaks the quiet, and into the hall strides the embassy of the bearkings.

"Apologies, my lords and ladies," the princess says. "You again neglected to consider the thousand and a half stairs my poor, earthbound body would have to climb to get here."

Adorned from head to toe in silver jewelry embedded with thick cuts of amber, Princess Freanna is wild-eyed with a crown of chestnut-colored hair that she leaves unbound and free. Just eighteen years old, she is the only surviving child of the First Bearking, the first two having died in an accident several years before.

"They were chasing a stag," the princess had said over some dinner where she'd gotten into too much wine. "The dull-minded cubs didn't see the rotted wood of the tree beneath them."

Spoiled and stubborn, Freanna takes as much pride at digging in her heels on matters of state as she does sparring with warriors in her bear form during her spare time.

Freanna slumps into her chair. She wears a dress the color of moss and belted with chains of silver studded with claws. Of the five bearkings, Freanna's family is sovereign right now. Their kings rotate every ten years. Despite her attitude, Freanna's voice is needed here.

Even she will see reason, I tell myself. *She must.*

The horselords' ambassadors are right behind. Stern as ever,

Lord Cambor greets us with a stiff bow. Dressed for practicality, the only hint of his status is an intricate silver breastplate, the metal having been worked so intelligently that it looks as if it is made of woven reeds. There are three horselords in all, each with equal power.

Cambor's wife, Lady Marradoa, similarly acknowledges us with a curtsy, her dark brows pulled together in knowing concern. Her eyes flick around the room, taking in every detail as she would if she were in her equine form. In my experience, she keeps her words and thoughts close to her chest, choosing to listen rather than speak, but in private conversation, she is warm and tactical. The food supply for the Four Kingdoms has flourished under her guidance.

A chime sounds, and I stand without thinking. "Their royal highnesses, King Kharo and Queen Laianna of the Leonodai."

My heart thrums. Skies, I've shared bread at their table on more than one night, but the sight of our people's monarchs still steals the breath from my lungs.

King Kharo's dark attire is visibly simple. *Pious,* I think. He is a king, but today he will try to get his way without straining relationships with the other kingdoms.

The queen's gown matches that of her husband: a rich blue so deep it would have appeared black in another light. Her circlet rests intertwined in her hair, which has been arranged in a warrior's style: braided down to her neck, then tied off in a low ponytail. The other ambassadors may not make the connection, but to any Leonodai present, the choice speaks volumes— everyone in the Four Kingdoms must be ready to fight.

They take their seats, with the rest of the room following suit.

"It's nice to have someone in that seat again," Queen Laianna whispers to me. "I'm sure you will do wonderfully, Sentinel Shirene."

The king speaks before I can respond, but I nod my thanks.

"Esteemed ambassadors," the king begins. "I thank you for your time and will not waste it with minced words. Last week, I called you here to discuss a sickness that has since killed several Leonodai children, with no signs of stopping. The only cure known to us is a flower that grows deep in our enemy's lands."

"It would have to, wouldn't it?" Freanna mutters. "My grandfather kept journals. He said humans stripped the land at Garradin. Who knows how many miles of destruction there are, now, a hundred years later?"

My hands clench. Everyone in the Four Kingdoms, from child to elder, knows the story of the fifth magical race: the fox-kin.

Since the beginning of time, the fox-kin had thrived on Balmora while the other four magical races lived on Vyrinterra—it's how we all spoke the same tongue, though on the Heliana we simply refer to it as Leonodai. When humans first made their way across the continent, they didn't present an immediate threat. But years turned, and the humans wanted to settle the coast. The fox-kin refused to share the land, and the tensions rose. The fox-kin called on the other kingdoms for aid.

Only it came too late. The fox-kin weren't armored and didn't have means to defend themselves. The humans attacked in the daytime, when most fox-kin were sleeping. They poured water, sand, and refuse into the tunnels of the fox-kin's underground city.

In that horrible act, Garradin became a tomb, and our war with the humans began. The first king and first queen used all their magic to split the Heliana from rest of Vyrinterra, raising her to the skies to fight and defend against the threat. We've been fighting ever since.

The king, however, doesn't need a history lesson, and he ignores Freanna's whispers. "Together, we agreed to offer the humans a lasting peace in exchange for the cure, or at least safe passage to where it grows." The king pauses, and I feel the blow before it comes. "The humans have refused."

Princess Freanna lets out a groan. "Typical. We shouldn't have attempted to bargain with them in the first place."

"Indeed, Princess Freanna," Hammond cuts in. "We put too much faith in the humans' desire to reach Vyrinterra. Now they know that the Leonodai are vulnerable. And they will expect us when we go looking for the cure."

"You have already decided?" Rhys says inquisitively. "I thought we were called here to give our opinion."

"I doubt," Lord Cambor cuts in, "that King Kharo has to give any more than a moment's thought as to whether or not to save the youngest generation of his people. It is what any of our sovereigns would do." The ambassador's stormy expression is made sterner under his heavy brows, pulled closely together. "Besides, we all rely on the Leonodai's protection."

"We don't," says Freanna. "Our fortresses are built to withstand any attack—like the one that we are about to invite thanks to the Leonodai's lack of prowess in the healing arts. That is why I suggested we look for the cure on Vyrinterra before going to the humans," she finishes. "But if you recall, I was overruled."

"The Leonodai children dying several floors below your feet do not have the luxury of time," snaps Sentinel Renna, voice rising with years of practiced authority. "We don't have time to be pulling weeds up in the mountains. We must rely on what we know."

"So far," the king says slowly, letting the room calm, "the disease has only affected children, but we don't know if that will change. We must act fast. Sentinel Hammond, if you please."

To my left, the Second Sentinel straightens up.

"Tonight," Hammond's voice booms, "we will send out teams of Leonodai warriors to Balmora. Only the most trusted will be chosen. No one will know their mission except them.

The teams will seek out the panacea and return it to the Heliana."

"And what is it you are asking of this council?" Alys asks, drawing a long lock of hair forward and twisting it around her finger. "Our people already defend from the seas as you defend from the skies. We've taken down nearly two dozen large ships this year alone."

Hammond bows his head. "And you have our gratitude, Lady Alys. From the sea-folk, we are asking only greater vigilance. The humans know we are weak, so they may ready a stronger attack."

Rhys cleared his throat. "We need not consult our Queen for this," he says. He shares a glance with his sister, who nods at the same moment he does. "We know our sovereign's will dearer than our own. The people of the sea have the most to lose if the shores of Vyrinterra are corrupted and polluted by humans should the Leonodai not defend us. I will request that patrols be increased."

"The humans may try to go around the Heliana," Renna notes.

"The Queen sees all," is Lady Alys's immediate reply. "She knows every shadow that crosses the horizon and which of those do not belong. She will know, and we will fight."

"Thank you," says King Kharo.

An awkward silence follows. I steel myself. Faera would never have allowed a lull during something so important, even for a moment. She would lead the ambassadors to where she wanted them to go.

"Lord Cambor. Lady Marradoa," I say, meeting Hammond's eyes for a moment. He gives me a tiny nod. "Of the horselords, we ask you to strengthen your city's defenses. We would also seek to bring some of your healers to the Heliana, on the chance they can teach ours something to delay the disease's onslaught."

"A reasonable ask," Lady Marradoa replies, eyes ever watchful. "We can agree to that. The defenses on our shores will be strengthened, and our most vulnerable evacuated should the humans attack. That said, we would return to Vyrinterra as soon as possible to inform the other lords of the plan directly."

"Thank you, Lady Marradoa. The boat will be readied immediately, and a team of warriors will help lower it to the sea whenever you are ready."

I turn, looking Princess Freanna in the eyes. "Princess, we ask the most from you. You know the Leonodai rely on metals from your mines. We'd ask that not only you provide us with additional materials, but your blacksmiths as well."

Freanna's eyes go wide. "The bear-kin do not share their secrets of weapon making."

"Princess—"

"No," she says sternly. "You may have metals, but I won't order our smiths to leave home for this. As I mentioned, the bearkings need not fight at all. You are in our debt."

A hundred years of protecting your hides so your people could get lax up in the mountains, and this is the thanks we get? I grit my teeth. "Yes, we are. If you need more time to consider, please take it. But for now, the Leonodai graciously accept an increase in raw materials."

Freanna sits up. "I will return with the other ambassadors to inform my father of what has occurred and ensure the supplies are sent promptly."

"Skies keep you all. Thank you," says the king. He rises, and those gathered do the same. "We will waste no time. At the hour, Sentinel Shirene, call the warriors to the Tower. We will send the teams that Sentinel Renna has chosen tonight."

"Yes, Your Grace." I bow my head. Then, for a moment, I doubt. "The High Summer festival is our people's most revered day. The citizens will know something is wrong should we interrupt it."

"The citizens will know soon enough when they notice children missing," the king replies solemnly. "At the hour, Sentinel. Sound the bells."

3

CALLEN

Rowan is with Ox when I finally find her in the High Summer festivities. Her hair is braided to her neck with the rest of it flowing down her back. I've never realized how much I liked that style until now. Practical, but pretty, too.

Focus, warrior.

My heart thunders in my chest, and no amount of training for war has readied me for what I am about to do. I was up before dawn, restless with the rumor Exin casually mentioned last night as we were eating dinner. Around us, members of our own cohort and the younger warriors-elect mingled with excitement and anticipation in their eyes, eager for the reprieve that High Summer would bring us.

"So. I heard Rowan's been visiting Ox's room at night," Exin had said, the edge in his voice clearly seeking more gossip. My friend's implication was in no way subtle, and I nearly choked on a mouthful of fish.

"Wh-what?"

"Just what I heard." Exin resumed poking around his plate. "I thought you might know something, though. Crazy to me that you two never got together."

I shook my head and tried to push past it, unable to think of anything to say. There was no way he'd meant anything by it, but Exin's words stung worse than a burn, and my heart pounded as if I were in the middle of an intense sparring match. Questions spun in my head like buzzards—when was the last time Rowan and I had hung out in the evening, outside of practicing for the Four Gates race? Was there any truth to this?

After dinner, I went to her room. When no one answered the door, I flew up to my own room and slammed the door behind me.

I should have told her how I felt months ago.

I slept restlessly and woke up with my heart low in my chest. Still, when the sun rose, I'd gotten myself together enough to get out of my room and ready for the race. I'd trained for weeks, after all. Rowan helped me memorize the course. She knew that winning the Four Gates race was a surefire way to grab the city's attention—and that of the sentinels. It is the ultimate goal of a lot of warriors to become a sentinel someday, and I was no different. What's more, the honor would surely be enough to bring back some semblance of my father's former, proud self.

He wouldn't be there to watch the race. These days, he and my mother rarely left our family quarters in the lower levels of the palace. I don't remember the last time I visited, and they've never once come to see my room at the Warriors' Hall.

The image of my father's hollow gaze and the desperate hope that Exin was wrong weighed on my wings like anchors as I did a few laps around the Hall to warm up. No matter how hard I tried, I couldn't shake how I felt. A stronger warrior may have been able to overcome his emotions, but I couldn't. I didn't want to.

So when the time came for competitors to check in for the race, I didn't go.

Back in the present, I step back into a sheltered archway and try to gather my wits. I run a hand through my hair and try to shake my nerves. I'll have to get her alone somehow. I press the pads of my fingers into the stone wall behind me.

Then, before my courage leaves me, I round the corner and call out her name.

It's Vera who sees and greets me first. "Hey, Callen, happy High Summer!" She cocks her head to the side. "It's a shame you didn't race today. I was all ready to cheer for you."

By this point, Rowan has seen me, too. She waves, letting go of Ox's hand as she does. "Hey," she says, greeting me with a hug like she always has. Only it feels different this time. "You okay?"

"Yeah, why?"

"You didn't race," she says. "It's all you've talked about since last winter."

"Yeah, actually," I reply. "It's nothing important. But I did want to talk to you, really quickly. If you have time."

"Oh." She gives me a look, but nods. "Yeah, okay."

She parts with the others, saying that we'll catch up. I try not to grin with vindication at how quickly she agrees to come with me. We've been best friends since we were kids—even now, that connection is strong. I still matter to her.

Once it is just the two of us, I turn toward the palace. I take a shortcut through a narrow alleyway. The shouting of children above us makes me look up.

There are three of them, two girls egging on a third to make the jump from one rooftop to the next. They are about five or six years old—just old enough to be growing into the full extent of their magic, including shape-shifting for the first time. Each of the kids is dressed in what I guess are their best festival dresses, but the dirt on their hands and elbows tells me exactly what they are doing.

Rowan sees where I'm looking and smiles. "We used to do that," she says. "Remember? Jumping and trying to change into a lion at the same time."

"To see if we had enough magic to shape-shift, yeah. I remember," I reply. "I also remember you insisting we try on a wider gap than this one."

"And we both made it across fine, even when we couldn't transform yet," she says. "We're alive."

"Yeah, yeah," I reply, wishing my heart weren't racing as it is. I run a hand across my brow and through my hair, cringing at the nervous sweat.

"So," Rowan asks, adjusting the sash on her waist. "Where are we going?"

A great question. It took me a while to think of the right place to get this off my chest, but somewhere around dawn, I landed on it. "The grotto."

"During High Summer? You're feeling bold." She laughs, but she takes her lioness form anyway and starts for the entrance we discovered years ago. "Weird. I was just thinking about that place."

We fly over to the secret entrance. The spot is concealed off by the shadows of the palace on one side and mossy boulders on the other. I lift the blanket we use as a door and as camouflage. I let her go first, then take a deep inhale as I follow behind.

Already, the air is cooler. Rushing water sounds in the distance. *Skies.* Will the water be too loud for us to talk? I should have picked somewhere quieter. But it just felt right to do this in a place that was already ours.

Rowan slows as we get closer to the spring, sensing the same hushed reverence we felt when we first found it. I stand beside her as we look into the restless, glowing waters. Above us, the cave arches sharply into a high, domed ceiling. Dust clings to the green-glass lanterns affixed above the four tunnels where each of the rivers—Sun, Moon, Crescent, and Wind—flow outward. Magic pulses through the air like blood through veins.

Rowan's mother, Talla, told us this is where the first king and queen of the Leonodai used their magic to break the Heliana from the coast of Vyrinterra when Garradin was destroyed and the threat of the humans became real. Doing so took every bit of their magic and ended up killing them. For their service to the magical races, the then-divided families of Leonodai banded together into one kingdom.

The current king, Kharo, is a direct descendent of that first king. I wonder how that feels, to have to live up to such expectations. With a general for a father, I only have a drop of that pressure, while the king had a rain.

I glance over at Ro, watching the glowing reflection of the spring dance in her eyes a moment before she catches me staring.

"What?" she asks.

"Nothing." I look back to the spring. "Just been a while since I was here."

"It's the same as it's always been," she says, and I pick up on the hint of annoyance in her tone. Is it annoyance or impatience? Does she want to get back to the festival? To Ox?

It's now or never. Skies keep me, I have to do this. "Ro, I wanted to talk to you."

She leans back against the wall of the grotto. "You already are."

"Hilarious," I reply. *Inhale, exhale.* "I just . . . I wanted to tell you something."

Her expression changes, eyebrows raising just a little in concern. For once in her life, she doesn't say anything. I send a prayer to the first king and queen, hoping they're watching over me from the Endless Skies. Whatever magic lifted the Heliana into the skies, it has to be enough to say this.

"I love you," I say. "I love you, Ro, and as way, way more than a friend. I'm in love with you." Her lips move, but no sound comes. I swallow hard. "I just really wanted you to know."

She looks away from me. "Callen, where is this coming from?"

"I've wanted to tell you for months," I say. "But I didn't have the guts until I saw you with Ox."

"So you only wanted me because I was with someone else?"

"No, that's not it."

She avoids my gaze. "Well, that's how it sounds."

"I know, just . . . wait a second." I lean on the wall next to her. She moves away. Rowan never shies away from me. We're different. We're *us*.

I can barely hear my voice over the sound of my heart pounding in my ears. "I've wanted to tell you for so long. You're funny and smart, and you're going to be a really great warrior. I know you think I go easy on you in sparring, but I swear on the skies I don't."

"Okay . . ."

"And you're so beautiful, Ro. I can't believe I never told you. You should see how the other warriors look at you."

Sand scrapes beneath her feet as she shifts. "So?"

"So. It just felt right, when I realized I wanted you in a new way. When I realized I loved you."

Rowan starts to pace, her hands touching the hilts of her throwing knives like I know she does to focus. "I can't believe this is happening. What did you expect me to say, Callen?"

"That's not . . . Come on," I protest. "I was hoping you'd want what I wanted." My hope sours to bitterness. "Haven't you ever looked at me like that, even once?"

Finally, Rowan's eyes meet mine. Dark brown, with flecks of gold as all Leonodai have. "Of course I have," she says. "Of course I've thought about it. I just think I want something more. Something different." *I don't want you.* That's what she wants to say, she's just too kind to say it.

I put my hands on my hips. "Great. Got it."

"Look, I gotta go, Cal."

The sound of my nickname breaks me. I let out a bitter laugh. While I call her by hers all the time, she only uses *Cal* when she is frustrated about a bad training session or thinking about her father. When she wants to be alone.

"Okay, go then," I reply. "I'll just go throw myself in a river or something."

She sighs, exasperated. "Callen."

"Rowan."

We stare at each other a second, but it passes like a lifetime. I think of every time we must have touched: hand in hand climbing rooftops when we were children, or swimming in the rivers with Vera and our other friends after sparring days. I want so badly to hold her now. To go back to how it was between us just minutes ago.

She turns abruptly and heads back the way we came. "I'm sorry, Callen. I have to go now."

I follow behind her, giving her a wide berth. *The Sun River,* I think. *That will be the best one to throw myself into.* All at once, Rowan's steps get faster. She throws back the blanket covering the entrance and dust flies into our eyes.

I curse. "Rowan, what the skies—"

"Listen."

Then I hear it, too. Bells.

I count the tolling, ready to decipher whatever signal is coming from the palace, but it's too early in the day for the closing ceremonies. Even if it weren't, the High Summer festival calls for highest bells, the ones that spark curiosity and joy.

These sounds are low, each one a different shade of midnight. In seconds, wings are lifting from the streets in the distance as warriors and warriors-elect answer the call.

Grief and fear drum together in my chest, alternate beats of the same instrument. Rowan turns to me, sunlight making the gold in her eyes glow with fire. Determination.

"We have to go," she says, referring to the Glass Tower. Because of our ranks, she'll be in the back half of the Tower, and I'll be with the other warriors up front. "I'll find you. After. To talk about . . . this."

"Okay," I reply. "Let's go."

She takes her lioness form. Wordlessly, I call my magic and do the same.

There is one thing every Leonodai, every warrior, places more honor on than anything else: loyalty. Loyalty above all. Rowan may not be a warrior in name, but she is one in soul. She must answer the bells' call.

We are being called to our king, and we cannot wait.

◆

Rowan breaks away from me toward where the warriors-elect gather, whereas I go to my place closer to the thrones. I beat my wings forward to slow myself as I cross beneath one of the palace's hundreds of white stone archways.

The Glass Tower never fails to make me feel small. Windows and mirrors line the walls in an alternating pattern. The floor is a polished marble gifted to the Leonodai by the bear-kings of old, before their kind became as reclusive as they are now. The light gray stone nearly glows, appearing to contain a depth of light and swirling patterns like the ocean's surface. The first time I saw it, I was almost afraid to step onto it—it looked as if there was nothing to catch me.

At the end of the hall are the thrones, two high-backed chairs of dark wood inlaid with gold. The thrones themselves are empty. Instead of the royal family, the current sentinels wait for us in front of the dais. Such a sight would usually inspire pride in me, but to interrupt the High Summer festival with bells so low and foreboding . . .

"Hey," calls a voice. Exin comes over to me. "Missed you earlier at the race. Where were you?"

"Dealing with something . . . else," I reply. "I'll tell you later."

He indicates his head toward the sentinels. "Any idea what's going on?"

"No clue."

"Whatever it is, it's enough to worry the citizens," he says. "We're never called like this." Exin glances around, then nods toward a group of warriors-elect who just flew in. "Maybe the king's moved their ceremony up a day?"

"But why?" I reply. "Besides, none of their families are here."

Near us, in a group of seasoned warriors six years my senior, I spot Sethran. He was involved in my third and fourth years of training, and after his classes ended, I sought him out for one-on-one mentoring. With a keen mind for strategy, he doesn't always fight in tournaments, but when he does, he is an absolute spectacle to watch.

Sethran sees me and nods, touching his hand to his shoulder. I do the same, spirit rising at the sign of respect from him. Then I spot Rowan in a group of warriors-elect behind him, and my excitement vanishes.

I should have kept my mouth shut. At least the bells gave us something to focus on. She said she'd find me later, and I have to respect that. If she wants to find me, she will. The tiny spot of pale blue stands out against the dark of her hair. Almost reverently, I touch the matching earring and rub the metal between my fingers.

Then I notice Ox breaking through the crowd toward her. He says something to her and then, with a touch at the small of her back, makes his way over to the other warriors.

It's such a tiny gesture, but it takes all I have to remain upright. Blood pounds in my ears as a chime rings out. Years of conditioning force me to take a knee, and I stare blankly into the depth of the stone that reflects my own stupid face. I was—am—way too late. If she wants to be with Ox, there's nothing I can do about it.

We wait for the king and queen to enter. It won't be the first time I've seen them. The pair make appearances here and there, sometimes simply walking among the citizens in the marketplace. But lately, they have become more private, devoting themselves to raising a strong heir.

The magic threaded throughout the Heliana relies on the vitality of the royal line. Prince Tabrol, as the heir, is referred to by many as the lifeblood of the city. The very city will fall if the royal line fails, so the scholars taught us. Throughout our history, the royal family has been extensive. But sometime in the past forty years, the line began to fail. A royal cousin was killed in battle, another by infection. Kharo's older sister is rumored to have taken her own life, but no one knows for sure.

Prince Kharo, as he was then, wasn't raised to rule. He became king and quickly took his warrior queen. Crown Prince Tabrol's birth three years ago was such an occasion that even training was canceled. Rowan and I spent that day relaxing with our friends, then watching the sunset near the Western Gate. She'd put her head on my shoulder for the first time, but I didn't love her then like I do now.

I could kick my past self for not seeing it sooner.

Shaking myself from my memories, I wait with the others for the king and queen to make their entrance. Only they never do.

Instead, the Ninth Sentinel steps forward, clearing her throat. I glance at Sethran and see the pride in his expression. A sentinel and a warrior in love—they're their own kind of royalty. Sethran told me they've stopped taking walks together in the daytime because they get so many adoring looks.

Sentinel Shirene takes a breath. "Honored warriors, today you have been summoned at the request of Their Graces King Kharo and Queen Laianna, the sovereigns of all Leonodai." Her voice does not shake, but I sense a weight of worry behind it. "The king commands your discretion as to not alarm the citizens of the Heliana. Nothing you are about to learn leaves this room."

For a moment, her eyes flicker to her fellow sentinels, from which she gains some sort of reassurance.

"Two weeks ago, the healers brought to the king's attention an illness among several children for which the usual remedies proved ineffective. The healers and scholars have searched their books and believe that it is a human's disease brought here by the dead birds that have been found throughout the city. As of now, two children have died." Her voice sticks on the last word, and I can guess whatever the Ninth Sentinel is feeling right now is the closest she has ever been to true hate. "The healers treating the children are unaffected, and at this time, we believe it only affects the youngest Leonodai."

I resist looking for Rowan behind me. Her mother runs a school in the northern district. She, Shirene, and Matron Talla love those girls like they are family.

"Horrible as the disease is," Shirene goes on, "there is no reason to panic. The scholars also found record of a cure—a flower—that grows in the heart of Balmora. King Kharo has commanded that twelve teams of four warriors will go into the humans' lands, find the cure, and bring it back. You are to exercise caution to go undetected as long as possible."

Thoughts spin and twist and fight for space in my mind, suffocating me. No one has been sent into Balmora in years, since long before I even began training. It is horrible that kids are sick, but something about this still feels bigger than that.

"The warriors will leave tonight at the eleventh bell, when we won't be seen by the humans," says Shirene. "Each team and their respective commanders will receive additional instructions from the Fourth and Sixth Sentinels. Hammond?"

The Second Sentinel, Hammond, comes up beside her. "We want to avoid an unnecessary panic. We also want to keep the disease from spreading. We know many of you have younger family members. As such, the king has postponed the ceremony for warriors-elect tomorrow."

Instantly, there are murmurs of protest from the warriors-elect, and this time, I don't stop myself from seeking out Rowan.

The look on her face shatters me. That ceremony is all she's wanted for so long.

"Quiet, please," Sentinel Renna calls out. Obedience and training bring the room back to a tense silence. "Upon the teams' return, the warriors-elect will take the oath as normal."

She inclines her hand to Shirene, who unfurls a scroll. The Ninth Sentinel's large, pale blue eyes scan the paper for the briefest of moments. "When I call your name, please stand. Teams will join Sentinels Carrick and Hammond in the antechamber and wait for the remaining warriors to be dismissed before receiving instructions."

Next to me, Exin turns, and we lock eyes. The names and faces of the warriors in our cohort flash in my mind as I think through who might be picked. Exin—he's a swift flyer. *Sethran will go,* I think. I pray to the skies that I'll be on his team.

The sentinels cannot go themselves. During their swearing-in ceremonies, they vow to always remain on the Heliana as a sign of their devotion to the king. It's the same reason they are not allowed to marry while in the king's direct service. So long as he lives, he is their highest priority.

A looming dread creeps into my mind. The Heliana's magic is strongest close to the city, and it drains like water from a leaky bucket when we're too far from it. If I'm chosen, my wings will only carry me so far into Balmora. Eventually, the magic will run out. We will be confined to our human forms and forced to make our way on foot.

The Ninth Sentinel calls out the names.

4

ROWAN

Shirene's voice echoes around the Glass Tower, strangely familiar and unnatural at the same time. "She's the King's Voice," I whisper. "I can't believe it."

"He needed one," Vera replies. "It's a great honor."

I nod my agreement. It's the kind of thing Shirene would never ask for, though. I wonder which of the other sentinels spoke up for her, or if the king chose her blindly.

Teams fill up between hushed cheers. As groups of four file out of the hall together, my heart sinks like a boulder into a river. No warriors-elect are being called. Stealing glances at my peers, I'm met with concerned expressions and furrowed brows. The ones with younger siblings find strength in one another's gazes.

"We should be allowed to go," says a deep voice that is unmistakably Bel's. Skies keep him, he is not great at whispering. "We can take the oath now." I turn my head a tiny bit so he knows I heard him and agree.

My heart pounds. *Ox. Callen. Ox. Callen.* I don't want either of them to go—but how selfish is that, when I would love to be on a team?

"The final team," Shirene calls out, "will be commanded by warrior Sethran."

"Oh no," I whisper.

To Shirene's credit, she doesn't so much as flinch. She's always been cool under pressure. It's one of the things I respect most about her.

"Next, warrior Callen."

Callen stands. He is not so far from me that I don't notice the pale blue earring on his left ear. *No.* My heart lurches—first he tells me he loves me, and now he's leaving.

Skies, he'd better come home. My mother loves him like her own son. *And me?* It's Ox who makes me feel the most alive, the most free . . . but Callen is steady. He has always been there for me. I would have no idea what to do if he died.

I'm too caught up in my own thoughts to realize that Shirene's called the next name. His silhouette is contrasted by the sun, sending his shadow so far that it almost touches my feet. Cheers of support rise at his name. Ox.

"No," I whisper. "Not all of you."

"They'll be okay," Vera says quietly. "They'll be fine."

I swallow, trying in vain to believe she's right. Going into the humans' lands is dangerous enough as a lion. Magic wanes as you go farther inland. It's why most of the battles between Leonodai and the humans happen at sea or near the Cliffs. Fighting in your human form has spelled death for Leonodai since the humans created guns.

Shirene adds Exin as the final member of their team, then closes the scroll. "Remaining warriors and warriors-elect, you are dismissed. Remember, the king compels you to remain quiet. The city knows you were called, but you are not to give the specifics of your fellow warriors' mission. The city's healers and teachers have been made aware so they can help in containing the disease, but no other citizens need know. An urgent need calls warriors to Balmora. That is all."

Teachers, I think, drawing a small sense of reassurance from that knowledge. At least my mother will know, then. At least I'll have someone to talk through this news with.

I list their names in my head again and again. Seth, patient and commanding. Exin, eager and battle-ready. Callen, careful in a fight and my oldest friend. Ox, with his arrows and wit.

They are going. And I am not.

The rest of us are dismissed, and some Leonodai not on team fly out right away, eager to reach loved ones and check if they're all right. Turning, I seek out Bel and head over to him.

"Hey," I say. "I'm with you. Let's go ask if we can take the oath early. All we need is the king to speak the words." I don't need the songs and pageantry, though a part of me aches at the idea of going without them.

"The teams have been named," he replies sullenly. "Look, I know. But we can be useful here. Keeping the citizens calm while still being ready to go if asked is as honorable as being put on a team."

My shoulders drop. "You really think so?"

"Yes, and you know better. The king commanded that warriors be sent," he says. "And warriors are going. We're needed here. If the humans catch one of the teams, then they may launch a counterattack. And without all of the warriors, they'll need us. We can all play a part. Loyalty above all."

I give Bel a smile. "Way to drop our people's motto on me."

"It's going to be fine," he says, with a touch to my shoulder— the Leonodai sign of goodwill. He flies out with the other warriors-elect, but something in my gut makes me linger. Vera waits for me, but I tell her to go on ahead.

Everything Bel said is true, but I can't stop from thinking about one last-ditch effort. The Glass Tower is nearly empty now. A few warriors remain, trading words of encouragement with the sentinels. I see who I'm looking for by the Second Sentinel, her fingers still wrapped around the fateful scroll.

I march determinedly up to my sister. "Lady Shirene."

She turns at her name and frowns. "Warrior-Elect Rowan, I do not have time."

"Lady Shirene, please." I touch my right hand to her shoulder. "Let me join a team."

"What?"

"Please. Just consider it."

Her lips purse, but she exhales in defeat. "Meet me at the Princess Garden. On the hour."

5

SHIRENE

One of the palace attendants offers me a glass of water, and I take it eagerly.

I feel bad for snapping at Ro, but she was out of line. At least when we're like this, sentinel and warrior-elect. I outrank her. Still, Rowan's always been eager to help, even if that help isn't asked for. I put up with her following at my heels for years. Not being on a team must be killing her.

But you're a sentinel, I remind myself. My loyalty is to the king and the citizens first. Besides, Rowan's not the only one in pain.

I look over at Seth.

His arms are crossed as he waits with his team. Callen keeps close next to him, his hand to his chin in concentration. The other two, warriors Ox and Exin, speak quietly to each other, the former taking in the other teams and the latter with his hand firmly on his broadsword.

The four of them will do well together, I reassure myself. *Seth will be just fine.* When Sentinel Renna presented her thoughts on the teams, she carefully described each individual's skills to the king. As head of all the warriors' training, she spoke with a level of certainty that no one else on the Heliana could match.

I had wanted to mimic her confidence today in my own speech to the warriors—but my feet ache, and it feels like a lifetime since I didn't have bags under my eyes. Too many urgent meetings with the king, the healers, and the scholars. Too many hurried steps from one end of the palace to the next. Too many haunting cries from mothers and fathers whose children are overheating with fever.

Sentinels Carrick and Hammond quiet the group and call everyone to attention while Renna makes her way around the room and hands out scrolls to each of the commanders.

"Each of these contains a detailed map of Balmora, as we best know it," says Hammond. "Still, you will be going farther than that."

"Lord Hammond, sir," calls a voice. Warrior Io, with her shaved head and fierce glare, gets his attention. "How many children are sick?"

Hammond pauses a moment. "There are fifteen presently in the healers' care."

A hushed gasp sweeps the room, and I feel the sting of Hammond's words strike close to home. Literally.

All my training couldn't prepare me for the sight of the familiar Storm's End insignia on the dead girls' shoes as their places in the sick room were cleaned up. The Heliana has three schools, each with a slightly different approach to care and lessons. My mother, Matron Talla, ran Storm's End, which focused on the arts like music, pottery, and writing. For Rowan and me, that care was a way of life until we were each thirteen and followed in our father's footsteps to warrior training. Storm's End is *home*. I know sure as the skies that Mother is strong enough to cope with almost anything. Anything but watching her girls die.

Hammond continues. "Also on the scroll is a drawing of the cure you seek. I know it does not appear to be much," he says, "but the scholars are sure of its power. They say each child will need a 'petal a year, a stem a season.' We don't know how many children will get sick, so when you find the cure, you're to collect as much of it as you are able."

"What of the crown prince, my Sentinel Hammond?" I recognize Callen's voice and find him standing next to Sethran. Callen shifts his stance, arms folded and head held high. "Skies keep us, but the prince is young. What will be done if he, too, gets the disease?"

Hammond considers this. "Your question is one that I'm sure many others share. But to put your mind at ease, the crown prince is not sick." The very walls seem to exhale. "Crown Prince Tabrol has been quarantined in the royals' private chambers. Every precaution is being taken."

Callen bows his head again and steps back. I wonder how Rowan feels about him being on a team. The day they met changed our lives—he and Rowan took to each other like flowers and summer rain. Part of me always suspected he was in love with her, but the rumors of the Warriors' Hall travel far. I would have heard of it by now.

It's Carrick's turn to speak. The red-haired sentinel goes on to explain the flight pattern the warriors will take. Noam told us the cure used to thrive on the southeastern side of Balmora, and that is where we are sending the teams. "We have reason to believe the flower may be inside the human city called Ramsgate," says Carrick. "Should you not find the cure outside the city, you are to sneak inside. But do your best to remain undetected. We want to give the humans no reason to provoke us or the other kingdoms."

Again, we leave Noam out of the conversation. It was Renna who had first suggested keeping him out of our message to the warriors and the other kingdoms, but I seconded the plan. The city needed focus and simplicity. There was no point in relighting embers of gossip that had been put out months ago.

Hammond and Carrick take more questions from the teams.

"How long will the journey be?" someone asks.

"We estimate no more than ten days' time," Carrick replies. "Five days to find it, five days to return. You should pace yourselves accordingly to ensure you last the whole journey."

More questions ring out, but I know the answers already, and my gaze wanders to Seth. He knows the weight of responsibility he and the teams carry. Callen was right to worry about the price, but if the disease begins to strike adults as well . . . At the rate it kills, our people could be decimated in a matter of weeks. I shouldn't think like that, but I can't help it.

When the questions ebb, Carrick and Hammond dismiss the warriors to a mixture of murmurs and hushed whispers of reassurance.

"Lyreina, Shirene," says Sentinel Renna. "Stay here and give the teams support as needed, but don't linger long. Afterward, make your presence known to the citizens. It'll help keep the people calm to see us enjoying the festival, for however long we can." She exhales, straightening up farther, though I know she's been awake at least as long as I have, if not longer.

When she goes, I walk an arc through the room. The team leaders speak to their reports about strategy. Seeing so many warriors ready for battle eases my worry. We have trained for this. They'll be fine.

"Sentinel Shirene," calls Seth, and I am undone.

"Warrior Sethran," I say, using his full name purposely. "What is it?"

He bows his head. "Congratulations on being named the King's Voice."

"This is hardly a moment for flattery, warrior." I exhale with a smile. "You have to ask me a question."

"Is the cure what the scholars say it is?" Seth asks.

"Skies, I hope so."

"And will you wait for me?"

I can't keep back my smile. "Yes, of course."

Seth smiles, and I try to memorize the kindness in his eyes, the stubble at his chin, and the thin scar near his left eye that I gave him early into our training days. I felt awful about it back then, but now that I've traced it with my fingertips on many moonlit nights, I thank the skies he didn't take care of the wound as the healers instructed.

"Will you have a moment," he asks, "before we leave?"

"I have to go into the city now," I say. *Well, the Princess Garden first.* "But there should be time. We will have time." To say goodbye and to make him promise to come home at any cost.

The love of my life smiles. "We will have time."

6

Rowan

I go to the spot right away, though I know Shirene won't join me for a while. I need answers.

Sheltered from the ever-present winds, the Princess Garden is a beloved place for Leonodai. Today, families wander through the lush greenery while couples find solace in the garden's shady alcoves. Sprigs of violet flowers jut into the air between dots of soft yellow blossoms. Pale green stalks reach their fingers skyward, their sturdy blooms curling outward.

I take a seat on a low stone wall that divides one part of the garden from another, shifting so that I remain in the sunlight. My mind spins as I try to build up my argument for Shirene, just as children build up castles in the coarse sand on the banks of the Crescent River. I have to go with a team. I have to do something other than sit still.

I wait for the better part of an hour. Finally, Shirene appears, stepping around the corner with the fine fabric of her dress flowing like water behind her. We share our parents, but that's where the resemblance between me and my sister ends. Her fine, pale blond hair falls straight to her shoulders, while my dark brown waves go nearly all the way down my back. Where she can hold her tongue, I never want to. With seven years between us, we aren't as close as some sisters are, but she is all I have.

"Shirene," I say, the desperation rising in my voice as I hop off my makeshift seat. I don't use her title. Here, she is just my sister. Here, she is my last chance. "Put me on a team. I can help."

"We have to do as the king commands," she replies.

I wave my hands, like, *Come on.* "We both know those names did not come from the king. You and the other sentinels know the warriors better. You paired everyone in teams that worked well together. Was Renna in charge of it? I noticed her at training this week." It wasn't hard to spot the older sentinel's uniform as we ran drills. I hadn't thought much of it until now.

I had figured it all out while I waited. Beyond having compatible skill sets, Callen would follow Seth anywhere. It felt like every time we hung out in the past months, he'd talk about some amazing thing Seth had taught him and how much it was fueling the fire of his goal to become a sentinel someday. And while Exin may be Callen's friend, Exin and Ox are cousins, and family ties go far. They all balance one another. *Or at least they will, so long as Callen and Ox's feelings for me don't come up. . . .*

"There are plenty of other teams just as good among the warriors-elect," I say.

"Rowan—"

"I could go with Vera, Bel, and Maurin," I say. "Renna can pick a warrior to lead us, if she wants. You just have to ask the king to let us go."

Shirene exhales hard. "I already did."

"What?"

"It was the Second Sentinel's idea, actually, not mine. But I supported his motion. The sentinels know the warriors-elect are ready. But the king has much to consider. Nothing like this has ever happened before, and we all know he is thinking of Tabrol. The king is sending the best we have."

I scoff. "And we're not the best?"

"Skies, don't be so selfish, Ro. You know what I mean."

"Yeah, I do. But what if—"

"I know, Ro." The finality in her tone gets to me. "What if."

It's one thing if *I'm* worried about the city, our people. It's a whole other thing to see the fear in Shirene's eyes and to know that my sister is just like me. Afraid.

"Please," I say. "You have no idea how it feels to be helpless right now."

Shirene takes my hand and gives it an encouraging squeeze. Her fingers are cold. Look, "I'm sorry. But if you heard what Noam said of the disease, you would know that we don't have time to question what's already been decided. We have to send the teams we have right now."

"Who's Noam?" I ask reflexively, but already something is dawning in my mind. Why did I know that name—*oh*. "Wait, Noam? The sentinel who deserted? The one whose place you took. What does he have to do with anything?"

Shirene curses, and my curiosity soars. I haven't heard her swear since the first time I cursed in front of our mother, and I confessed it was Shirene who taught me how.

"Skies. Okay. Let me explain, and don't interrupt." My sister's glossy hair moves in waves as she talks. "There is a human village in the mountains of Balmora. Not many humans go themselves because it's too far. After he left, Noam sought refuge there. The humans welcomed him, and he's lived there ever since."

I think back to the announcements the sentinels had given last year as the search for Noam's replacement was underway. "But the sentinels said they weren't ever able to find him."

"They couldn't tell anyone they had," my sister replies. "It would have created more gossip. They—we—let Noam stay in his exile until now. Noam told us and the king what the disease was. How *bad* it may get, Rowan."

I lean back. "How can you trust him?"

"At the end of the day, he is Leonodai," she says. "He knows that, still. Otherwise, he wouldn't have been so eager to help us when we went to him for answers." Her tone gives her away. When she's thinking like a sentinel, Shirene knows to bottle up. But with me, she forgets.

"You're worried," I say.

"Of course I'm worried," she fires back. "Children are dying." She straightens, asserting the few inches of height she holds over me. "Just . . . keep quiet for a few days, okay? Noam's role in this may come to light after we are through this crisis. Not before. Can you manage that?"

"Hey," I reply, "I'm not stupid, Shirene. If you weren't supposed to tell me about him, then that's on you. But yes, I can keep a secret. I'm a warrior, too."

"No, you're not. I am a sentinel, and you are a warrior-*elect*."

A lifetime of shrinking back against Shirene's anger takes hold of me. For a moment, it's like we're kids again and she's telling me to stop following her around, to leave her alone.

She turns from me. "I shouldn't have even had this conversation. Don't share what you've heard until you hear it announced formally. That's an order, Warrior-Elect."

"Understood, Sentinel," I reply before immediately turning and launching myself off the garden wall, taking my lioness form before Shirene gets a chance to see me cry.

My sister has never pulled rank on me before. Ever. I guess being a sentinel is more important than our shared blood. *It's her duty,* my mind whispers, and I know that's true.

But in my chest, my heart drags toward the sea. I hardly see her anymore, and when I finally have her for a moment, this is what I get? What kind of person is she becoming?

For a moment, I contemplate going back, but when I look around, Shirene's already gone. *Fine. Go back to doing errands for the king.*

I swoop down low and take my human form on the Heroes' Path. The paved trail twists along the sheltered side of the palace ridge, where the strong northerly winds can't reach it. It's here we keep records of our past, both in statues and inscriptions in bronze. Citizens, especially older ones, walk up the path as I walk down. Some carry flowers, food, and other baubles in their arms to leave them at the feet of the great Leonodai who came before us.

I know each statue and story well. King Exin brandishes a long spear that points toward Balmora, an ever-present sign of defiance to the humans. Scholar Islaine's hand—made of pure gold—shines from wear. She copied the entirety of the Leonodai's oldest texts so that they'd withstand the test of time. To this day, new scholars in training still gather at her statute to touch her hand as a blessing.

I pause in the shadow of a woman dressed in the simple, practical clothes of a healer. Queen Rowyn, my namesake. Mother says she always preferred the other spelling. Queen Rowyn is known as the Soul of the Heliana, a queen who aided her husband as his mind deteriorated early into their reign. Loyal to the end, she is said to have humbly dressed as a healer so the king would not fear her after he'd forgotten her name, their love, and any echo of his former power.

A touch on my shoulder pulls me from my reverie. "Callen."

"Hi," he replies. Strands of light brown hair have escaped the bun at the back of his head, leaving him looking as defeated as I feel. "I know you said you would find me. But that was . . . before."

"I know." I turn away from Queen Rowyn and her watchful gaze and meander down the path. "It's okay. What did the sentinels have to say?"

"We have until the eleventh bell," Callen replies, following. "But I saw you didn't fly off with the rest of the warriors-elect. I wanted to see if you were all right."

Skies keep him, I know in my gut that Callen is not talking about our exchange in the grotto earlier. It isn't the first time we've had a fight—if you can call what happened a fight—and it isn't the first time we've both silently agreed to ignore it because of where we are or who we are around. He just wants to know how I'm doing after the news.

"Of course I'm not okay," I say, then lower my voice to a whisper. "How could I be?"

"I know." He gazes out at the city below us. The Heliana's gentle arches, curved pathways, and pale stone faces make her glow in the sunlight. Our city is beautiful, but the sight of it doesn't make me forget the silent threat currently threading through her streets.

Callen shakes his head. "I can't wrap my mind around it. Have you heard from your mother? Did she already know?"

"I'm going to go to Storm's End now," I reply. "That's all I can do. Because of a stupid oath I haven't taken, I have to stay here and . . . what, do nothing? This is a chance, Callen. This is what I've been training for."

"I'm sure the sentinels have their reasons, Ro," he says. "They always think things out."

"Well, they didn't think out this one," I mutter. "How are you doing? Did they tell you how long you'll be gone?"

"Ten days, at least. No one's been that far into Balmora in a century. Since before Garradin."

We both look outward onto the city. My heart aches.

"I'm scared," I say. "The people have no idea what's coming."

The truth comes so easily with Callen. Years of having no boundaries with each other will do that. *Well, you kept some boundaries,* I think, trying in vain to push it from my mind again. *There are bigger things to worry about than your best friend telling you he loves you.*

Except that the same best friend is right beside me.

"Rowan, any one of us could die," Callen says. "If I don't make it back—"

"Don't say it," I cut in. "You're coming back. Everyone is coming back."

"But you know what I'm getting at."

I do. My pulse quickens as my stomach spins like a child's toy top. There's almost no telling how far they'll have to travel and if they'll come back. I don't want to say the wrong thing, but I have to say something.

"Just never stop trying to come back," I start. "Okay? No matter what happens over there. Because, skies alive, Callen, if you don't come back, I'm going to go there and find you myself."

"And give me hell for it."

"And give you hell for it," I echo.

A heart-wrenching roar sounds from above us. It's another healer, different from the one I saw this morning, and he's flying fast for the palace. Fear weighs down my stomach as if I've been swallowing stones.

"I have to go," I say. "My mother will need me."

He nods. "Okay."

"Okay. Great." I step forward, but something stops me. Maybe it's our ancestors' eyes on us. Maybe it's something else.

Turning, I touch his shoulder. His armor warms beneath my fingertips as I linger. On any other day, it would mean nothing. Today, it's all my heart can muster without making a bigger mess of a problem that needs to wait until the sick children are better. Until we have the time and space to work things out.

I step back and shift into my lioness form, flying high and far away from him before I can hear him say anything else. Before I have time to wonder why I am so reluctant to say goodbye.

7

CALLEN

I watch her go and feel bits of myself fraying, unraveling so far that they won't ever be fixed. Skies alive, I can't die on Balmora now knowing the last word I spoke to the most important person in the world to me was *okay*.

I have to give her time and space, for real this time. And nothing says space like the miles of open ocean and enemy territory that will keep us apart for over a week. With a quick touch to my blue stone earring, I take my lion form and circle the city, heading to the Warriors' Hall. The massive, U-shaped building's glass roof shines in the sunlight as I get closer. I tilt my wings and aim for the second floor, where my room and the rest of my cohorts' rooms are.

As I land in one of the Hall's open entryways, I catch a glimpse of Ox and Exin leaning over the railing opposite my room. Ox sees me and gives a polite nod. I return it, a feeling in my stomach twisting like I've eaten something bad.

He's a strong fighter, I remind myself. Warriors are trained in all manner of weapons, and Ox favors a bow. An archer is a solid asset to have if we encounter humans and want to avoid an outright battle as the sentinels instructed. I have no doubts about his loyalty to the king or to the city, but if I could pick a different member for my team, I would.

I glance down at the lush greenery and reflection pool on the Heliana's lowest level, the Underbelly. A handful of warriors-elect linger in the walkways, their heads low as they sulk together. The excitement about getting to move up a level must have soured. I don't envy the frustration every warrior-elect must be feeling.

I go into my room, drawing the bolt firmly across the door behind me. I wash my face and body, then re-dress in a clean uniform. The long cobalt tunic falls to my knees, going over my underclothes and pants and then secured in place by a belt. The open triangular cuts on either side leave room for my legs to move freely. Intricately embroidered wings and feathers line the hems, and at the center is a re-creation of the Glass Tower, just as light hits it. Sunlight in the form of gold thread spills out from it.

It's similar in style to the warrior-elect uniform, though theirs lack any decoration and are made in a rougher cloth. This uniform has to be earned, and I would earn it twice over on a mission like this.

I collapse back onto my bed with a sigh. Someone knocks at my door, maybe to congratulate me or say goodbye. Either way, I pretend I'm not here. My mind still echoes with the sound of Rowan's disbelief in the grotto, and the pain of knowing I embarrassed myself for nothing.

At least I have the mission to focus on now. Find the cure, bring it back.

The journey will fill my thoughts, and the days apart will give Rowan and me the space to move past what happened. Best I can hope for now is that we'll go back to just being friends. We never have to talk about it again.

My pounding heart says otherwise.

8

Rowan

The door of Storm's End is locked when I arrive. My hand rests on the round iron handle a moment. All my life, these doors have been open, even at night. I didn't think my mother still had the key.

Luckily, I know of the side entrance through the school kitchen. Making my way around the side of the building, I brush aside some overgrown vines to find the latch on the gate. I scoot way down the small alley between the school and the adjacent building, then let myself in.

The kitchen of my childhood feels smaller as I cross its terracotta tiles. The tables and counter have been swept completely clean, and the arched windows overlooking the courtyard have been let open wide.

Past the kitchen are the classrooms. The halls of Storm's End usually ring with laughter and songs, but today, the sound of my sandals on the ground is the only haunting melody.

I slow as I near the last room by the staircase that leads to my mother's private living area. The nap room is lined with six beds on either side. Plush rugs and blankets are normally strewn about, despite my mother and her assistants' attempts to teach the children to be tidy. Heart low, I step inside.

Each bed is made up and the pillows fluffed, ready to send the Storm's End classes into sweet dreams. Well-loved stuffed toys are delicately propped up on some of them.

"Mother," I whisper. This is a new pain. My mother loves

to teach, loves to have kids under her wing. But now I envision her fussing with the pillows and blankets, unsure of how to fill her time without the kids actually there. Storm's End is never supposed to be this immaculate, or this quiet.

Without waiting another moment, I turn and climb the stairs two at a time. I knock twice on her office door before entering. When she doesn't answer, I let myself in.

Talla An'Irina stands with her gaze turned to the balcony. Just as I carry her name, she carries her mother's. It is the Leonodai custom to trace lineages through matriarchs. Light glances and twists off the glass panes of the balcony window as the summer wind makes the curtains flutter.

"Mother?" I say, and she turns to me finally. We meet halfway across the room and linger in a firm embrace as long as we can. "When did they tell you?" I ask, my question muffled in the folds of her shawl.

"All of the children were sent home yesterday afternoon for the holiday," she replies. "The sentinels came by here this morning to let me know not to call them back."

"The sentinels said there were two children who died," I say. "Were they . . . ?"

"Yes," she says. The crack in her voice breaks me in two. "They were both my girls. Such sweet kids."

I tighten my arms around her, but it's she who lets go first. My mother keeps quiet for a moment longer, then beckons me close. She draws her arm through mine and pulls me in tightly. I lay my head on her shoulder.

"We haven't been preparing for this," my mother says. "We've been preparing for a war where every Leonodai has a lust for battle and the desire to protect what is ours. We haven't readied for one where little ones die."

I frown. "This could help us fight. To remember how much is at stake."

"Or it could blind warriors to reason," she counters. "Desperate people make bad decisions. I'm glad the king is keeping warriors-elect here. He's being careful in case we are attacked."

I open my mouth to retort but close it again when I realize just how right she is. It's the same thing Bel said in the Tower. She turns from me, and I imagine the wheels of her mind flying ahead to what she must do.

"We must burn their things. Their blankets, their spare clothes. Just in case." Her gray-streaked hair, piled onto her head and fixed with a beaded cord, shows her age, but it doesn't shake the strength rooted in my mother's soul.

The fourth bell tolls. A flash of light illuminates the room as the sun aligns with the mirrors in the Glass Tower. The light melts away my other thoughts. The beams tell the humans that we are here. We are strong. And we are not going anywhere.

My mother strides toward the doors. "We have work to do."

❧

Out in the school's courtyard, I arrange some heavy blocks of wood into a pile. Beside me are clothes and blankets and even a stuffed sheep that is clearly well-loved. It was the last of these that broke my mother. When she brought out the girls' belongings, the doll rested on top. My mother handed it all to me and let out a shuddering breath. "Burn the basket, too."

I gather my resolve and strike the flint against stone. Sparks rush out and catch against the dried reeds at the base of the firewood. I work quickly and silently, moving between the courtyard and nap room to make sure nothing is missed.

Mother leaves to go consult with the other leaders of the Heliana's schools, Oak's Heart and Moon's Shadow. When word of the disease breaks, they will not have time to themselves for many days and nights. Worried parents will need their questions answered. Grieving ones will need much more.

Smoke drifts from the firepit, stinging my eyes. I take a step back as the small folds and embroidery of a dress are engulfed in black. When it's all but ash, I add more wood and more of the girls' belongings. As I watch several pairs of small shoes burn, I fight the nausea in my stomach. A disease that only kills children. I didn't know anything under the skies could be so cruel.

Heat kisses my skin until I'm sweating, but I don't stop until the possessions are all gone.

The coo of birds carries from above me. Their talons curl around the windowsill as they huddle together and try to keep out of the twisting smoke. I focus on a ruddy-colored bird on one of the perches above me and start to call it. Though their Knowledge has been gone for centuries, ancient magic connects Leonodai to all birds. The practice of capturing short messages in magic and sending them on borrowed wings is taught to Leonodai children early. A lump forms in my throat as I realize that practicing with the birds may very well be what exposed the children to the disease in the first place.

It takes a tug of magic to link the bird's mind to my own. The bird turns and focuses on me, a high-pitched *whrrl* sounding from its small chest. A low whistle from me seals it.

"Ox," I tell it, picturing his face clearly in my mind as I do. Then I add my message, "The rooftop. Ninth bell."

I snap the connection like a taut thread. The bird ruffles its wings, and then it goes.

9

CALLEN

The lack of sleep from the night before gets to me and I doze off. I'm awoken by the sound of fourth bell. With a stretch, I sit up and give my room a once-over.

There's little else I'll need for the mission besides my armor. The sentinels will have food and other supplies prepared for us, but I will need a cloak for camouflage as much as warmth. I had to be ready to face the enemy, as well as the elements.

Thumbing through my modest closet, I settle on one lined with thick wool from Vyrinterra. The horselords take extreme care of the other animals there and only sell a limited number of these cloaks per year. My father got it for me as a gift, but there hadn't been any heart in the gesture. It didn't matter that he drank most of our family's money away after having been relieved from his duties as a general following a catastrophic loss against the human soldiers five years ago. What mattered was that I looked like a general's son, the kind who would prove himself enough to make the city forget about the losses we suffered that day.

For a moment, I contemplate going by the palace to say goodbye to him but quickly decide against it. Since starting my training, I've lived in the Warriors' Hall while he and my mother live in the palace's lower levels—the last echoes of my father's former station. My parents haven't come looking for me after I took the oath last year. They had stayed in the back. *At least they came,* I tell myself, and not for the first time. *They were there.*

My parents still hear the palace news. They probably already know where I'm going. If they'd wanted to say goodbye, they would have sought me out by now.

Besides, they're not who I really want to say goodbye to.

After determindly rustling through a storage trunk, I manage to find a piece of parchment. I start with her name.

If there's any chance I don't return, I want there to be a testament to how I feel. Something she can hang on to that isn't just memories. I scratch out words, cursing under my breath that I didn't think out what I wanted to say before starting. Halfway through, I remember to try to keep the scrawl that Rowan's teased me about for years neat and legible.

The light outside starts to turn from yellow to gold as the sun sets, but there are still hours until the eleventh bell.

When the ink dries, I seal the letter with wax and fly toward Storm's End. The afternoon's festivities are in full swing despite the interruption of the bells. Below me, the citizens light lamps across every alleyway and in every window, keeping with tradition. The light of the summer sun must last as long as possible.

The windows at Storm's End are similarly lit with candles and wide open, even those of the Matron Talla's private quarters. Landing softly on the matron's balcony, I take my human form. Straightening my armor, I knock twice to announce my presence.

"Come in."

Inside, the air laced with a citrus scent, emanating from candles. Flowers on the mantelpiece. And books—the matron of Storm's End kept a library in here, though most of the books are too lengthy to keep the attention of the children in her charge, but not her daughter. Rowan has practically worn through the volumes containing legends of the heroes of old taming beasts of sun and sky to create the world.

Matron Talla leans on her desk, her back hunched. Her hand rests at her lips, as if she is fervently wishing for the right thing to say. She doesn't rise in greeting or, truly, do very much at all. Light reflects in her eyes as they stare blankly at the door that leads to the rest of the school.

My chest tightens as I put it together. "They were your girls. The ones who died."

"And another four of mine were quarantined this afternoon."

"I'm very sorry." Tentatively, I place the letter on her desk near a glass orb meant to hold down papers on windy days.

"Thank you," she replies. Finally looking to me, Matron Talla frowns, bemused. So much of Rowan's stubborn, confident demeanor comes from her mother—and I see it now. "What's that?"

"A letter for Rowan." I swear inwardly as I realize I might have made a huge mistake. "She's not here, is she?"

"She is downstairs still, I think, getting rid of . . . of the girls' things. I just returned. Why? I can call her up."

"No, that's okay." *Rowan didn't say anything about the grotto. Talla would mention it.* "I was hoping you'd give it to her if . . . if I don't come back."

"They are sending teams, then." She sees my look and waves her hand idly. "I knew what the sentinels were planning. Is Rowan on a team?"

"No, ma'am. They are only sending warriors."

Matron Talla exhales a laugh. "I imagine that didn't sit well with her."

I match her smile. "No, it didn't."

"When do you leave?"

"After the sun goes down. We don't want the humans to know we're coming."

"And you know where the cure is?"

I nod. "We know where to start looking."

"That's good," she says with another sigh. She gets up and opens her arms for a hug. "Come here, Callen," Talla says sternly, in the way all Leonodai mothers do when they want your attention.

Like any good Leonodai child, I obey. Her embrace has the strength of a hurricane, and I let it rock me for just a moment.

She lets go, but keeps both hands on my shoulders. "You're a fine warrior, Callen. And a good soul. If it were up to me, I would welcome you as my son." She laughs at my embarrassed look. "Oh, I've known you loved her since before you did, I imagine. It's not up to me what happens next, but I've always thought of you like my own. I'll keep hoping for your safe return, no matter what." A wry smile crosses her face. "If anything, for my earring back."

My hand flies to the stone as if it burned me. "If you—"

"No, no. Keep it," she says, drawing me in for another hug. "Just bring it back."

"Thank you, Talla. That means a great deal to me."

"Your parents did you a disservice, not keeping you close."

"It only meant that I had more time here. You always welcomed me." Lots of children on the Heliana run amok among houses. When everyone knows everyone, it's hard to get lost. Still, those children had parents who would check if their sons came home from playing. Mine never did.

Matron Talla reaches up on her tiptoes to kiss the top of my head. "Come home, Callen," she says. "That is all I ask. Come home."

10

Rowan

The rooftop of the Warriors' Hall glows from below, save for in one spot. At the junction where the Hall meets the palace ridge, the builders used stone instead of glass to connect the two.

It's there that I meet up with Ox. He's already there when I arrive, even though the ninth bell is still sounding. With his eyes fixed on the stars, I am sure he doesn't see me approaching, but the sound of my wings gives me away.

"Hi," he says, waiting for me to take my human form and sit down next to him before putting a muscled arm around my shoulders. He kisses my cheek. "You smell like smoke."

"The sick kids," I answer. "Two were from Storm's End. They didn't make it."

"Oh. I'm so sorry."

"Thanks," I say. "I was helping my mother make sure it doesn't spread to the other girls. They'll all be staying at home for a while, but better to be safe."

He smiles. "You look pretty."

"The scent of smoke?" I say, tugging at my clothes. "That does it for you?"

"No," Ox replies with a nudge. "Just . . . you. You worked hard all day, and yet you still have that light in your eyes."

"That's the starlight reflecting," I reply.

"Not all of it."

I frown. "You seem very sure."

"I counted all the stars while I waited," he says. "There's an extra one in your eyes."

Skies. Alive. Ox makes me feel so light, like one of the stars themselves. "Okay, fine, you win." Gingerly, I lean back and lie down on the chilly stone. Ox does the same, finding my hand as he does.

A clear summer's night and a handsome boy holding my hand. Any other time, I would feel giddy, or at least content with having him close. Instead, I feel I only want to look at the stars—to dive deeper into them, higher and higher.

Right then, I miss my father. He would have known what to say in this situation. *Well, not this exact one,* I think, feeling the warmth of my fingers interlaced with Ox's. But he would have known how to help me when feeling split in two, while pressed by the weight of the secret the sentinels have asked us to keep.

"Are you afraid?" I ask.

"Warriors don't ask each other about fear." His tone tells me he isn't exactly serious, but he isn't totally wrong. If anyone else were around, I have no doubt that Ox would lie—but here, in our secluded place, it's just us. Just Ox and me.

So he tells the truth. "Yes."

"I should be going," I say. "I hate that I'm not."

"I know." He props himself up on his elbow. "It's not fair."

"I'm a day shy of being a warrior. A day."

Ox goes quiet. With the glow from the glass rooftop and from the stars above, I can see my reflection in his eyes. "I can't decide," he says finally. "I don't know if I should be angry you are not going or relieved that you will be safe."

I sit up, too. "I don't want to be safe, Ox. I want to be fighting."

"I know, I know. And you should be.

"You have to find it."

"I will."

"The humans have guns," I whisper.

"Sure, humans have guns," he says. "But we have a city to fight for. And I have a lioness who is braver and stronger than I am who I must come back to."

He leans in, and I meet him halfway. His hand curves around my head as his lips press urgently into mine. Nothing held back—nothing ever is with Ox.

When we pull apart, he tilts his head skyward. "Race you to the moon?"

"What?"

"Balmora's no more than a quarter hour's flight. Besides, we won't be flying once we get there." His expression softens. "One last flight. You and me."

I stand in response, and he grins as I help him up. "Fine," I say. "Only if you promise it isn't the last."

With a swift kiss on my cheek, he steps back and takes his lion form. I'm right on his heels. Stretching my wings into the cool grace of the night, we soar directly skyward. The Heliana shrinks to a dark diamond beneath us before being obscured entirely by moonlight-kissed clouds. Ox slows to let me catch up, but then we're back to it—wings beating in near unison as the temperature around us slips from chilly to cold, to nearly unbearable. The clouds form a blanket below us until it's as if nothing exists but us—us and the stars.

The pinpricks of light are out in force, as if they had readied themselves for us to be here. A thicker streak of light blue cuts from one end of the sky to the next. Some say it's the entrance to the Endless Skies; others say it's only the start of the path to them.

I close my eyes as the night air rolls over me. The Endless Skies are a myth, a story like that of the Wise Horse and the Heron, or the legendary Exin the Great for whom Callen's friend is named. Still, it is a beautiful thought. That this life isn't the end, but the short wait until eternity.

The air gets short in my lungs, and my magic tugs at me impatiently—the Heliana's power can only reach so far. Wordlessly, we both dive. Every inch of me feels dizzy with joy and the feeling of unmitigated freedom. Anything's possible up here.

Ox and I fly in lazy spirals around each other, twisting closer and closer as we fall. Every time we pass each other, I see an unrelenting wildness in his expression. He loves this as much as I do.

But wildness knows its limits, as do we. We are warriors first, and when Ox dives back down for the Heliana, I follow. He has to be ready by eleventh bell, and despite his confidence, I know the flight to Balmora won't be as easy when he is carrying the hopes of the city on his wings.

Worse yet, there is nothing I can do to help carry that weight.

11

CALLEN

Leonodai don't believe in ghosts. Ghosts and fairies are for the bearkings and their lore. Still, as I fly over the Heliana one last time with the echoes of the tenth bell swirling through the air, I feel as though I am already gone.

I sail through the night air as easily as a fish in water. The stars dress the sky in a glitter of silver and blue, bright against the sliver of the moon. The summer air is just the right amount of cool. By the time I see the sun rise, I'll be far from here. Far from the lights and laughter of the marketplace, far from the soothing rush of the rivers.

Far from home.

Voices carry from the open arches of the Glass Tower as I land and take my human form —I'm not the only one to arrive early. Another friend from my core group, Jai, leans against the doorframe, his longbow strung across his back. He gives me a nod as I approach. There's something bundled in his hands.

"Say all your goodbyes?" he asks, giving me a quick hug in support.

"As many as I need to," I reply. "What's that?"

"A gift from my little sister," he replies cheerily, raising the small doll he has clutched in his hand. "I don't think she understood what was happening. But she understood that I was leaving." For a second, I catch him tightening his fingers around the doll. *She could be the next one sick,* I realize. I can practically see the thought as it winds and twists around my friend's mind.

"Skies keep you, Jai," I say. "Meet you back at the Warriors' Hall. Last one back has to kiss Scholar Orr."

A small smile. Scholar Orr is as infamous for his age as he is for his endlessly long lectures on Leonodai history. "You're on, Cal. Thanks."

I spot Sethran across the room and walk over to join him. Over his cobalt robes, Sethran wears a leather breastplate with the Leonodai insignia embroidered on it in gold thread to denote his status. Beside him, Ox sits on the ground with his back to the wall, hands resting on his knees.

"Is Jai okay?" Sethran asks, touching his fist to my shoulder in respect.

"About as okay as the rest of us, Commander," I reply, returning the gesture. "Waiting on Exin?"

"And on the signal. We have time." Sethran inclines his head at a group of sentinels at the center of the Tower near the thrones. Sentinel Lyreina pushes back her short dark hair as she goes over the map of Balmora with warrior Io, while sentinels Renna and Carrick make rounds among the warriors. There is an unusual slowness to Renna's steps. As lead trainer of the warriors-elect, she's known everyone by name for years. But it's not the thought of fondness that makes me worry.

It's the thought that maybe, in her mind, she's saying goodbye.

The Ninth Sentinel stands apart from the rest of them, keeping a watchful gaze on the room. Shirene and I used to eat dinners together at Storm's End along with Rowan and her mother— back then, it was a reprieve from warrior training for Shirene and a glimpse at the future for me. Shirene wasn't one to talk a lot, but she was always receptive to my questions about her training. Unlike her sister, Shirene fits into the city's expectations like a key to a lock. I was not surprised when she was chosen as sentinel, and it is reassuring to know someone similar in age to me can make it.

The sentinels call all of the commanders over for a moment. Ox watches Sethran as he goes, then clears his throat.

"Hey, Callen," he says. His voice is steady, though I can't shake the feeling that this moment was rehearsed. "I have a feeling you don't like me very much. And I think I know why." *Gee, I wonder.* "But we're on this team together, and I know you want to save those sick kids as much as I do. Loyalty above all. Out there, we won't have time for anything else."

Anything else—like the girl we'd both fight for. I don't want to hear her name on his lips or think about who he's spent his last hours with . . . but he is right. If our team is to succeed and find the cure, it means working with—and not against—each other.

Rowan has to stay here, both in heart and in person.

"Loyalty above all," I reply, offering my hand. "The mission comes first."

He takes it. "Thank you, Callen."

"Skies alive, you two are making me look bad," Exin cuts in as he walks over. He claps a hand on my shoulder. "We had until eleventh bell, didn't we?"

The four of us have all leaned into our strengths: Exin's brought his broadsword, which I know he favors. With Ox's bow, Sethran's longsword, my axe, and all of us with shields and secondary weapons to rely on in a pinch, we're a well-balanced team. We can do this.

Our commander returns with waterskins and small satchels for each of us. The shiny buckles on each are imprinted with special markings that told me these were no ordinary bags. These had been crafted with magic in mind, and would transform to suit our lion forms as our armor and uniforms did. The type was hard to come by, unless you were a healer or messenger. The Sentinels are giving us the best of the best.

Inside, dried meat and fruit are packed in expertly alongside herbs for pain and wound care. "Remember, the sentinels say even a small amount of the cure will do," he says. "'A petal a year, a stem a season.' A six-year-old would only need six petals."

"Just one flower," Ox notes. "That much for each child can't be hard to find, right, sir?"

"Skies, I hope not," our commander replies.

We wait for the rest of the stragglers in a hushed, humming quiet. Voices carry and find one another, trading words of strength. I catch myself hunching and straighten up, holding the crown of my head high like the instructors taught us in our years of brutal training.

My thoughts turn to the sick kids. Two already dead, and who knows how many others under the healers' care. They don't have much time, and neither does the city if things get worse. The sentinels never say the name *Garradin* out loud, and neither will I. But I can't be the only one thinking about it.

The unspoken truth everyone knows is that a hundred years ago when the humans poured water and mud into the tunnels of Garradin to kill the fox-kin, the ones lucky enough to escape had their magic snuffed out instantly, like flames blown by storm winds. When the Leonodai's and bearking's forces finally pushed the humans back, they found only ordinary foxes, their Knowledge taken from them completely.

The scholars had known animals could lose their Knowledge. After all, even at the time, there were only five peoples who could still shape-shift. But to have witnessed the historic loss was a turning point. The Four Kingdoms came together, with more fervor than ever, and had kept a united front against the humans ever since. My father used to tell me that the reason the bearkings stay on Vyrinterra now is because they are afraid of losing their own magic.

How many Leonodai would need to join the Endless Skies before the losses begin to affect the Heliana's powers? If too many kids are lost, or if adults start to get sick, we could become the next Garradin.

"Fear or no fear," the Second Sentinel shouts as the eleventh bell begins to toll, "you remain proud! Proud of your blood, proud of your people. Loyalty above all!"

We echo the words back to her. It is our city's children on the line. Ours is a mission of legend, of the kind that Rowan longs to be a part of.

You can be the hero of this tale, I think. *You can be the hero of hers, too.*

The sentinels give the signal to take flight.

—

Cold wraps around me like a shroud as my paws lift from the Heliana. Sethran takes us into the headwind while the rest of us form a line behind him. All around me, the other teams take the same formation, each of us saving our energy. We'll split up at Balmora, but for right now, we take the most direct path to the Cliffs.

In the decades since that fateful day, the humans had claimed the spot where the fox-kin's city once was and turned it into a fortress. In a natural split in the Cliffs is a sheltered cove that the fox-kin and sea-folk used to use for trade. The humans scarred the land, cutting a zigzag path into it. Above it, they constructed pulleys and machines to get their resources from the height of the land above and onto the shore below. It's the place where they launch their ships, and understandably, it's the most guarded place on Balmora. Every few months, they test a new iteration of ships. One with cannons mounted. One with metal in the base so the sea-folk can't sink it. They try whatever they think will get them to Vyrinterra, once and for all.

Below us, the dark sea rolls in an ever-shifting rhythm. Here and there, the ghostly shapes of sea-folk come and go as quickly as breaking waves, patrolling the waters for enemy ships.

It's a quarter hour's flight to Balmora—not a far distance by any means, but it feels longer without the promise of a quick return. We glide most of the way, saving as much energy as possible. I focus on my breathing, the way we've been taught. In what feels like no time at all, the restless churn of waves becomes a roar. We're approaching the Cliffs.

Teams begin to break away, each aiming for a different part of Balmora's western shores. My senses are hit with a wall of smells I've come to associate with Balmora from my past scouting missions—smoke and dirt, earth and metal.

Out of nowhere, a watchtower blazes to life, the flames throwing harsh shadows over the broken landscape and shocking my vision. Moments later, another one lights up in the distance. Humans and their shadows pour out of the earth. As my eyes adjust, I see their hidden bunkers among the barren earth and tree stumps just as bullets begin to fly. Roars intermix with the sharp fire, and I instinctively swing higher to get out of range. We're far from the human fortress. They shouldn't be this far south. Is that what they've been doing these past months? Building out defenses to span the entire coast?

Sethran banks sharply to the right, roaring for us to follow. "We need to take cover, quickly." From behind, I hear a roar as other teams do the same. "Ox, the tree!"

"I see him!" To my right, Ox responds by taking his human form. Just as his armor transforms, the bow he has clipped to his chest plate as a lion dissipates into sparks of magic, re-appearing on his back. He pulls it forward, nocking and then loosing an arrow with a practiced deftness—a move that I've never mastered, no matter how hard I tried.

But the strain is evident on his face as he takes his lion form again, golden sparks flowing over his body noticeably slower than they would at home.

"Dive!" Sethran shouts. "Get to the ground, now!"

Exin drops, and I follow. I lower my head so my helm takes the hit of the branches and leaves as I try to land, claws scraping against the bark. As I come to a skidding halt, I take my human form. My axe—held in place with metal loops on my lion armor—falls to the ground as my form changes, but years of practice tell me exactly where it landed. My hand wraps around the familiar, heavy weight as I lift it. Sethran roars a command, but I've seen what he is warning me of. I launch myself at the human who's emerged from the direction of the watchtower, sword in hand. Parrying his strikes, I use my shield again and again until the human's panting hard from exertion. Swinging around and under him, my axe meets his rib cage, and his body falls.

Breathing hard, I take in the battle around me. By now, the entire coastline is alight. Roars and gunshots, screams and shouts clatter in the air. They weren't supposed to see us coming, not like this. The humans were supposed to be isolated at their fortress.

"Exin!" I shout, realizing I've lost track of him. I call his name again, waiting for his answer but instead hear him howling for me, just ahead to the left. I run in his direction and find him sword to sword with a human. The man is bleeding out of his arm, and Exin from his leg.

I adjust the grip on my axe and yell, as loudly as I can in this form, as I lunge at the human. It's two against one, and the human is wounded. Exin takes the killing blow. He sits up in triumph, chest heaving and glistening with sweat—but when he tries to stand, he falters. I let him lean on me as he presses down on the wound, air hissing between his teeth.

"Go on without me," he says. "I'll slow you down."

"I'm not going to just leave you," I say, adjusting his arm around my shoulders, but he pulls it away. "Give me your arm."

"I'll slow you," he repeats. "Go."

"Exin—"

"I'll buy you time." He shoves me in the other direction. "Loyalty above all. Go!"

I stagger back, trying to make my friend's words make sense, but they don't. His wound continues to bleed, and in my gut, I know he does not have much time. But I can't leave.

Then Sethran calls my name from the trees. My commander.

Years of training rush back like a river let run wild. With one last look at Exin, I join my commander. Ox appears out of the smoke, face shiny with sweat and marred with dark droplets of blood.

"We retreat now," our commander says. "We have to get out of here."

I follow after him, and that's when a pang of pain jolts my chest. I surrender to it—the last of my magic leaving me. The three of us make a break for it, staying low as we head directly away from the closest watchtower. At the rear, Ox slings arrow after arrow into the fires and chaos behind us.

Guilt weighs in my gut like a stone over leaving the battle so quickly, but Sethran is right. Our orders are to find the cure and save the city's children. And to do that, we need to stay alive.

We race through the underbrush, the roars of our comrades fading to screams and more gunfire. Sethran takes us due south, and with a startling suddenness, the rage of the battle disappears. I focus hard on the feel of the ground beneath my feet, putting one foot in front of the other like it's the only thing I've ever known how to do.

A truth burns brighter in my chest than the fires we leave in our wake: now that the humans know we are here, there is no turning back.

12

CALLEN

When the land around us has been silent for an hour, Sethran lets us slow our pace. I sip at my waterskin carefully, conserving it as best I can without passing out.

We walk in silence for a few miles, until the underbrush starts to reemerge and green peeks through the otherwise barren soil. Sethran spots a rocky outcropping in the distance with decent camouflage from surrounding trees and brush. My legs grow heavy with fatigue as the adrenaline of the battle dissipates. We finally reach the outcropping, and our commander calls for a rest.

Sethran leans against a boulder, pounding his fist idly into the rock behind him. "What happened to Exin?"

"He took a bullet to the leg," I reply. "It all happened so fast."

The blood pulsing out of my friend's leg is an image I won't soon forget. In the battles against the humans, I've seen my fair share of cuts and gaping wounds. The sight or scent of blood doesn't scare me—rather, like a blacksmith's tools, it sharpens my senses. I have learned which wounds can be mended and which can not. Exin was bleeding too much, too fast . . .

"It would not have healed, not without a healer's attention right away," I say.

Sethran takes my meaning. "Skies keep him and everyone else who may have been lost. The humans were ready for us."

"They came from underground," Ox says. "Are there tunnels that we know of?"

"There are mines at the base of the northern mountains," our commander responds. "But that would be too far. Warriors haven't been called to battle in what, six months? The humans must have been planning and expanding their hold, while we sat idle."

Ox takes a seat near Sethran, resting his elbows on his knees. "The king and sentinels probably saw the break in the fighting as a sign of victory."

"Well," Sethran replies, his tone bitter, "they were wrong. And it cost Exin his life." He paces for a moment. "I'm going to go look for water."

I look skyward. The moon is waxing, which works in our favor if we are to travel by night. Still, there isn't much of the land that I can make out clearly. A dark mass that may be a forest calls in the distance. That will give us the best cover and best advantage, and we know how to fight in the trees. Part of the third year of warrior training takes place largely on Vyrinterra, in the forests controlled by the bearkings. We'd spend days in the trees, practicing avoiding detection and seeing if we could make it all the way up the mountain without being caught. If you were, you were sent back down to start over.

As Sethran goes, Ox stands back up and stretches his legs.

"Are you okay?" I ask him.

"Never better."

"I meant are you *wounded*."

"Not physically," he says, putting his leg back down. "Exin was my cousin, you know."

"Yeah," I reply. "And my friend." The Warriors' Hall would be quieter without his laughter lighting up the place from Underbelly to roof. When it comes time to clear out his room, I'll volunteer myself to help. It is a solemn duty, but one that warriors do themselves as an act of service to one another. "How do you feel about this mission?"

"I'm in favor."

"Skies. You know what I mean," I retort. "Don't you ever give a straight answer?"

He shrugs. "Only when I want to."

My frustration gnaws at me. There was only one answer I really wanted. "Well, are you and Rowan together?"

"Sounds like something you should ask her. Besides, I thought we agreed to focus only on the mission," he says. "'The mission comes first' and all that? Was it just for show?"

"No," I reply. "But I'm waiting for you to start acting like less of an ass all the time."

Ox laughs. "This is me, Callen. Take it or leave it."

"What reason do you have to act like this if it's not about her?"

"Well, for one thing, it's pretty entertaining."

I exhale hard, trying to fight my desire to punch Ox in the face. With his short dark hair and quick mouth, he is the opposite of me. Even our choice of weapons contrast with each other. Ox can fight from a distance, whereas I have to get close to my enemies. Maybe that's what Rowan meant by wanting something different—but that is too literal for her. There is something in Ox that she likes, but I don't exactly feel up to the task of finding out what it is.

"To be honest," Ox says, more quietly, "I'm still wrapping my brain around all this. I'm so angry at the humans, and leaving someone you care about behind is easier said than done."

I flinch. Is this another game to him? Or does he actually mean it?

"I'm angry, too," I reply finally. "None of this is fair."

Ox nods and gazes skyward. His expression relaxes as he takes in the sky. "I'm sorry, Callen. I forget how I can seem to people I don't know well." He comes over to me and touches my right shoulder. "Let's let it lie, shall we? We can talk about something else. What is your favorite Exin story? Skies know I have a few gems."

Ox and I are both chuckling at the time Exin tricked Scholar Orr into cursing in front of everyone, when Sethran comes back. "No luck on water," he says. "What the skies are you laughing about?"

Sethran's confusion only makes us laugh harder. It feels good to feel something other than guilt. Exin told me to go. He knew his role in this fight had shifted and, in the perfect clarity of acceptance, had known to try to free me of any guilt. That was so like him. No number of practical jokes could shake his ultimately kind soul. Telling me to go was his final act of grace.

I draw a deep breath, letting the night air cool me from the outside in. Rowan, as much as she hates being left, is safe, at least. Exin has given me a chance at staying alive, and I have to take it so I can get back. I have so many reasons why I have to keep my eyes on the east, toward the cure.

To save the sick kids. To serve my king. To keep Matron Talla from bearing another loss. And to have the chance to make things right with Ro. I look idly to Ox, then turn away again.

I can't control where her heart will fly, but I can control mine.

13

ROWAN

Dawn breaks over the rooftops. Citizens will be in their beds past their regular hours, sleeping off the night's festivities.

From my childhood room at Storm's End, I am alone with the birds. They murmur and whirr to themselves as the sun whispers from the east, telling a story of promise and panaceas, cures and celebrations. The small bench beneath the window was made for a child, but I still found a way to wedge myself onto it.

Last night, while most of the Heliana had their attention on the bonfire at the heart of the marketplace, I was looking skyward. The teams' armor glinting in the moonlight was the only betrayal of their presence as they left.

Vera, who watched and waited up with me, had nudged my arm. "You okay?"

"No."

"Yeah. Me neither."

When we couldn't see them any longer, Vera headed back to the Warriors' Hall while I stayed at Storm's End. I didn't want to wake up in the Underbelly—it would only remind me that today was supposed to be our day. To have my dream put on hold was too much to deal with on top of my fight with Shirene, worrying about the teams, and trying not to count how many of the Storm's End girls may be in sick beds by the end of the week.

"Please," I had asked the stars, "please let them find it. Bring it home."

I doze off, only to be woken again by the birds stirring on the panes by my mother's balcony one room away from mine. Her voice carries in the morning air as she sings to them.

Careful not to make any noise, I sit up to try to listen better. Goose bumps sweep over the bare skin of my arms and midriff. I'd slept the summer night in a sleeveless linen shirt and pants, but it's not the morning chill alone that causes the sensation. To hear my mother singing is one of my favorite things in the world.

I only remember one of my mother's performances. It was shortly before she gave up singing to teach. She led the chorus at a celebration of my namesake, whom we can still see in the stars closest to the moon. I don't know the words she sang. All I remember is a flash of a rose-colored dress and the sound of bells as she moved her hands. Charging melodies rippling along with the sound of the other singers.

I am grateful to have the memory and even more grateful for every moment I've spent with my mother since then. Someone like Bel was not as fortunate. Both his parents were warriors, and both went to the Endless Skies on the same night my father did ten years ago. Bel was taken in by his relatives, but things kept going wrong for him. His aunt, warrior Ellian, was reported lost during her mission the next day. They never found her body.

The history of the Leonodai is built on the names of lost warriors. I don't want the next chapter to be built on the names of lost children.

Back in the present, my mother switches to humming, then after a beat, I hear a low whistle. Two sparrows take flight. I bet they're going to the healers to see if there's been news. A few minutes later, she knocks on my door and lets herself in.

"You'd sit out on the window bench like that when you were little." She holds out a cup of water, and I take it. "I thought you'd outgrown it."

"Oh, I have." I push back with my shoulder and sit up, swinging my legs down where they can fully extend. Pinpricks and goose bumps travel up my shins.

"What a lovely morning," she says. Beyond us, the clouds are wispy, whipped by the wind of the skies above. "Makes you forget."

"I watched them go."

"I thought you might," she replies.

"I should be with them."

My mother sighs. "We can't always do the things we want to do. Besides, there is much more work to be done here. Have you heard from your sister at all?"

"I talked to her yesterday," I reply, undoing my braid and combing it out with my fingers. "She's been named the King's Voice."

When my mother doesn't immediately reply, I look up. Her expression tells me all I need to know. "Oh, skies," I say. "Did Shirene not tell you?"

"I'm sure she's been very busy."

Too busy to send one bird? I try to recover. "She did seem pretty tired and stressed," I add. "I'm sorry you heard it from me, though, and not her."

My mother picks up a comb from my nightstand and deftly moves her hands to restart my braid into a four-strand one that I can't ever do on my own head. "She'll come visit when she can," is her reply. "I know she will."

She's tying off the braid at my neck when bells sound from the Glass Tower. My heart rate shoots up, and I count the tolling. *Warriors summoned to the Tower.* It's not a call to arms.

"Get going, darling," my mother says. I tug on my uniform, dressing completely in less than half a minute's time. With a final tug on the belt that holds my throwing knives, I take off for the Tower.

I land with the others, greeting sleepy-eyed members of my cohort as we gather in front of the other warriors-elect. I spot Bel fly in, hastily stuffing a half-eaten meat bun in his mouth.

He sees me notice and shakes his head, embarrassed. I wave it off with a smile before finding Vera at the edge of the room.

"Hey, Ro," Vera says. "How's your mother doing?"

"Okay, I think. All the kids are staying home for now. Let's hope this is some good news," I say, inclining my head toward the front of the Tower where Shirene and Sentinels Renna and Carrick have just walked in.

Vera leans in. "I heard the sky in the east was gray when the sun came up," she says. "Gray like smoke."

"What does that mean?" I ask.

"Not sure," she says. "But I don't think it's good. Who's that?"

A pair of figures dressed in pale blue come in and take their places alongside the sentinels. Their attire is so simple, yet they stand with our most respected leaders. Both wear capes split in two, trailing down their backs and onto the floor. *Almost like* . . .

"They must be sea-folk," I reply. "I've never seen them on land."

"Each of the other kingdoms has representatives here. I've met Lord Cambor of the horselords once," Vera says, nodding her agreement. "He came to watch a training. But I've never seen the sea-folk."

The chime sounds, and we kneel. For a brief moment, I forget why my view of the sentinels is so much better this time. Nearly a third of the warriors are gone.

"Honored warriors," Shirene says. "With our numbers depleted, we must shift our tactics in case the humans try to attack Vyrinterra by sea before the teams return. The other kingdoms have agreed to ready their defenses at the coast and send additional metals for us to forge extra weapons. As warriors and warriors-elect, you already are asked to be ready at all times to fight. Starting today, each of you is asked to remain in the Warriors' Hall unless on official duties, as to eliminate any delays if you are called to arms. No one should be leaving the Hall unless given permission."

Sentinel Renna steps forward. Her gray-blue eyes sweep over the room like a winter storm. "I know the warriors-elect are eager to take the oath."

I suck in a hopeful breath. Is it just me, or did Shirene's eyes seek me out as Renna spoke? Did she speak out for us? For me?

"However, as you can imagine," Sentinel Renna goes on, "the king's days are long, and he doesn't have room in them to speak the oath over each of you." Sentinel Renna lets the disappointed murmurs make their way through the room before continuing. "For now, our focus must be on the sick children and keeping the disease from spreading. You will each be assigned a section of the city to inspect for more signs of infected birds. The scholars say even a touch can spread the disease."

Not the scholars. Noam. My sister made it clear that they were relying on Noam for information. If the scholars had a clue of what to do about the disease, the sentinels wouldn't have gone looking for a deserter. But why don't they share that with us? We've already been tasked to keep one secret. What's one more? Leaving Noam out of this conversation is a choice.

My curiosity nags at me as Renna continues with the instructions. "Once found, you will carefully gather them. From there, teams of warriors will take the bodies and bury them on Balmora. That is your mission."

At least we'll have something to do, I tell myself. I know it should be happy to serve, but wandering around the city doesn't feel like enough. Sentinel Renna takes questions, and my heart drums as some warriors in the front speak up.

"Do you know how long the disease takes from first signs until death?" asks a blond-haired warrior I don't recognize.

"Ten days, according to the scholars," answers Sentinel Renna.

One of the younger trainees goes next. "And is there no other medicine? Nothing works?"

"The healers are doing everything they can to keep the children's symptoms at bay," the sentinel replies. "But the scholars are confident in the cure from Balmora."

One after another, Sentinel Renna's answers lean on the knowledge of our scholars. I keep waiting for her to mention Noam, or to mention at least that we got help from outside the Heliana . . .

But the moment never comes. Renna dismisses us to get our assignments. My peers rise around me, but I am frozen to the ground as if a frost has seized my limbs. Something isn't right. I press my fingertips harder into the floor as my body tingles with uncertainty and doubt.

The sentinels are lying to us. And I'm the only one who knows.

❦

I wait with the others to hear what section of the city I am to search. I'm matched with Bel and another warrior of our cohort whom I don't know as well. Before I go, I let Sentinel Carrick know of the bird I found yesterday.

"Thank you, Warrior-Elect," he says. "I will let that group know." Something in my gut roots me to the spot, and when Carrick puts his tired eyes back to me, he raises a brow in question. "Yes, Warrior-Elect Rowan?"

"Sorry, sir," I say. "I'm just wondering how the scholars determined it was a human disease if it's never been seen before on the Heliana."

Carrick scratches his ruddy-colored hair and gives me an almost imperceptible shrug before regaining his composure. "The scholars' libraries are extensive. Thank the skies they found any answer."

I fake a satisfied nod and move out of my place in line. Vera, waiting for me by the front doors, tilts her head in question. I wave off concern. "Just making sure he knows where I found a bird yesterday, before I met up with you."

The warm summer winds rush over the both of us, our matching uniforms waving in the breeze. Vera wrinkles her face as we turn for the balcony.

"What a glamorous duty we've been assigned," she says. "Necessary, but . . . ick."

"The faster you find them, the less gross they are," I say. "Where are you covering?"

"I'm at the fields," she says, referring to the small area of vegetable fields on the eastern side of the Heliana. "You?"

"I'm near Storm's End, actually. Northern district along the Crescent."

"Okay," she says. "See you later? You can come to my room and commiserate once we're done." She pulls me in for a hug. "I know you're worried about your mother and the girls. Even if you don't say it."

I nod into her shoulder. "Thanks, Vera. I want to stop at Storm's End once we're done looking, but I'll find you before dinner."

"I heard it's all the leftover festival food," she says. "All the food, none of the prices for us warriors-elect."

"That's the dream, isn't it?" I say back, forcing a grin.

I take my lioness form and glide down to the northern district, but my mind stays in the Tower. I'd pressed Carrick for a reason. He backed up Renna's lie, which means the sentinels planned their explanation of how they learned of the disease. But why not tell the truth? Even the loyalest of citizens would be hard-pressed to hate a deserter who helped our city in her hour of need.

There has to be something else.

Finding a clear spot in a nearby street, I land and retake my human form. Bel will tease me for being late, but I need a moment to think. Callen said the sentinels do everything for a reason, and I agree. Which means lying to the select group of Leonodai to whom you have already trusted with the secret of the disease is . . . not good.

I rack my mind, wishing I could have someone to talk this out with. There isn't any way Shirene will be able to find time for me again, and I'm still really hurt by what she said. Callen and Ox are gone, and my mother has too much on her mind already. I'd have to put the pieces together myself.

As I walk, citizens mill about, tidying up after the festival and trading stories of what new clothes they bought . . . or who they spent High Summer with. It isn't an official tradition like staying up all night or lighting candles in every window, but it's inevitable that I will hear of new couples and passionate flings in the coming days. Dances, wine, and the day off from warrior training tends to do that.

I blush, thinking of how Ox and I never got our dance. I'm not sure I would have been able to after what Callen said, anyway.

Skies, he had terrible timing. I hadn't lied to him—I *had* thought about us before. Callen is as handsome as any other Leonodai warrior, his tanned frame lean with muscle. His messy gold-brown hair is longer than how most of the other male warriors keep theirs, but it just feels right for Callen.

Since he is a year older, he began his training ahead of me. He changed so much and was so busy in that first year that our off hours together were precious. That was when the first rays of a sunlit crush rose inside my chest. Once I wasn't seeing him every day, I started to notice how much better everything was with him around. Still, he never made any sort of move. He was my best friend, and that was all I really needed. Now his confession is making me wonder: What is it that I *want*?

At last, I spot my fellow warriors-elect waiting in the shade of a tree near our assigned location. As I expected, Bel shrugs off my tardiness once I make up an excuse about going to Storm's End first to check on my mother.

"I'm glad the sentinels told your mother and the other schoolmasters," he says. "It's important they know what's going on. I think the whole city should."

We split up to search our assigned area. The sun beats down on my back and neck as I pore over the ground, but the sound of the nearby Crescent River helps me focus.

If the sentinels aren't telling the truth, I'll have to go find it myself. And in order to do that, I would have to find who *they* were talking to—the deserter, Noam. He must be somewhere hidden in the palace, close enough so that the king could call for him at any time but not anywhere that would draw attention.

I've never gone into the palace by myself. It is off-limits unless you are assigned a post there, and those are reserved for fourth- or fifth-year warriors. A warrior-elect like me would have no business there. I could lie and say I was looking for Shirene, but on the chance someone took me seriously and found her for me, what would I say then?

Thankfully, the skies see fit to interrupt my nonsense. Bel calls me over to a pair of sparrows just a few feet apart from each other. Using a shovel, we place the birds and dirt beneath them into a tightly woven sack. Bel offers to fly it up to Carrick, and I go back to the Warriors' Hall. After washing up in my room and changing into a fresh uniform, I head to Vera's room as promised. We get an early lunch and talk for an hour or so before I make up an excuse to go to my room.

"I'm exhausted for some reason," I tell her. "I'm going to take a nap."

"Sleep tight," she says before turning for her own room on the other side of the Hall. First- through third-year trainees share rooms, partly to strengthen connections and partly so everyone fits in the Hall, but as a fourth-year trainee, I have my own space.

All the rooms in the Hall are the same. Next to a simple bed, I have one square window, a washbasin, and a trunk to store my things. Over time, I added a rug to keep my feet off the cold stone and a few other trinkets: books from my mother, a collection of candles for light, and a speckled ceramic cup I bought one year at High Summer. But none of that is as important as what I keep hanging on the wall, ready at all times: my armor.

Leonodai believe that every warrior should have one piece of armor that is crafted specifically for them. For me, that is the vambrace for my right forearm—my throwing arm when I use my knives. My breastplate, helmet, knee guards, and everything else were crafted for anyone. But the vambrace is for me.

I pick it up now, feeling its familiar weight and letting the metal warm to my hands just a little bit. I've dreamed of wearing it into battle so many times. And I will, still.

But first, I have to go find the deserter.

14

SHIRENE

The sight of so many small bodies in the sizable beds of the palace sickroom is almost more than I can bear. This place wasn't meant for them.

Afternoon air swirls over the sound crying and coughing, bringing a chill to my skin. Beside each bed, parents curl protectively over their children. Here and there, I see the cobalt uniform of a warrior, their head hanging low.

So far, not a single person over twelve has gotten the disease, despite the children living in larger households. Noam had said as much, that it only affects the young. *Cruel, cruel, cruel,* I think. But at least it means the children's families can be here. The room next to this one has been prepared for the parents, so they are never more than a few steps away. The healers, too, sleep in shifts nearby. I feel the heaviness in their hearts whenever they speak to me, and sometimes from a look alone. They've trained for years to help others, but in this moment, there is nothing to do but keep the disease at bay.

It isn't healing. It is stalling.

But duty is duty, and being the King's Voice meant my presence here brought some reassurance with it. With an exhale, I walk over to a young mother holding her son's hand. I crouch down next to her, and for a moment, she's startled—then she's right back to tired.

"Is there anything I can get for you?" I ask her gently.

"No, my lady. Thank you," she replies. She pulls at the sleeves of her shirt. Fresh tears slide down her face as she blinks rapidly. "He's my only son. It took us so long to have a baby, almost as long as we waited for an heir."

I get her meaning. With the magic of the Heliana sustained by the royal line, kings and queens usually waste no time expanding their families. For King Kharo and Queen Laianna, it took nearly eight years. The bells that sounded Tabrol's birth seemed to push the very Heliana higher into the sky.

The young mother before me suddenly puts her face to my shoulder, a guttural sound escaping her throat. "I don't know what to do. I feel so helpless."

I bring a hand to the back of the woman's shoulders, curling her in a moment's safety like my mother used to do for Rowan and me. "Being here is all you have to focus on," I reply. "Each time he wakes, he'll want to see his mother's face."

She sits back up, wiping her face. "Do you have children, Lady Shirene?"

"No," I answer honestly, missing Seth so badly it is as if he's been gone for years. "But I want them."

"I thought raising a child was the hardest thing one could do in their lifetime," she says quietly. "But this is. This is the hardest thing."

"Hold fast to hope," I say, though my words feel hollow as a burned-out tree. "The warriors have been sent. They know their mission well. They will return in a few days' time, I swear it."

When I part ways with the woman, I turn to find Hammond watching me from across the room. The Second Sentinel smiles softly, the kind of smile I imagine my father would give me in that moment. "How are you holding up, Lady Shirene?"

"As well as I can be," I reply.

"You are doing very well."

"Thank you," I say. "I wish I had your confidence."

A shuffle of movement at the door, followed by the slam of it banging against the stone wall, makes me jump. Sentinel Renna stands in the doorway, her expression flooded with alarm.

She doesn't need to say a word. Hammond and I cross the room, joining Renna in the hallway. One of the more practiced healers is beside her, a basket of healing herbs and tonics gripped tightly in her left hand.

"Come," Renna says. "Hurry."

We wind through the hallways of the palace. Maids and other palace workers duck out of our way, sensing the urgency in our steps. We pass the generals' quarters, whizzing by a pair of girls who must be daughters of someone on the king's war council. As thanks for their service, generals and their families are given living spaces here in the palace, the same way sentinels are.

Only we are not allowed to have families, I think bitterly, remembering the young mother's question from earlier. It was the hardest part of volunteering myself to be selected as a sentinel. Seth and I talked for hours, but we both knew the incredible honor it would be to serve the city so intently. I can serve as long as I want, and we'll have our family when we are both a little older.

"Renna, what's this about?" Hammond asks as we continue to climb staircase after staircase to the higher levels.

"Not yet," she replies curtly. Then she adds, "The king has called for us."

The rules don't allow for Leonodai to fly while inside the palace, though there are emergency exits built into the walls in case of a fire or other disaster. My legs burn, but it isn't my first or last time climbing from the lower levels to the royal family's quarters below the Glass Tower.

At long last, we pass the guards on either side of the one staircase that provides access to the royals' wing. Normally, they'd have stopped the healer, but when flanked by three sentinels, anyone would be let by.

Catching my breath, I trail behind the others as Renna turns left toward the queen's quarters. The scent in the air changes from the honey warmth of the palace candles to the light smell of jasmine, the queen's favorite. A handmaiden dressed in pale purple and pinks nods to Renna as we approach, and we're let in without being announced.

The queen sits on the bed with her head in her hands, sobbing. The king kneels before his wife, speaking in soft tones, but I don't make out what he says. Both of the royals snap to attention as we bow our heads in respect. The healer gazes around the room in awe. While the opulence of the palace has become normal to me, I forget how it feels to witness it for the first time. I reach my hand and touch her free arm to give her some assurance.

"Thank you for coming," the king says. The queen shifts, facing us, but she does not blot her eyes when fresh tears come.

"Your Graces, what's happened?" Hammond asks.

"The worst thing that could happen," replies the queen, her voice tight with bitterness. "My child is sick. He has it."

My heart seizes. Beside me, the healer gasps.

"Let Prena see him," Renna says quickly, indicating to the healer. "She tended to warriors yesterday, and has not be exposed to any of the sick children."

The king moves toward a door on the far side of the room, leading to the nursery, but the queen cuts him off. "I will get him."

We wait in a desperate silence until she reappears with Tabrol's small frame situated over her shoulder. Prena steps forward gingerly to examine the boy's flushed face, but I'm overcome.

I've never seen Tabrol so closely before. Just three years old, his curly, gold-blond hair is lighter than that of either of his parents, but his hazel-and-gold eyes are unmistakably his father's. The small prince shifts away from Prena, putting his face determinedly against his mother's neck. The queen closes her eyes, gripping him tighter and bouncing him on her hip.

"Well?" she says, so quietly that if the room weren't shocked in stillness, I'd have missed it.

Prena straightens up, a braver Leonodai than I am being in this moment. "I'm so sorry, Your Grace. But I believe he has the disease. I'm so sorry."

"The fever only began this morning," the king says. "There is more than enough time."

Slowly, gently, I reach for Tabrol. Something in my heart says I have to know for myself.

"May I?" I ask the queen. She nods.

I reach out two fingers and put the back of them to the prince's forehead. The sensation is so sudden that I have to keep myself from flinching. The boy's forehead is far too hot, as if he's been playing for hours in a midsummer sun. If only a cool drink or swim in one of the Heliana's four rivers would cool him off.

A feeling beyond words stirs in my stomach. I am no mother and can't be as long as I am a sentinel. I've accepted that—but looking at Tabrol and seeing the roundness of his cheeks and the soft way he fits in his mother's arms strikes me like a sword meeting a shield. In a way, Prince Tabrol is the city's child. He is our hope and our future. I feel the weight of his life press into my very bones. *He is just a little boy.* It's unfair enough that he's going through physical pain. It is impossible to comprehend the thought of his life being cut so short . . .

"This is our fault," Queen Laianna says suddenly, with a quiet violence that shocks the room. The warrior in her comes surging forward as she turns to the king. "We should have said yes."

"Laianna . . . ," the king replies gently, but heartbreak has taken hold in the queen's eyes.

"We should have said yes months ago," she says. "Then none of this would be happening."

What is she talking about? I look at Hammond, my brow raised, but he avoids my gaze.

"Forgive me, Your Graces, but the prince should be in a room with lots of air," Prena interjects. "I will stay with him, if you let me."

"Please," replies the queen, gaining some strength from having something to do other than despair. "Come. I will help you open the windows."

The two go into the nursery. As the door shuts behind them, Renna turns to the king. "Should we send more teams?"

The word pulls me back to the moment. "The warriors-elect are ready," I say. "I know you already considered it, but that was . . . before. They can take the oath another time but still be sent."

"No," the king replies. He sits on the queen's bed. Bowing his head, he removes the gold circlet from his brow and shakes out his dark-brown-and-gray hair. "The threat of an attack has never been more real than it is now. If my son dies, the Heliana's magic will fail. The city will fall and the humans will be able to reach us by sea." He sighs. "They know we are weak, and they are fueled by the fury at our prior refusals. If they assemble their numbers, we will be overwhelmed. We must ready for war. Not a battle. But a war for our lives."

Renna hesitates, but bows her head. "Yes, Your Grace. I will prepare the remaining warriors."

"The citizens will need a place to go," says Hammond. "We should empty the Keep below the palace. It is the city's safest stronghold."

The king nods. "Do all that you think is right. You need not wait for my approval."

We bow to the king. Closest to the door, I lead us out of the queen's rooms toward a common area where a group of hallways meet. To our left, a staircase winds upward into the ceiling—that's how the king typically enters the Glass Tower. Bookshelves waist-high line the adjacent walls below massive tapestries depicting the forests of Vyrinterra. The halls are empty save for us. Only the royal family and sentinels are allowed on this level.

"Skies keep us," Renna says finally. "The crown prince."

"I don't want to believe it," I say. "But the king is right not to send warriors. If—"

"Time is already against us," Renna says, cutting me off. "If the prince had more time, we could try to make amends. The humans have the right to be angry."

The confusion must be clear on my face, because just then, Hammond lets out a deep sigh.

"Renna, my old friend," he says. "Shirene doesn't know."

The other woman turns sharply. "What?"

"She doesn't know," he repeats, looking at me with that familiar fatherly expression. Only this time, it is mixed with something else. Regret? Worry?

"What don't I know?" I ask. "What's going on?"

Renna sinks into a nearby chair. "Do you want to tell it, or should I?"

"I can," Hammond says. "Do you want to sit down?"

"I'd prefer not to," I say. "Please. What is going on?"

The older sentinel pulls out a chair and takes it himself. "A little over a year ago, the humans began leaving messages in bottles that they put purposely out to sea. The Sea Queen's ambassadors brought them to us after their people found them floating in the water. The messages were simple, but clear. They even wrote it in our own language, skies know how. The humans wanted peace."

"What?" I gasp. "Why?"

"A famine," he says. "They offered peace so they could feed their people with the food from Vyrinterra."

I start to pace, my body seeming to know this information is too much to process while keeping still. "Why did the king refuse?"

"All four kingdoms did," Hammond replies as Renna lets out

a bitter scoff. "We couldn't trust the humans to keep their word. It could have been a trap. Besides, we had been successful at keeping the humans at bay for decades. It wasn't on us to help the humans when we were comfortable keeping things as they were."

"Warriors still die in battles out at sea and at the Cliffs," I reply. "How can you say that's 'comfortable'?"

Renna gets up, her arms folded. "We cannot change what was decided back then. I'll get to the point that this one keeps dancing around." Her words are sharp, but she and Hammond had the benefit of working together for many years. A few barbs are nothing between them. "When Noam learned of the humans' peace offer, he advocated for the kingdoms to take it. No voice was louder in favor than his. Time and time again, he argued to all four kingdoms' ambassadors, and to the king, that it was an opportunity to establish goodwill and a lasting peace. Ultimately, when the Four Kingdoms rejected the idea of peace, he was livid."

Hammond makes a *hmm* sound in agreement. "He abandoned his duties to live with humans on Balmora for good. He thought that if they welcomed one Leonodai, they would welcome more."

"Why wasn't I told any of this?" I ask, my voice rising in a way that I wouldn't have dared just a few weeks ago. That Shirene would have kept her composure and probably held her tongue. This Shirene was changed, exhausted in body, mind, and heart. I have every right to be angry—and now I understand why the humans do, too. "I have been a sentinel for nearly a year. No one thought to tell me this? That the humans know our words *and* that they wanted to stop the fighting?"

"I don't think it was a conscious decision," Renna replies. Her storm-gray eyes, lined with age and fatigue, bore into mine. "There was so much else to teach you. More important things for you to focus on. Besides, it was already done, a book opened and closed."

"Except now it's open again," I say. "That's the real reason why we haven't announced Noam's return, isn't it? Not only because we have more important things to do, but because if the citizens knew he had returned, they'd want to know why he left."

Hammond nods. "Yes. The people cannot know, Shirene. They can't know their children are dying simply because their leaders were too proud."

His words shake the very stone we're standing on. The lifeblood of the city is sick, and if he dies, then the Four Kingdoms will have no one to blame but themselves.

Wordlessly, I turn away from them and trudge back to the infirmary. My peers follow, murmuring to themselves, but I don't listen. Right now, I can make myself useful by staying with the families. That much is true, that in this moment, it's also enough. We're halfway back when I see the Chief Healer climbing the stairs toward us, taking two at a time despite her age.

Renna goes to her. "Is something wrong?"

"Sentinels," she says. We wait in agony as the poor woman catches her breath. "I was looking for you. You or the Chief Scholar." Her eyes dart around, but there is no one else in the hallway.

"What's wrong?" I ask.

She keeps her voice low and quiet, but not so much that I don't hear her next, horrible words. "We've lost another child. An eight-year-old boy."

"Skies keep him," I say, with Hammond and Renna echoing the same. By the look in the Chief Healer's eyes, she's far from done.

"He was only in my care four days," she whispers. "His mother said he wasn't feeling well before, but even then, that makes it five days *total*." Her voice racks with pain. "Don't you see? The disease is moving faster than the scholars warned. They told us we had ten days. Now you see it is half that."

The three of us share a look. Hammond's expression is as close to panicked as I've ever seen it. Renna looks ready to murder.

"Go back to the infirmary and comfort that family," I whisper. "Tell no one. We'll consult with the Chief Scholar and come to you as soon as we can."

She shoots me a look like she resents being told what to do, but she goes anyway. When she's out of sight, Renna pivots and strides determinedly down the stairs. I know exactly where she's headed.

"Noam said ten days," I say as we head toward his room.

"The *deserter* lied," she fires back. "And the prince is doomed because of it."

15

ROWAN

The chimes of fourth bell ring out as I cross from the Warriors' Hall and into the palace. The two buildings are connected by a walkway with the honey-colored glass in the windows and supported by sturdy stone arches underneath. I'd picked one of my nicest outfits—a pale yellow dress that was fitted nicely to my frame. My mother had had it tailored to me for Shirene's sentinel ceremony, but it hasn't seen any use since. I had left my long hair down, but at the crown, I braided it to the side and secured it with a single gold feather hairpin. I had enough to worry about without my hair getting in my face.

At best, I hope to pass for the daughter of one of the military families. The only part of the palace I've been to regularly is where Callen's family lives, though I stopped going years ago when Callen did. I hope that if I walk there with confidence, it will quell any curiosity from watchful guards. Anyone stationed in the palace will be several years my senior and may not know my name, but they'd notice someone who looks completely lost.

For better or worse, everything appears to be moving more or less normally in the palace. The Leonodai who work here don't have the luxury of taking a day off after High Summer. Still, it is a beautiful place to work and call home. Built into solid stone, an ample number of candles and sconces line every hallway. Stairwells wrap around the walls, leaving the center open and welcoming. Here and there, multicolored windows cast sunset-like patterns of light on the plush rugs. Palace attendants carry baskets of laundry or messages from one end of the hallway to the next. One gives me a second glance, but I duck out of her view and up a staircase.

Walk confidently, I remind myself. I know where I am going, at least for now.

On the next level, scholars in training study together over polished wood tables, the books stacked next to them nearly taller than they are. Just like warriors, they are expected to know their craft inside and out. On this level, numerous bookshelves run from wall to wall. Near them, candles enclosed in tall, thin glasses wait to be lit. No matter the time of day, a scholar can navigate the maze of tomes at their leisure, but the high glass limits risk of fire.

Feeling out of place on this level, I take the first staircase I see. Already, my legs are warming up as if getting ready to run drills or spar.

The third level is the last one to be built into stone, before the palace clears the top of the ridge, and is home to the king's war council and the fully fledged scholars. Somewhere on this level is supposedly a grand ballroom, and though I am dressed for it, I don't have time to explore. In the corner of my eye, I see the bright blue of the warriors patrolling the hall. They aren't there to keep out enemies—after all, none have ever reached here—but they are meant to prevent inquisitive citizens from roaming around.

I fight the urge to quicken my step, lest it make me more obvious, but I turn quickly toward where Callen's parents live. The hallways look more familiar, and although the color of the rug is duller than I remember, the interlaced vine design is exactly like it was when I was a girl.

"Not the time for reveries," I whisper to myself. If I go any farther, I'll wind up at a dead end. Pausing for a moment in a corner out of the way of the main walkway, I try to think like my sister and the other sentinels. Noam would be kept somewhere close to the king, but not too close. That meant this level, or perhaps the one above would be ideal. But it's not like I can just go knocking on doors.

I decide to lean on my warrior training and do some reconnaissance. Grabbing a book from a nearby shelf, I find a reading nook by a window and scoot myself into the corner. Hopefully, I won't be seen at all, but if I am, I can pass for a bored palace girl. I open to a random page, keeping my eyes and ears open.

On the levels above me comes the rolling of a cart and a pair of voices. They pass directly overhead, but I catch sight of a green healer's uniform reflecting in a mirror. *Okay, so healers are up there.* That means the sick children might be, too. A moment later, I swear I catch the sound of crying. I swallow nervously, returning my eyes to the borrowed book when a tall figure rounds the corner.

"Rowan?"

My heart jumps to my throat, but as I look up, it's not my sister or a guard who's caught me. It's Callen's father.

"I thought that was you," he says. "Looks like I can still get some things right in my old age."

He says the last words with spite. In truth, the former general isn't that old, but he looks it. A sallow sadness has taken hold of his formerly commanding gaze, and he's gained some weight since I last saw him.

"Sir," I say, hastily setting the book aside. "It's good to see you again."

"And you," he says, but it's just a formality. I can sense the question of what in the skies I'm doing here coming, so I beat him to the punch.

"I'm looking for my sister," I say. "She hasn't answered any of my birds." *Or she wouldn't have, if I'd sent any.* "It's a . . . personal matter. I hoped she'd hear it from me but I haven't been able to get ahold of her."

"The sentinels have to put the king and royal family before their own," he responds. "I'm sure it can wait."

Sweat builds under my arms as I try and fail to think of another lie. *Breathe,* I think. *Make whatever you say believable.* "You're right," I say. "I'll just leave her a note, then. One of the scholars downstairs will have parchment and ink. Thank you."

Before he can say anything else, I hurry down the stairs. There's so much more I could say to him, like, "Why didn't you ask me about your son?" but now's not the time. Once out of sight, I follow through on my words and ask a nearby trainee scholar to borrow some of her writing materials. Once Callen's father's shadow disappears, I hastily hand them back.

"Sorry," I say. "I've changed my mind. Thanks, though."

The sound of rumbling wheels makes me turn. A palace attendant pushes a small cart with a pitcher of water and a few other odds and ends down a hallway and out of sight. The smell of a hot meal lingers in the air, drawing more curious looks than just mine.

"Where's that attendant going?" I ask.

"That's Sentinel Faera's old quarters," the trainee replies. "You know how she was a scholar first. She asked to remain in her old room when she became a sentinel."

"But who's in there now?" I ask, trying to keep a curious tone without being too obvious. The only thing this scholar has to believe is that I am a gossip-driven girl, nothing more.

The scholar shrugs, flexing out her writing hand in a stretch. "I'm not sure. I didn't think anyone was there, if I'm being honest."

"Weird," I say, but I don't take my eyes from the spot. I wave a hasty goodbye to the trainee, who reburies herself in her book without a second glance. Walking aimlessly over to the hallway, I pretend to inspect books while the attendant with a now-empty cart passes by me. When I'm sure no one is looking, I make my move. The short hall leads to a rounded door that's been left ajar. Without wasting any more time, I knock and go in.

"Leonoden," he says, using our word for *countryman*. "Can I help you?"

The deserter is somewhere around my mother's age, maybe forty-five years old. He's in what I suppose are human clothes—and I don't know why I expected anything different. Given that he is wearing a long-sleeved cotton shirt and vest and plain pants and boots, I may not have known who he was at just a glance. But the gold of his eyes is unmistakably Leonodai.

"Hello," I reply. I pick a name at random. "I'm . . . Prena. I live here in the palace. My father is a general here. Can I come in?"

He indicates I can sit, and I take the chair across from him. The room still bears traces of Sentinel Faera's stay. A bookcase holding dusty volumes sits in the corner, and I spot a white uniform hanging in the wardrobe. Other clues tell me Noam has made this room his own. The bed is pushed to the far corner, presumably so the table fits next to the window. The room faces southwest toward open sea, a shallow outcropping with a handful of potted plants just below the pane.

"So, Prena," he says. "I will presume that you didn't pay a visit to a *deserter* because you want to share this view. If you have questions, please ask."

I sit back. "You're very . . . forthcoming. You don't even know who I am."

"I have nothing to hide," he says.

I wait for him to swallow a mouthful of his lunch while my own turns in my stomach. I exhale determinedly—facing Noam is a new kind of battle. Strange and without weapons, but a battle nonetheless. I had to leave here with what I came for.

"The sentinels aren't telling the citizens about you," I say. "I found out through listening around. They're telling everyone they are getting their knowledge from the scholars. Why?"

Noam wipes his mouth on a napkin. "They don't want any-one looking for me."

"And why not?"

"Because they can't let the truth get out," he replies. "The sen-tinels are losing a battle they brought on themselves." He pauses, his dark brown eyes reading my expression. "I doubt that the sen-tinels ever shared that the humans offered peace a long time ago."

I grip the chair beneath me. If I had my knives, I'd go over them with my hands to steady myself, but for now, the chair will have to do. "I don't understand. The humans have never wanted peace."

"Oh yes, they have," Noam replies. He sets down his fork and leans back, folding his arms. "Balmora has been suffering a fam-ine for years now. Around the time I left, humans offered peace in hopes we'd help feed them. But we refused."

"How do you know?"

"I was there, of course," he replies. "I implored the king to accept the offer. Think of all the warriors that this city has lost to battles with the humans. We had the chance to end it, but the king and the other kingdoms chose not to."

I look out at the sea, not sure how to process all that I am hearing. "You say that like you know everything." I ask. "How can you be sure?"

Noam smiles, but not kindly. "I was a sentinel myself. I know how they think. The sentinels like things the way they are," he goes on, confidence ringing in his tone like a Tower bell. "They always have. They will always choose stability over change. I wanted to give change a chance, so I left to live with the humans in one of their villages in the mountains. There, they welcomed me. Gave me shelter and let me stay. I proved my point that some humans would work with us if we tried. But it's too late now."

"You left to live with our enemy. What about Garradin?" Noam flinches at the name. "What about your people, your family? What about loyalty?"

The last of these comes out as a shout, leaving a louder silence in its wake. I bite back the apology that rises in my throat. I'm not sorry. I'm furious, and confused.

"I get that you're helping the sentinels now. And that's good," I add on half-heartedly. "But that doesn't change the fact that you deserted."

"No, it doesn't." He sighs. "You are young, Prena. But with luck, you may have a chance to follow your own path like I did."

I straighten up in defiance. I would never abandon the Heliana. "When the sentinels came for you, were you afraid?"

His expression changes to one of bemusement. "No."

"Well, weren't you scared of punishment?"

He laughs. "The sentinels have always known where I was.

I shake my head. "No, I remember the announcement a few days after you left. They said they didn't know where you were."

"If they were ever going to punish me, they already would have. They especially can't do so now that it was I who told them about the cure to begin with."

"The sentinels should have told us the truth," I mutter. My leg bounces idly, but I try to refocus on what's really at stake. "Is it real, the cure?"

Noam nods without hesitation. "Yes."

"Why don't you have any of it?"

"It's not a common disease, and the cure has never grown in the mountains," he replies. "All the village leaders knew of it, though, from when they lived in the larger cities, like Ramsgate."

"Ramsgate?" I repeat.

"The humans' capital city," he says. "It lies due east from the Heliana. That is where the cure is said to still grow."

There is something unsettling about how Noam talks—it draws me in, and he seems so sure, but a huge part of me still wants to doubt him.

"How can you trust the humans so much?" I ask. "Aren't you afraid they'll lie?"

"I have no reason to," he replies. "My friends in the village are not monsters, just people like you or me. They would give the prince a whole field of the cure if they had any. The human leader, General Marchess, is the one who refused to help. And from the little I know of him, he will not yield."

Prince? With one small word, Noam stops my world from turning. I don't say anything at first, hoping I heard wrong.

"Prince Tabrol has the disease," I say quietly, half a question and half praying that he'll jump in and correct me. "I . . . I didn't know."

At last, Noam seems to break. He looks out to sea, a true sadness lingering in his expression. "I didn't expect you to. But you seem like a smart warrior. I think you can handle it."

"I'm not a warrior," I stammer, but Noam looks at me flatly, like, *Come on.* "How did you know?"

"No palace girl would just barge in here and sit down with a deserter. You came in with fire in your eyes. You have a sharpness to you. That's training, and spars won."

I open my mouth to retort, but he waves me off.

"Prena, the king cannot let his son die. He'll need to ask for the Four Kingdoms' permission to offer peace again, maybe make the deal even more enticing to General Marchess. But skies know how long that will take to get a message sent and returned."

"That will take forever," I say, my heart racing with a sudden, new realization. "The warriors who were sent don't know about the prince."

"No. But for a child, they wouldn't need much," Noam says. "The humans I spoke to have a saying: 'A petal a year, a stem a season.' Tabrol would need less than one flower to live."

Less than one flower for the lifeblood of our city, for our entire future. Every Leonodai from child to elder knows the royal line has to remain strong; otherwise, the Heliana will fall. The scholars—and my mother, since she taught me herself—drilled that into my skull since I was a girl.

Everything I've worried about is true and yet is also worse than I feared. I've never thought about how the sentinels must pick and chose information like choosing fruit at the market. They only tell the city what they want us to hear.

I have to get to Shirene. I have to apologize for yesterday, then tell her that I know everything. I can try to convince her that the other warriors and warriors-elect—skies, even the citizens—need to know the truth.

Loud voices sound from the hallway like an old bickering couple. But I recognize the stern tone of Sentinel Renna.

"I have to go," I say, then immediately realize that the only exits are the hallway and the window.

Launching ungracefully out of the chair, I push myself over the windowsill and out onto the outcropping below. I duck to the side just in time. The hinges of the door let out a blaring squeak as it's pushed open, and I'm about to fly away when Renna's angry shout hits my ears.

"How dare you lie to us!" the Fourth Sentinel snaps. "You said the disease takes ten days. Ten. The healers have just told us another child who only became sick five days ago has died."

The wind buffers me, pushing me against the palace walls. I look skyward, heart drumming, hoping that no patrol is circling above me. My dress flies up in a flurry around my knees, and I grab at it, bunching it in my hand to keep it from giving me away.

I should go. I should absolutely go. And yet . . . I don't. Closing my eyes, I listen hard toward the room behind me. Noam has given me part of the truth. Something in my gut says I am about to get the rest.

"I didn't lie," Noam protests earnestly.

"Then your human friends were not honest," Renna replies. Her voice is heavy with rage.

"You are sure of the number?" says a new voice, but one that I've known my whole life. Shirene is far from calm, but at least she's not shouting.

"Yes," Noam says. "It must be because the disease is new to Leonodai. I was assured it took ten days."

"The warriors have been sent already," says Shirene. "They think they have more time."

A final voice, a deeper one that I guess is Sentinel Hammond's, speaks next. "We must go to the king at once."

"You, too," is Renna's reply. The scrape of a chair against the floor tells me she's been talking to Noam.

My hand cramps from how tightly I've gripped my dress, but I don't move. The sun presses into my skin as I keep totally still. The minutes tick by. Whether I am being careful to not get caught or paralyzed by the revelations of the last few minutes, it's hard to tell.

Prince Tabrol has the disease, and now the children are dying too fast. The warriors who were sent were told to take every precaution—and precautions can come in the form of longer rests to avoid detection, or sleeping a full night to make sure their weary selves can make the full journey. They'll want to make it home as quickly as possible, of course, but not every commander will take great risks. Someone like Seth surely won't, unless he knows what is truly at stake.

I have to help get the news to them. But how? I have orders to stay at the Warriors' Hall. To go find a team . . . that means I will have to go without anyone's permission.

My body sways with the thought. Skies keep me. Have I really just considered leaving the Heliana, like Noam? Only it isn't like Noam. He left to prove a point. I'll be leaving to save my city.

No. This is crazy. I am just a crazy girl standing on a roof-top, not thinking straight. But my breath is skimming in my chest for another reason, too. How can the sentinels believe they always know best? It isn't fair that they are keeping things from the citizens. Doesn't "loyalty above all" include honesty with the people who look to you for guidance?

I groan aloud. Unsure what to do, I take my lioness form and fly low around the palace and back to Storm's End. My mother will have something for me to do, some new way of helping her and the other schools. If I keep my hands busy, then maybe I'll be able to forget what I've just found out long enough for the teams to return with the cure, and everything will be fine.

I go to my mother's balcony rather than the side door, knowing she'll probably be in her office. I land and am about to call out her name when I hear a small, soft sound that cuts me worse than a new blade.

I hold my breath as I carefully lean forward, enough to see but not enough to be noticed. My mother sits hunched at her desk. The shine of her tears reflects in the nearby candlelight. She cradles something in her hand, and I move forward ever so slightly, trying to get a better look as my eyes adjust. The blackened shapes are familiar, but I don't realize what they are until I notice the soot clinging to her fingertips.

It's one of the dolls that I had burned—or thought I had. She must have taken it from the pile at the last second. She holds it as if it is an injured bird. Something fragile and precious. A black dress and shawl hang on a wall hook behind her. Just as the yellow dress I am in hasn't seen much use, neither has that one. But I recognize it on sight. It is the one she wore the day that we sent my father to the Endless Skies, his body burned on the pyre with the other fallen warriors.

I pull myself out of sight again, biting back my own tears as I press into the wall. *Mother.* She is the kind of lioness to rouse a person's spirits with a song, or offer her help before it is asked—a formidable woman but of a softer, kinder strength. The loss of my father nearly broke her, and it took years before she came back. Losing two of the Storm's End girls has stirred that despair, and now it is rushing forth like a river.

Once news of Prince Tabrol's illness breaks, she will drown.

I don't know how long I stand there. Bells ring to mark the hour, and I let the sounds crash into me as I think of what to do. I can't go inside, put on a brave face, and lie that the children still have a good chance when I know they don't.

They will have to send more warriors, but a decision like that can take time, as Noam said. What's more, I can still see them deciding against sending more teams. If Tabrol dies, we'll need people here to defend the city from the humans if they attack by sea. No, not *if* they attack. When.

I refuse to stay idle.

If I am going to do something on my own, it has to be now. There isn't enough time for me to wait and see what the sentinels and king decide. The small prince can't afford for me to.

Closing my eyes, I go through everyone I know, trying to find some clarity. Seth would never entertain the thought of leaving. Callen would take time to think it out, considering every angle. Ox would rally someone else, or at least have someone agreeing with him before deciding. But I'm not any of them. I'm not even a warrior.

I am Rowan An'Talla, and I have to decide on my own.

I go over the facts in my mind. I am the only one who knows of the children's worsening illness and of Prince Tabrol's. If I leave now, I will still be serving my city in a way. To find the teams and renew the urgency of the mission is, in a way, doing my part. But selfishly, I know if I leave, it also means I get what I want. Can I live with that? Will my intention be enough to absolve me of a charge of desertion when I return? I don't know.

What I do know is that the sound of my mother's crying will haunt me until the end of my days. If I can spare her any amount of pain, I will.

Mind spinning, I take to the skies. Warm sunlight makes the gold of my wings shine, and I stretch them out, farther and farther until I'm straining to hold the position. I need the sunlight to give me courage. A lot of courage.

I have to make a choice, but in the pit of my stomach, I know that I already have.

"Skies keep me," I say to no one. Maybe to the first king and queen, or to my father watching over me. Maybe to the Endless Skies themselves.

I am going to help my city, and I am going to do it on my own terms. Even if it means disobeying the king. Even if it means risking my dream. It is the right thing to do, and it is what I want to do.

Now I just have to hope the risk will be worth it in the end.

16

ROWAN

It takes me until sixth bell to gather my armor and my wits. Along with my knives, I choose a lightweight shortsword and set it on my left side. I run by the dining hall and pack as many dry foods as I can, ignoring any curious looks. I sling my now-heavy pack over my shoulder and head for one of the exits, but a tug in my gut makes me pause.

Looking over my shoulder, I take in the glow of the Warriors' Hall one last time. From the reflection pool and earthy foliage of the Underbelly to the glass rooftop and every proud archway in between, I love the Hall. I've worked so hard to get here, to earn a place for myself. Skies willing, I'll be back in just a matter of days. But it still feels like I am leaving so much behind.

"Thank you," I say, touching a hand reverently to the wall. "I'll see you soon."

Then I turn to the east.

I don't know the flight paths the warriors had been assigned, but Noam said Ramsgate is due east, so that's where I'll fly. I cradle my determination like a candle flame—I have to protect it, or I'd lose my nerve. *Just get to Balmora,* I tell myself. *Once I'm there, I'll feel better.*

The sun lingers above the west, but the first diamonds of stars are beginning to appear overhead.

The entire sky is mine. Taking my lioness form, I rise to meet her.

On the first day of training, one of the older warriors instructed us to fly into the frigid sea. Then he called us back up to the Heliana to dry in the sunlight. Then he sent us back to the water.

It went on for an hour: sun and sea, warmth and icy cold, until our spirits broke and our skin forgot how to mend. I remember vomiting onto the grass, hating every bone in my body and swearing I would never feel so low again.

Deserting feels a lot like that.

I fly straight down from the city, until I'm skimming the sea's surface. A quiet thrill thrums through me like a harp string finally played. It has been years since I rebelled in any way, let alone in an enormous way like this. My first weeks of training were spent doing extra drills and cleaning dishes as part of numerous reprimands. I had a smart mouth, as my mother was quick to remind me. Years of training had helped instill a deep sense of respect for the warrior ways, but even now I have to actively hold back when an instructor's tone rubs me the wrong way. It feels good to have this little piece of myself back, especially now that I know what the sentinels did and are still doing.

The sight of the ocean rushing past me as I fly brings my mind back to the glowing waters of the grotto. I miss Callen so much, more than I expected to. He would have helped me think this out step by step. Would he have sided with me, maybe even come with me? *Of course he would have,* my heart whispers. I know that now. Ox would have said yes, too. At least I think he would have.

The waters churn more violently as I approach Balmora. At the Cliffs, I fly into the most shadowed part of the rocky surface and swing my body upward. Here and there, my longest feathers brush on stone, but I keep going. Cresting the ridge, I fly low and try to stay hidden as much as I can, but the land is covered only by sparse sea grasses and weeds. Still, I don't want to gain any height. My magic could start to fail any second. . . .

It comes quickly, like air being sucked from my lungs. I use the last moments to drop my bag from my jaws and tuck my body into a roll. I tumble into the grasses, a rock embedded in the ground colliding with my hip as I do, and I let out a sharp yelp as I finally come to a stop.

I lie there for a minute, panting. I've done it. I've made it to Balmora.

Save for losing my magic, everything feels right. The dirt under my elbows is just dirt. A strange, droning sound that I can't place carries from the mountains to the north, but closer to me, the birds and insects sound the same here as on the Heliana. I welcome everything that feels familiar.

I get up and dust myself off, then retrieve my bag. The Heliana is a gray blur over the sea, too far for me to make out any of her buildings. I have left everything I've known behind, and I can't turn back. I've made my own mission: tell the teams about Tabrol, and help them find the cure before it is too late.

"Hang on, little prince," I whisper. "Just hang on."

The teams have a day's journey ahead of me, but if I press forward as long as I physically can and minimize my sleep, I may just have a chance of finding one. Any of the warrior teams would do, but I'd be lying to myself if I said I didn't have my heart set on one in particular.

Seth would look after me, as he always did. As for Ox and Callen . . . I'd be happy to be beside either of them.

Skies, I wonder if they've talked about me. They'd have to talk about *something* when taking breaks or resting for the night. If I came up at all, what would they say? Have they realized that they have feelings for the same person?

Enough, I tell myself. It doesn't matter if they've talked about me. That is the last thing I'll bring up when I find them—that is, if I find them.

My heart can wait. My fears about deserting—and my dream of becoming a warrior—can wait. I turn for the east and don't look back.

17

SHIRENE

It's silence that does it.

Finally, alone in my quarters with nowhere to be, and no one looking for me, I break. Or at least I try to.

Pounding my fists on my bed, I beg for tears, and none come. If I'm going to cry, it has to be now. Who knows when I'll get another moment's rest?

Someday, when this is all behind us, I'll come clean and start again. But for now, no one can know. The citizens can never learn that it was us who turned down peace, us who fanned the hate in the humans' hearts. We are the reason they deny us help now, victims of a pride that has endured for generations.

Now, like a hunter caught in his own trap, we have no one to blame but ourselves.

I sit back on my knees, defeated. Seth. What if he doesn't come back? What if the prince dies before he does?

Eighth bell sings out from the Glass Tower. I push myself to my feet with a sigh and light one of the citrus candles by my bedside. It is from the same maker as Mother's candles, and as the room warms with the scent, it takes me back to Storm's End's halls, when I was just a person and not a voice for the city. The moment's reverie doesn't last. I can't let it.

The palace maids have already tidied up my room, but I smooth out the bedspread I've wrinkled, savoring the soft feel of the fabric. Warrior training emphasizes tactile feeling: know your weapon, know the ground you keep low to, know the difference between familiar and unfamiliar. Even in my exhausted state, old habits die hard.

With a quick scrub of my face, I let down my hair only to redo it again in a twist of twin braids knotted at the base of my neck. I tie it off with gold thread, denoting my status. Renna will scoff at the look—the hair of a palace maid with the status of a sentinel—but for once, I'm able to shrug off what Renna might think.

Satisfied, I take my lioness form and make a long, circular sweep of the city. A few citizens wave their hellos, and I roar out in response. Keep the people happy, keep the people safe. I want so badly to succeed at both.

Heart hammering with love for my city, I angle downward to Storm's End. I'm guessing, but Rowan won't go back to the Underbelly after yesterday. Impulsive as she can be, she shows her hand more than she thinks. When things get hard, she goes home.

I trust her not to spread what I'd told her, but that isn't why I want to see her. I pulled rank on her, on my little sister, just as I told her I never would. I let her down.

My shadow crosses over Storm's End, and I'm about to fly for the matron's balcony in the back when I see the crowd gathered outside the front doors. *Oh no.*

I land and take my human form. A group of people, men and women alike, crowds the doors of the school. I recognize the woman closest to me, a fisherman's wife whom I know from the market. Her eyes widen when she sees me.

"Lady Shirene!" Her words are half-exclamation, half-sob. "Is it true? Are there children dying?"

I had rehearsed this moment in my head so many times. "We are being careful," I say smoothly. The crowd parts, and

I see Mother's deep magenta dress. Her expression shifts when she sees me. "The king and sentinels have heard the rumors as have you. And we are being careful. Now please, let me through."

Still, the questions tumble into one another.

"Are we safe?"

"I saw healers flying from the palace!"

"What's causing it?"

My heart clamors in my rib cage—there are too many people, and so many questions. I have to stall as best as I can.

I am the King's Voice. This is my job, now more than ever.

"I just came from the palace. We must work together to keep calm until the king and scholars tell us what to do next." There's more grumbling and whispers, but my title and calm have done the trick. "Matron Talla, if you will."

She unlocks the doors to Storm's End and ushers me inside. Just before the door closes, I see a pair of women reach out and hug each other. No words, just an embrace. The murmurs behind us quiet as the doors click shut. I don't think I've ever been so grateful for its protection.

Mother opens her arms and draws me in for a hug. "I'm so glad you came."

"I'm sorry I couldn't get away sooner," I reply. "I'm so sorry about the two girls."

"We can only look forward," she says, but she avoids my gaze.

"Skies. Rowan told you."

"And the fish vendor outside." Her shoulders drop. "Congratulations, my sweet girl. The King's Voice. I'm so proud of you. Your father would be, too."

I struggle to hold back my tears. "Thank you, Mother. I'm sorry you didn't hear it from me. I'm just . . . so busy."

"Come on," she says. "Let's rest."

"I don't have much time," I reply, but I follow her, anyway. It's strange to see the circular classroom empty and clean. A pang of sorrow strikes me as I imagine my mother spending her High Summer here, putting everything away. Alone.

"Is Rowan here?" I ask.

"She came by yesterday."

"Was she okay?"

Mother laughs and waves me toward the kitchen. "She was upset about not being put on a team. Other than that, she seemed fine."

"Good." I didn't expect Rowan to say anything about Noam, but she kept our fight to herself, too. I'm not sure how to feel about that.

Here in the kitchen, the wooden countertops lie bare and the sink perfectly dry until my mother spills a little bit of water from the kettle. Three tall, thin windows at the other end of the room give us a view of the adjacent house, where a family has kept their High Summer lamps on and is having a makeshift dance.

"I miss this place," I say absently.

"You know you're welcome anytime. You and Sethran."

I exhale a smile. "You can call him *Seth,* Mother. It's been long enough."

"Oh, fine. I just like the full sound of it." She sets the tea down, and for just a moment, I relax.

The noise that interrupts my peace is unholy. It begins as a buzz, like if I pressed my ear against a beehive and managed to escape with only the memory of the sound. It grows into something more like thunder, but without any of the beauty and only the malice.

My mother goes to the window, her voice thick with uncertainty. "What is that?"

Scrambling up as quickly as I can, I dart back out through

our small kitchen to the nearest hallway that leads to open air. "What in the skies . . . ."

The machines fly in arced paths, circling the city. A half dozen shadows trail behind them—warriors already on their tail. The sound grows unbearable, and I see the warrior flying in the rear dive sharply, engulfed in a belch of black smoke. From the lower levels of the palace, somebody screams. I squint harder, struggling to see in the evening's fading light, but I don't need to see what's going on to know the horrible sound of bullets being fired.

"Mother, get away from the window!" I cry. "Go to your room and close the doors. Now."

My mother, with her caretaker's soul, is no fighter. She obeys without a word.

I dash through Storm's End, practically barreling into the door of my old room before wrenching it open. Bless Mother, she's left it alone just as I hoped. My old set of warrior armor lies as I left it in a storage trunk. Though not as fine as my sentinel ones, I don't have time to go to the palace.

When I'm ready, I take my lioness form and follow the sound of the machines. I beat my wings feverishly to catch up with the others. *What are they?* They had the wings of a bird, and lines streak their span like those of bats, but they don't move like ours do. My ears are stuffed with their endless droning, and my head swerves as I try to count them in the dim light. Five. No, six.

Gunfire peppers the air, countered by deep roars of pain. The smell of blood meets my senses like a fire to dry brush. Immediately, the warriors scatter, one of the fighters falling too fast before someone else swoops to grab her. Screams sound from the streets as I hear others echoing the command to take cover.

The Heliana is under attack. *The king.*

A sentinel's first job is clear: protect the king at all costs. Flaring my wings hard, I fly directly at the palace, but the Tower is blessedly empty, and every light has been snuffed out. The royal family will use the emergency tunnels in the palace to shelter in the stone Keep deep within the ridge beneath the palace. They will be safe.

Banking away from the Tower, I find the closest of the machines and head toward it. I swoop up high so I'm above the machine, but I struggle to keep pace with it. A human protected by a glass dome sits at the machine's controls. I swoop lower, readying to roll onto my back. Wind, smoke, and the unforgiving smell of the humans' metal makes me gag, but I push the roiling of my stomach away. If I can hit the glass with my armor, it might shatter.

A roar sounds right behind me. A warrior whose name I don't know materializes by my side, her slim frame keeping better pace with the machine than I ever could. Better yet, attached to her armor between her forelegs is a sturdy bow and capped quiver. An archer. Her piercing blue eyes meet mine, sharp with resolve.

"The glass!" I roar. "Let me break it!"

"Go!" she growls back.

She slows a beat, giving me the clearest shot. With a roar, I curl around and fold my wings against my face and limbs, exposing the unforgiving metal of my armor as I let my full weight fall towards the machine.

The glass explodes, and the human cries out in surprise.

My hind legs bounce off the machine as the machine dips. Suddenly, it pitches upward, slamming into my body before I can get away. Lights swirl in my eyes as the wind is knocked out of me. A tangle of cords and cloth releases from behind the human's seat, catching my wing like a net.

Wind rushes by as the machine plummets, this time without any sign of recovery. I pull back, but only manage to tighten the ropes around my right wing and leg. My claws scratch feebly at the side of the machine, and I beat my free wing away.

But the human is strapped in, and the cords stuck with him—and me. The sea rushes toward us as my heart seizes, and I bat away furiously, sharp golden feathers splintering . . .

Desperately, I shift to my human form. My wings disappear in a burst of gold magic, and as they do, the cords loosen. I roll backward onto the wing of the machine, vision spinning in a rush of air and black smoke. Moments later, I'm in a free fall toward the sea.

I retake my lioness form, right wing throbbing with pain, and fall back as I watch three warriors slam into the machine's left wing at once. The machine pitches angrily, the smoke spewing out in sputters. The droning intensifies, and the human screams as the warriors force the machine down into water.

Mindful of my strained wing, I fly in slow arcs as the machine sinks and gradually fades from my sight. Already, I see the sea-folk surrounding it, making sure it never sees the skies again. The other machines fly off in retreat, making wide U-turns until they're headed back for Balmora. The warrior who aided me flies over, out of breath.

"Thank you for helping me," I say. "Are you wounded?"

"No, Sentinel," she replies with a quick dip of her head. "You?"

"I'm fine," I reply. "I must go to the king."

"I saw Sentinel Renna fly to the king's rooms when we first heard them," the warrior responds.

"And they would have gone to the Keep," I reply. I dive, heading straight there. She dives with me, gliding over the rooftops. Here and there, groups of healers huddle around citizens lying in the streets. My stomach flips. We weren't fast enough. I didn't protect them.

My lungs still burn from the machine's smoke. It moved with fire. How is that possible? And how many more are there? The humans have always been clever in their weapons. Now they have made one to bring the Heliana to her knees.

All while our numbers are diminished and our prince unable to leave his bed . . .

I'm running out of reasons to have hope.

18

ROWAN

I wake at first light, my cloak wrapped securely around me. Last night, I traveled as far as I could, eating my packed food for energy, but when I stumbled over a rock that I definitely should have seen, I called it a night and looked for shelter.

There was no telling how far I'd gone, and without a map, I only have the sun to tell me I was going the right way. Pouring a bit of my water into the dirt, I mix and then smear mud onto my armor—even my special vambrace—to hide the shine.

Walking as quickly as I can while keeping a sustainable pace, I focus on every sound and smell, no matter how small. My stomach growls as the sun climbs, but I keep moving. There were only so many rations that could fit in the bag, and it could be days until I find another team. If I find another team.

So long as I was headed toward Ramsgate, I had the best chance of finding the others, but part of me was grappling with the possibility of having to venture into the city by myself. I can't let the fear of that stop me. I have to do whatever it takes to find the cure.

But it sure as the skies would be easier with some help.

When the grumbling from my stomach gets to be too much, I cave and eat a few slices of bread and an apple. A mission like this is about surviving both the way there *and* the way back, but only one way matters right now.

At least I'd left the barren land around the Cliffs behind me. The dense forest farther east brought with it the comforting sounds of insects and birds. Sunlight streams through the branches, illuminating the dusty forest air and casting a pale glow on the earth. I inhale deeply, then let out a quiet whistle, calling up to any birds that are hiding in the tangle of branches above.

Nothing happens, and I'm disappointed but not surprised. It takes less magic to commune with birds than to shift between forms, but it still takes something. I envision gold threads, the way my mother taught me to think of it, extending from my voice and into the air. What it takes is a bird finding that thread and following it back to me. I whistle again, and after a few moments two tiny brown finches flutter toward me.

"Hi, little ones," I say, smiling.

I tear off a bit of the remaining bread, leaving the crumbs on my palm. The birds land in my hand, their tiny bodies quivering as they enthusiastically peck at the bread. I brush my thumb across the feathers between their eyes, and they close their eyes in delight as I do. Another trick I learned from my mother. When they've eaten their fill, I call up the threads of magic again.

"Callen," I say to one, diving into the magic pooled in my chest. "Ox," I tell the other.

The birds hop uselessly from my hand to a nearby branch. I curse. Of course magic won't work this far from the Heliana. Or maybe they are too far from me that it doesn't hold. I'll have to just find them on my ow—

The first bird goes, and when the second follows, I nearly fall over in relief. Best of all, they fly in the same direction.

"Southeast," I whisper. "Well, southeast for me, too, then."

I alternate between jogging and walking as early morning

becomes midmorning. My legs and hips ache at the repetitive motion. Sweat slides down my back and hairline. There's less wind than up in the skies, and without the ever-present breeze, everything is unnaturally still. My lungs start to strain from the effort but I wait until I am starting to feel faint before I stop to rest again. Picking a choice tree, I climb up. Keeping an eye out for the finches, I pick a defensible position and catch my breath.

I'm swallowing a cool gulp of water when there is a chirp by my ear. One of the birds has come back. I thank it in my mind, mentally severing the thread that connects us. The bird did his best, but the forest below stays still, until—

"Rowan?"

I look down and find a familiar head of black-brown hair and dark eyes looking up at me. "Ox!"

A gentle smile betrays his disbelief. "Are you following me, Rowan An'Talla?"

"Not quite," I fire back. "One second."

I put the rest of my food back, painfully aware of the awkward silence. A wiser Leonodai might have planned out their lie, but well, I'm not that Leonodai. I don't want Ox to be complicit in anything. What matters is the prince's illness.

The fact that I've left without orders . . . that could wait.

Ox's arms are around me the moment my feet hit the forest floor. He plants a kiss on the side of my head as he pulls me close. "What are you doing here?" he asks. "Did they send you, too?"

"Yes," I say, remembering that someone once said the best lies are short—and so is our time. "Ox . . . Prince Tabrol is sick."

Ox puts his hands on both of my shoulders, his jaw slack. "What?"

"It's true," I say. "And skies, it's worse. The kids are dying faster than the sentinels thought. One boy died after five days. Ox, that cannot be Tabrol."

"I know," he replies.

"We have to find the cure right away," I say, the thoughts I'd bottled up during my journey spilling out of me. "We only have five days, total, and that's *if* the prince holds on that long."

"Okay, okay," he says. "I can't get past the prince. I'm glad they sent more people, but why are you alone?"

Um. "The sentinels thought sending each warrior-elect alone will help us get by undetected."

"Got it." He exhales, then leans in to kiss me again. This time, the move catches me off guard, and after a heartbeat of bliss, a shot of worry races through me. What if Callen sees?

And skies, why does it matter if he does?

I pull back. "Where are the others?"

"We took a defensive position on a hillside to the south," Ox replies, tilting his chin upward in that direction. "After Exin, Sethran is taking things more slowly."

"Exin?" I ask, but as the question leaves my lips, I read Ox's grim expression loud and clear. "Oh no. Skies keep him." My mind goes to Callen. Exin was his best friend. I never saw the guy without a grin on his face, cheering up everyone he spoke to. "Well, tell Seth we need to get moving."

Ox exhales a laugh. "You call him *Seth*?"

I pause. "Don't you?"

"He's my commander. I call him *sir*."

"Okay, well, *sir* has also been with my sister for a decade," I say. "Give or take a year. I know him, and he knows me."

"All right," Ox says, inclining his head for me to follow. "Just don't forget he outranks you. You have to do as he says."

"Well, we'll see about that, won't we?" I've already disobeyed the king and sentinels. What's a commander?

Still, Ox's words sharpen a truth in my mind. My sister's partner or not, Seth is a Leonodai commander. He is trusted for a reason. Could I convince him that my deserting was the right thing to do? Would he even look me in the eyes once he knew?

That I don't know. Which is why I have to do everything I can to make sure he doesn't find out.

19

CALLEN

For what feels like the tenth time this hour, I wipe sweat from my brow. "I'd give my axe for a strong ocean breeze."

"I'll throw in a sword," Sethran replies. "But at least we have shade and water."

We found the small stream late last night. It didn't run as clear as one of the Heliana's rivers, but it would do. We're still several days from where the scholars said the cure would be, but pushing ourselves past exhaustion would be stupid. Pacing ourselves is as much in our training as fighting past our limits.

I tip my waterskin up and am swallowing a deep gulp when Ox emerges from the underbrush.

Then I see her. She's got dirt on her face and mud on her armor. At her side, all six of her knives curl against her thigh like ivy grown into stone. Her hair is matted and flat against her brow that's slick with sweat, but skies, Rowan is here. On Balmora.

"Rowan?" says Sethran.

"Commander Sethran," she says, tone warm with relief. She runs toward him, and after a nod of respect, the two hug.

"I'm surprised to see you," Sethran says. "What are you doing here?"

"We were sent shortly after the warrior teams," she replies. "The situation is much worse now, sir."

Her next words are like a frost-in-summer—impossible.

"Prince Tabrol," Sethran says, shaking his head slowly. "But the king and queen were keeping him isolated. How did he get sick?"

"I guess it wasn't enough," Rowan replies. "We have time, but we can't rest. Especially because the scholars were wrong about how long it takes. We don't know for sure anymore."

Sethran puts his hands on his hips and turns away, thinking. "Were you sent alone?"

"Yes, sir. To avoid detection," she says. "The sentinels didn't want to give more reason for the humans to attack."

"Are you expected to return, now that you've found us?"

Rowan shakes her head. "If you are willing to have me stay, sir, I would like to stay."

We wait a moment while Sethran considers this new information. I catch Ox's eyes on Rowan, but she's focused on her commander.

"The sentinels sent us for a reason," Sethran says finally. "And we have to honor that reason. We'll reduce our breaks and limit our sleep. This situation demands the most of us, and it's time we rise to it."

"Yes, sir," I reply, with Ox and Rowan as my echo. The latter's chest lifts in pride. *This is the life she wants,* I realize. *To serve a commander, one as respected as Sethran.*

"Rowan, do you have the energy to keep up?" Then, seeing her frown, he corrects. "Not that I don't think you do. But you must have been up all night to catch us."

"I'll be fine, sir," is her reply.

"All right, then," Sethran says. Then, addressing all of us, "If anyone hears or sees anything strange, say something. And keep your eyes on the ground. If the skies are good, we'll find the cure sooner than the scholars predicted."

We move east. With the night's sleep and food in my stomach, my body is revived from yesterday's travels—but that's not the only thing giving me strength.

I cannot believe she's here. I try to push it down and out of my mind, but I can't deny that my mood has soared. It was horrible to leave Ro, especially with what happened at the grotto. If I hadn't confessed how I felt, this would be even better, but I'll take awkward time with her over no time at all.

After the four of us find an even stride, I slow my pace a little until I am next to Rowan. She's dulled her armor, just as we have, but I sense her excitement that she is wearing it at all— here, out on a mission like she's always wanted.

"Hey, Ro," I say. "I didn't realize you were serious about your promise to come get me yourself."

"I'm always serious about promises," she replies. "Besides, I didn't come for you."

I blush. "Right, right. The prince."

"Skies. Sorry. I didn't mean it like that," she says. She touches her fist to my shoulder meekly, an offering of peace. "I'm glad you're safe. Ox told me about Exin. I'm so sorry, Callen."

My friend's name is like a sucker punch. "We were ambushed at the Cliffs," he says. "I'm not sure how many other teams made it."

She walks ahead of me a little, getting between me and Sethran. "We'll light a candle for him at the grotto when this is all done."

My heart quickens at the unspoken offering behind her words. The grotto is our place. She isn't mad. She wants to go back, at least one more time.

"When this is all done," I echo.

We fall into a steady silence, and pretty soon, I'm panting from exertion, but there is no way anything is going to slow us down at this point. With Rowan at my side, things feel right, like she is supposed to be here to help us. And skies know we need the help.

Four days until Tabrol dies. Four days until the Heliana falls and life as we know it is lost for good.

20

ROWAN

I stay ahead near Seth with Callen behind me. Ox is last, the wide range of his bow giving us some safety. He shot a pair of rabbits earlier, and my mouth waters at the thought of a meal.

"Did you see your sister before you left?" Seth asks quietly.

I nod. "We had a fight, actually."

"Oh?" he replies. "About what?"

"Not being trusted to go on a team." Then quickly, I add, "It was before they changed their minds."

"You know nothing the sentinels do is personal," he says. "Believe me, I know it feels that way."

"I know." And I do. I was surprised how much he supported Shirene's decision to become a sentinel. Shirene loves kids the way our mother does, and I always figured she'd want to be a mother herself. Thinking of it now, I wish I'd just asked her, at least once.

"Well, for what it's worth, I'm glad you found us," Seth says, giving me a sincere smile. "Though I won't tolerate any of the back talk that you used to give me when you were little."

"You were a stranger dating my sister," I say. "The back talk was justified."

"So says you."

"Yes, I . . . says," I reply, and we both laugh. "I promise to only talk back in my head, or I'll vent it to one of them."

Seth looks over his shoulder. "About that . . ."

Oh, skies. "Please don't."

"I hear the rumors in the Hall, you know. They're both

good guys, Rowan," he says. "But I'll send you home if you can't keep your feelings in check."

"You would never," I reply, but his expression has shifted away from friend and back to commander.

He pauses, and I do, too. "I mean it, Rowan. We can't take chances."

"I know," I reply. "I understand."

Seth resumes the lead, while I slow a little to put some space between us. My legs tremble, and the space underneath my eyes feels heavier with every passing second. The crunch of twigs behind me pulls me back.

Callen comes up behind me, brow raised. "You okay?"

"Yeah," I say. "Just a little tired."

We keep walking together, strides matched, pushing through the ferns and underbrush. The terrain rolls in uneven hills and valleys, making the journey at times more arduous. The air is still thick between Callen and me, but remembering my words to Seth a few minutes ago, I grasp toward any topic that's not *us*. "What happened at the coast?"

"The humans built up their defenses these past months," he says. "That must be why the attacks by sea stopped. As soon as we got close, the coast lit up with gunfire. Sethran told us to dive, so I dove. Exin got shot in the leg. He told me to go," he says. "He knew he was going to die."

My chest tightens. "He did his duty, Callen. We can honor him by doing ours."

"Yeah," he says. "But it's still hard to forget."

Ahead of us, Seth stops short and raises an arm. He motions downward, crouching as he does. I drop and go for my knives.

A horrible, ghostly horn sounds near us, followed by a high scream. I flinch and look up in alarm, ready to run in the opposite direction, but Seth turns toward it.

"What is that?" I whisper.

"This way," says Seth, walking toward the sound. "Keep low."

The three of us follow behind our commander. Up ahead, the forest drops off into an open valley. Below us are trees—or what's left of them. Fractured stumps of what used to be thousands of years of magnificent pines and oaks have been left in ruin, the soil around them churned up.

A pair of straight metal rails stretches out farther than I can see, like twin arrows fired off into the distance. On it, less than a hundred yards away, is a black machine, gleaming menacingly like a hunter over a kill and smoking like a bonfire. Humans are moving quickly around it, loading heavy crates and bags of supplies. The horn sounds again, and the machine belches black smoke into the air. The humans move faster, waving to one another frantically.

"A train," Ox says. "This can help us."

"A what?" I ask.

"That machine. It's called a train," he replies. "They move humans in those boxes."

"How do you know that?"

"The warriors were told of it," Seth answers. "The sentinels keep it from everyone else because—"

"Because that's what they do, evidently," I mutter.

"Watch it. The skies are good to us. We can get on it."

"What do you mean 'get on'?"

"Those boxes slide open," he says, pointing at the wheeled boxes behind the one spewing smoke. "We can hide inside with the cargo. Those tracks are headed east. So long as it keeps relatively straight, we could save hours—days, even."

"Okay," I reply. "So what do we do?"

He looks down at the steep ridge. "Figure out a way to get down without dying."

"We could go around," Callen offers, inclining to the trees to our right. "The slope tapers off."

Ox frowns. "We can't risk it leaving without us on it. I say we go straight down the ridge."

"And if we each break a leg going your way, we won't even be *able* to get on it," Callen replies.

"Stop," Seth warns. He's in full commander mindset now, like when Shirene pulled rank on me. "We'll go down the ridge, but carefully. Ox is right. We can't risk it leaving. It's our best option right now." He looks each of us in the eye to make sure we understand. "If a human spots you, take them down quietly. We don't want to leave death in our wake, but we have to stay alive to find the cure. Understood?"

With a chorus of *Yes, sir*s, I fall in line behind Ox and Callen. The two of them exchange a glance, silently daring the other to go first.

"Skies," I say, pushing my way between them. "I'll go first."

Stepping forward, I angle myself over the ridge, leaning so the bronze guard over my shins is parallel to the ground. Before I overthink, I push off, skidding down the ridge on my left side. Loose rocks scrape at my boot. All at once, my leg muscle gives out, and I lose my form, crashing down onto my side. The gravel slices into my skin like teeth, but I push up with a gloved hand and keep stumbling and running over the remaining rocks. I grit my teeth tightly—I refuse to be the reason the humans spot us.

I reach the train and touch the side, thrown off by the overwhelming smell of metal. The others join me a few moments later, and Seth tells Callen and Ox to pull open the door while he and I push it from the other side. We give it a few tries, but it doesn't budge.

"Next one," Seth says, breathing heavily. "Quickly."

We move to the next car, this one identical to the first. The humans mingle on the other side of the train. A group of them hurries down toward the front car that's spewing smoke. I reach back for my knives. If a human sees us, I'll have to kill him before he has the thought to sound an alarm.

The ghastly whistle rings out once more. Ox and Callen put both their hands on the sliding door of the car and pull, while Seth and I shove it at the same time.

"Come on, come on," Seth mutters. I glance over my shoulder, keenly aware of how exposed we are. One good shot, and a bullet would take any of us out.

Then, finally, the door slides freely.

"Rowan, go," my commander says hurriedly. With a jump, I push myself up and onto the car's floor just as he puts his hand on my back, guiding me forward. I scramble up, knee scraping against the rough, unfinished floor. The flavor of the air around me changes—grains and leather, piss and the overwhelming scent of humans. Bile rises in my stomach at the smell, but I force it back as I scoot out of the way so Ox can climb in, too. The train lurches, and the wheels start to turn.

"We're moving," I say, just as Ox curses loudly. "Hurry!" I shout, reaching my hand for Callen.

He jumps, and I pull back with my full weight. His body lands heavily on top of mine, and heat comes unbidden to my face. Callen realizes it, too, and rolls off.

"Sorry," he says.

"It's fine!" I reply awkwardly, avoiding his eyes as much as he is avoiding mine. Meanwhile, Ox has taken my place at the door, leaning out to reach for Seth. Our commander leaps in just as the train really picks up speed. With a shove, Ox slams the door shut.

The group of us sits there, chests heaving as it settles in. We've done it.

"Everyone all right?" Seth asks.

"Yes, sir," I reply, with the others echoing my response. Gingerly, I examine the scrapes on my leg. One or two ooze blood enough for me to see it in the low light, but as I press my hands against the others, they feel shallow. In the back of my mind, I curse myself for not having the foresight to pack any healers' salves.

The four of us sit in the darkness of the car, letting the uneven motion of the train rock us. To my left, Ox inches closer to me as we lean against the wall. He touches his leg to mine, and the sudden warmth of his body makes me flinch. He draws back.

Skies. I curse inwardly. He has no idea why I am so jumpy. My stomach churns with a mixture of confusion, guilt, and nausea from the moving train.

"The skies were good to us, but let's not get lax," Seth says. "Keep your weapons close and be ready to disembark anytime. We don't know if this thing will stop or turn."

"I'll take watch, sir," says Callen. I look up. I can just make out his frame in the darkness across from me and Ox. He has his knees drawn up to his chest, arms resting idly on his knees.

I could be wrong, but it seems like he is looking at me with hurt in his eyes. *You made things awkward between us,* I think, wanting so badly to be mad. *You did this.* And we can't exactly work toward fixing it with the others around.

The fact that I am here, relatively safe and among friends, reminds me of who isn't. Curling my knees to my chest, I try to remember the last thing I said to Exin. We were never the kind of friends who spend time together solo, but we'd had more than our fair share of meals together with Callen and Vera in the dining hall. I do my best to memorize conversations and jokes he told, no matter how trivial. The words are all sharp now, dense with my desperation to remember.

The thought of sleep overpowers my restless heart. My muscles, fueled by fear and excitement, shiver with fatigue, and my stomach aches. Riffling through my bag, I eat everything that's left and try to get some rest. The train stops twice more, and each time the wheels screech and scream in such an ungodly way that I almost give up trying to get any sleep at all.

Sometime later, I wake up, groggy and sicker to my stomach than I was before. Afternoon light streams in through the slats of wood that make up the roof of the car, enough to help me see. Callen sees me awake and gives me a nod. A knife glints in his hand. I keep quiet as he pushes the tip of the blade into the soft pads of his fingers to stay awake. The train shakes like it's rolling over stones.

"What is that?" I ask.

Callen cocks his head. "It's been doing that sometimes. I don't think the track is as good here."

I must have fallen asleep again, because when I open my eyes, I'm slumped on the floor. Apparently, my body's need for rest—especially to overcome my staying up so late the night before—overpowers my desire to be helpful to the team. My arm is numb from how I slept, and it tingles as I sit up. Ox's cloak slides off my shoulders as I do, and I curl my fingers around the fabric. He must have put it over me as I slept. The warrior in question is on watch.

"How long have I been out?" I whisper, scooting closer to him.

"It's hard to tell," he replies. "No bells. No sky. But it is dark now."

"I can see that," I say lightly. "How are you?"

"Not great."

"Yeah, me too."

He sighs. "But I'm glad you're here. I'd rather know exactly where you are and that you're okay than have to be wondering if maybe you somehow got sick, too, or if you were sent out on a team after all."

Skies, there he goes. Catching me off guard with his kindness.

"But . . . ," he whispers. "And I know this isn't the place. But if there's something I should know, I want you to tell me."

My stomach flips. What does he mean? Did he see through my lie about warriors-elect being sent out? I was so careful to channel my inner Shirene and consider my words tactfully so as to not give it away. "What?"

"I know you two are close," Ox says. "And I'm not about to get in the way of that."

Oh. He's talking about Callen. I swallow hard. "We've known each other a really long time."

"That doesn't answer the question."

I turn my head so I can speak closer to his ear. "We're not together, if that's what you're worried about." Immediately, he tightens his arm around my waist.

"Good," he says. "Because you still owe me a dance."

"I keep my word." I try to match his lighter tone, but it's hard to forget just where we are and how much danger the city is still in. I didn't risk my dream for Callen or Ox, or even myself.

Loyalty above all.

This isn't the time or place for my heart to be deciding what it wants, but eventually, the time and place will arrive. I only hope my future self will know what to do, because right now, I am as lost as ever.

21

CALLEN

The sight of Rowan curled up against Ox's shoulder should bother me. But we're far from a home that may be falling to the sea with every passing hour as our prince gets sicker. We're tired. Hungry. Far away from the brethren we are used to being surrounded by.

I look away from them and out the side of the train car.

Wind stings my eyes as I watch the landscape move by in a blur of greens, grays, and browns. Dawn breaks over the east. Pale waves of light, straw-like plants roll in the wind. Rows of churned dirt spotted with dried plants—farmland. We have gardens here and there on the Heliana, but the bulk of our fresh food comes from Vyrinterra. I've never seen so much farmland in my life. How many humans would this feed? The humans have controlled Balmora for generations, growing and spreading farther than we know.

Then again, as we pass more and more empty farmland, it strikes me that I haven't seen anything green and growing, not even one field. Was summer not a fruitful season on Balmora? The land looked dark with water, so rain wasn't their problem, unless they were getting too much of it.

Sethran wakes up. Keeping a careful hand on the side of the car to steady himself, he comes over next to me.

"So long as we're moving east, this is our best shot at finding the cure fast," he says. "How long do you suspect we've been on this?"

"Ten hours, maybe more."

Sethran nods. "We stopped for a long while at what I guess was around twelfth bell. Still, we must be close to the cure."

I eat the rest of my rations, chewing the stale bread slowly and letting the jam inside it roll on my tongue. I'm still hungry, but being on the train car has given us the rest we needed. Keeping my hand on the wall like Sethran did, I stretch my legs. Ox and Rowan have woken, too, the latter following suit and stretching. I go back over to Sethran. Being at my commander's side is reassuring. *And it beats being closer to the two of them.*

Shifting, I press my face against one of the open slats, letting the wind rush over my face. If I close my eyes, I might believe I was flying. The pink sky overhead is dotted with birds. My heart rises, and I focus on one—yes! Not just birds. Gulls.

"Look," I say. "Gulls don't fly inland. We're near water."

Together, my commander and I crack the door open. Cold air rushes in, sending my hair flying and goose bumps appearing over every inch of exposed skin.

The sea.

I catch glimpses of silvery gray between the foothills. The rough waves churn the water white in some places. Keeping one hand firmly on the siding, I lean out as far as I dare and try to see where we are headed. I squint as the wind blows directly in my eyes.

"The tracks turn north ahead." I pull myself back inside. "The front of the train will veer sharply left, giving us a blind spot. That's when we should go."

"Are we close to Ramsgate?" Rowan asks.

"Skies, I hope so," Sethran says. "We've made it farther than any other team could have in this time."

We're the city's best hope right now. I share a look with Ro, who appears to have realized this, too.

My ears grow numb to the sounds of the train as we wait—the push-pull, then screaming and shrieking—that for a moment I think I'm going deaf when the rhythm changes as the train enters into the turn.

"We're slowing down," I say.

Sethran nods. "Then it's time we get off."

It's agonizing, waiting for the machine to slow. Restless, I get up and look out the opposite side of the train car.

"Look!" I shout over the din. Immediately, Rowan rushes over, and I try not to notice how close our faces are as she looks out.

"Skies alive," she whispers.

Even this far out, the human's city looks like twice the size of the Heliana. Spires point like jagged teeth into the sky. Smoke billows from their spouts in grayish black plumes. A haze wraps the city and blurs the air.

"Look at the sky," she says. "Nothing's flying over it."

"The birds must know something we don't."

"Or they know exactly what we do," she replies. "The humans poisoned the sky here. They poison everywhere they go."

"Callen," Sethran says. "You first. Get ready to jump."

I do as commanded and crouch by the door, bracing my body for the impact. The grasses below will provide some cushion, but not a lot. I wait, heartbeat after heartbeat, as the train continues to slow down. I watch the clumps of pale grasses and yellow flowers disappear from sight in a blur.

Then I jump. I do my best to roll and weaken my fall, but the impact rattles my body. My wrist lands awkwardly, and I can feel the blood rushing to the site and the swelling kicking in. As Ox tumbles to a stop a few yards from me, he scans the surroundings to see if we've been spotted.

Rowan pauses for a moment at the door, the wind sending

her hair flying around her face. She jumps and lands out of sight. Sethran appears last, half swinging, half falling off into the dense thicket of sea grasses and sand. I keep my wrist at my side as I join Ox, offering him my other hand to help him up. Both of our gazes drift over to the humans' city to the north. For a moment, we're united in a mix of awe and hate.

"That has to be Ramsgate," I say. "At least we know we're in the right place."

"And now we find the cure," Ox replies stiffly.

The group of us trudge along the shoreline. The Cliffs have no beach other than the cove the humans have claimed, and the shores of Vyrinterra belong to the horselords on the eastern side and the sea-folk on the western one. Here the water stomps on itself, white and frothy. The sound is like thunder, and I have to squint into the wild wind to see. The sand beneath my boots is coarse and dotted with a myriad of colors mixed with strands of kelp and other sea debris.

Ox wraps his arms around Ro to keep her warm, though I can see his own fingers shaking. I grit my teeth. I can bear this— and of course I'm only talking about the cold.

Just the cold.

Who knew the humans' lands could go from sun to storms so quickly? I scan the horizon for any kind of shelter. A cave, a cove. Some kind of cover.

"No one's seen it?" Sethran asks. We've all had our eyes on the ground, scanning for the red blooms.

"Maybe we're too close to the water," I say. "The winds are strong here. Not much is growing at all." I pull at a patch of thin grass next to me, and the fine strands come up easily, roots and all.

Sethran frowns. "We need shelter." He looks back toward the tracks. "Let's follow where the train was going. There will be settlements as we get close to their city."

We crest up a hill and survey the unfamiliar land. Pale boulders jut out from hillsides. It doesn't take long for us to find the tracks again, or for us to start really feeling the cold. Pain radiates from my ears, and I alternate between keeping my hands over them and keeping my hands inside my cloak. Soon my teeth begin to chatter. Tugging my cloak closer to me, I exhale down into the fabric, but the warmth only lasts a moment.

"There!" Ox says, loudly enough to hear over the wind. I follow where he points and make out the shape of a one-story house with light glowing from inside. A pale tower stands close by it, a huge beacon of light flashing at the top. The light flickers like a candle flame, but in a steady time. Light. Dark. Light. Beside the house is another darker building made of slatted wood.

"We should head to that barn," Sethran says just as I'm about to suggest it. "Hurry. This storm is coming in fast."

The scents of dust, hay, and refuse pour from inside the barn as we bypass the house. A lock rests on the front door, keeping the animals inside safely enclosed.

"Let's go around the back," Sethran says. We follow him until we're out of sight of the house. He nudges a loose board with his foot and tilts his head. "Callen."

It's an order, not a question. I bring my axe high and swing it low and fast. The wood splinters, and a few hits later, there is a space large enough for us to squeeze through. The others go first, and I climb in as the first droplets of rain hit my skin.

The barn is lit only from a lone lantern hung near the doorway. Above our heads is a loft stacked high with even more hay, and farther into the darkness is the murmur of livestock. A horse shifts in its stall, wary of our presence. Even without Knowledge, animals like horses and sheep can sense the inherent danger in Leonodai blood. The only part of Vyrinterra where Leonodai are not welcome is in the horselords' herds.

"Up," Sethran says. "If the humans come here, we can attack from above."

We do as we're told, and within minutes, we're huddled together in the almost dark, surrounded by heavy bales of hay. Droplets of rain leak in from the roof above, but it's as good as anything we're going to get.

Shrugging off my cloak, I spread it wide in hopes it'll dry. The straw itches against my skin, but I lie down anyway and feel the sleep threatening to take me almost instantly.

"Are we just going to sit here?" Rowan says.

"We'll wait until the rain clears," Sethran replies. "We don't have the resources to go looking now."

"But the prince—"

"Enough, Warrior-Elect. We are no use to the city if we get sick from wandering out in the rain. We're where we need to be for now."

Rowan goes quiet. I try to make eye contact with her, but she gets up and moves to a different area of the loft, fluffing the hay up in a show of her building a bed.

Part of me agrees with Rowan. I want to be out there looking for the cure. But I trust my commander. Going out in the rain without the proper gear wouldn't be the wisest choice right now. With one last look at Ro sulking in the corner, I close my eyes. Without the glaring sounds and constant motions, it was possible that we'd get some actual rest here, as opposed to the bursts of sleep on the train.

Hours later, with the same light unchanged as the rain continues to fall, the sound of steps on the floor below wakes me. A shiver dances across my skin. I sit up, my hand going to my axe.

Then, with a laugh that is equal parts exasperation and affection, I realize that both Rowan and my cloak are gone.

22

ROWAN

"You withstood four years of training," I mutter to myself. "You can get past a little rain."

Thank the skies Callen always has good cloaks—the expensive, well-made kind a general's son would be expected to have. Seth will have my head for leaving, but if I can come back with the cure, then he will have to forgive me.

The ground slopes downward toward the beach. A flash of inky black slips in and out of the waves. I watch the seal for a moment, missing the freedom of the skies that it finds in the ocean. A sound like a shout carries in the wind, and my hands go to my knives. Behind me, a figure running toward me, noticeably lacking a cloak.

"What the skies are you doing?" Callen says when he gets close.

"Searching," I say. "Tabrol doesn't have time for us to warm ourselves."

Callen pushes a slick lock of hair from his eyes, blinking rapidly as the droplets keep hitting his brow. "You know if you'd just said 'food' or 'better shelter,' I wouldn't be as inclined to report you for insubordination."

I shrug, like, *Fine*. "I'm looking for food or better shelter."

"Rowan."

"Callen," I return with the same tone. A shiver races down my back. "What?"

"Any warrior worth their keep would know it's foolish to go out like this."

"Like how?"

"Unprepared. Against orders," he returns, blinking out rain. "What are you going to do if Sethran wakes up and finds you gone?"

I shrug, my chest aching.

"What is it?" he says.

It's just us. Just *us*. I can't lie to Callen.

"The sentinels never sent warriors-elect." Rain batters my cheeks, my hair, my very bones. "I deserted, Callen. But I didn't mean to."

"How did you not mean to?"

"Let's keep walking, and I'll tell you."

We go back up the sandy ridge, and I tell him about Noam and the humans' past offers of peace, how the sentinels lied, and about my decision to leave. "I was the only person who knew everything, Callen. It would have taken too long to find my sister or to rally others around me. I had to help. And now I've found you all, so I am helping. You wouldn't know to hurry if it wasn't for me."

Callen nods, but his expression stays locked in one of concern. "Ro, when you don't report for duty—"

"I know. It'll look like I deserted." I look everywhere but his stupidly handsome, familiar face. "I can deal with that later. We have other things to focus on, anyway. It's fine. I'm fine."

"Rowan." He says my name like he really knows me, and of course he does. He knows the years before my father's death, before I decided to follow in his footsteps and become a warrior. He knows the side of me I don't like to show—the vulnerable side, the one that's absolutely crushed, leaving me feeling hollowed out.

Tears start to mix with the rain streaming down my face. "If Tabrol dies, the city will fall. But if we find the cure fast enough, it'll save him and all the other children. And, if skies are good, it'll be enough for the king to get over the fact that I left without orders. So are you going to help me look for the stupid flower or not?"

It shouldn't be so easy, talking to him. But I fall back into it like stepping into an old pair of shoes. The flow of our words together and how quickly I can predict his.

"Let's look," he replies. "Lead the way."

Rain lashes against my skin, the fat droplets whipped by the wind. We must have looked for an hour, and nothing. I pull Callen's cloak tightly against my body. It's little use soaked with the sea's spray, but it comforts me, anyway. Wind howls in my ears, and my head starts to hurt for how cold they are.

"Let's go back," I say. Beside me, Callen shivers. "Here."

I lift the cloak and awkwardly drape it around the two of us. Our boots will get wet, but at least he'll stop shaking. Callen uses his arm and helps, propping up the fabric like a little roof.

Is this a mistake? I just want him warm. Or do I want him close? I don't dare look at Callen, but I feel him—our limbs touching as we walk, the discomfort of my wet clothes forgotten in my racing pulse.

"You okay?" Callen asks.

"Yeah. Just tired."

When the barn comes back into sight, I sigh. "Seth's going to have my hide."

Callen shrugs. "We can tell him it was me."

"No, no," I return, wiping yet another slick lock of hair from my face. "You still have a reputation."

"And so do you," he says, turning to face me with our shared cloak overhead. "Even if they're angry when they notice you're gone. After we save the city there's no way that the king doesn't pardon you."

I pause. "Do you really think that?"

"Yes."

"It's nice to hear someone else say it," I reply. I've been so wrapped up in acting first, thinking later, that I haven't allowed much room for any logical thought—and Callen does love logic.

I finally look at him. In the moment, it's so easy to remember the past golden hours we spent together. Our whole lives, two pairs of wings soaring side by side.

Callen keeps very still, until I swear to the skies he leans in. Our breaths mingle, and I study his face, his eyes, his lips . . .

He pulls back abruptly, sending rainwater dripping down my head. "Hey!" I say as I catch the cloak at the last second and pull it back.

"Sorry," he says. "I just didn't think this was a good time to . . ."

"I know," I reply. "But . . . do you know what I thought when the teams were named?" He shakes his head. "My first thought was that you'd better come home."

Callen furrows his brow. "Okay?"

"And this isn't about me or you. *Or* Ox."

"I know."

"But if for one moment, it was about us," I start. His head snaps up, expression so full of hope. "Then I'd tell you that I don't know how I'm supposed to feel, and I'm not going to risk a lifetime of friendship on a chance that I'll change my mind." I know I'm falling short. I know my words aren't enough, but I have to say *something*. "If this was about us, then I'd tell you that you know I love you. Of course I do. How could I not? You're my best friend, Callen, and I love you for that. I just don't know for certain if I'm *in* love with you."

The pain in his eyes is enough to snuff out the sun. "Right. Okay."

"We have more important things to focus on," I say. "Let's find the cure. Then we can . . . figure this out."

He gives me a half-hearted smile. "Okay."

Then he hands me the now-useless cloak and turns for the barn. I watch him walk away, feeling as if I am trying to grasp at the sun long after it's slipped below the horizon, leaving shadows in its wake.

23

CALLEN

Ox is awake when we get back. His eyes follow Rowan as she waves him a quiet hello, collapsing into the hay without bothering to try to dry off. Sethran, thank the skies, doesn't stir.

"I can keep watch another hour," Ox says.

"Thanks," I reply.

We both know that it's my turn, but it's not like I got any sleep traipsing around outside. Unfortunately I doubt I'll be getting any more, after what Rowan said to me out in the rain.

I settle into the hay, heart still racing in a way that gives no promised rest.

I remember the exact moment I realized I loved her. Training had been brutal that day, and I was in a foul mood, but Jai and Exin got me to join them at an evening's dance with their friendly encouragement and a glass of wine. It was a good vintage, something Exin had haggled over for nearly an hour before getting it down to a reasonable price, and it did its job.

Across the room, Rowan and her friends danced together in a circle. A couple of bolder Leonodai offered their hands and soon everyone was pairing off. The music of the hall bounced raucously in my mind, its eager tempo egging me on.

Skies, I remember thinking. *What a perfect winter night.*

Rowan loves to dance. I could see it in her movements so plainly—the flow of her dress and sash waving elegantly as she moved with the beat. She grabbed Vera's hands, and they danced together, energetic as kids. She saw me across the hall and smiled—and that's when I knew.

No matter what happens, I know our history will bind us forever. What I don't know is if forever has us flying side by side, or skies apart.

⟍

A donkey's bray interrupts the morning. I flinch at the sharpness of the sound, but my eyes aren't on the animals below us. They're on the human.

He's up early. Dressed in dull brown garb, he walks to the far side of the house to a small box garden and an adjacent chicken coop. Carrying the fragile eggs in his hand, he goes back inside. Every now and then, his shadow passes in front of the warped glass of the window of the house.

Sethran gets up with a small groan as he stretches out his legs and back. He takes a knee beside me. "What do you see?"

"One human. No other movement within the house." Then, a moment later, "He's coming this way."

I scoot back from the wall and look at the bales of hay around us. We're hidden, but should the human come up to the loft, he'll see. Sethran rallies the others. Ox raises his bow and nocks an arrow.

"Only if he sees us," Sethran says. "We don't want the humans to know we're here."

Then doors groan open, sending a shower of dust upward. The human says something cheerily, addressing the horse in the stall. The humans' language is heavy, like boots stomping. The four of us watch and wait as the human shoves a saddle and bridle over the animal's body and head. I loosen the hold on my axe. He's leaving. I ease back over to the barn's side and peek out between the slats, checking for light or movement inside the house.

The human finishes readying the horse, then rides off. When the beat of hooves on the earth fades entirely, I get up.

"There's no one in the house," I say quickly, hands trembling with anticipation—or hunger, it's hard to tell. "There will be food in there."

Sethran adjusts the sword at his hip. "Are you sure it's empty?"

"Yes, sir."

"Then let's go."

As we crawl out of the same entrance we came through last night, the salty air settles on my skin in a fine mist. Sethran reaches the house first and tries the door, but it's locked. Rowan walks around the back and finds a window that's unlatched. After climbing in, she comes back around and opens the door for the rest of us.

Inside, the house is dark but blissfully warm. A clean table rests upon a worn rug with some mud tracked onto the edges and beneath the chairs. A bowl of yellow and green apples beckons from the kitchen. I grab one and hold it reverently for a moment before sinking my teeth into it.

Ox opens his satchel, and Rowan puts the fruit inside. It doesn't sit right with me that we're stealing, especially having seen so much muddy, empty farmland on the way here. Still, we have to survive. There's half a loaf of bread on the table, too, beside bits of cooked meat and cheese, and a few empty cups. I could eat it all by myself, but Ro dutifully divides the portions into fours. Ox goes through the rest of the kitchen for good measure.

"That's all there is," he says.

"No, it's not," she replies. Her eyes are fixed on a small cup on the table.

Ox strides over to her. "What?"

She holds out the cup. Inside is a flower with six petals, each a blazing red.

24

SHIRENE

"Is that everyone?" I ask Lyreina, wiping beads of sweat off my brow.

She looks up from the scroll laid out before us. "It's as close to everyone as we'll be able to get. The Keep is full."

We're stationed on the southeastern part of the palace ridge, where a massive pair of half-circle doors has been let wide, revealing the deepest tunnels below the palace. The Keep hasn't ever been used like this. We're lucky to have it. The more citizens we can shelter in its depths, the better, at least until the warriors return and we are at full strength again.

Typically, it houses the boat used to transport the ambassadors to the sea when they need to travel to and from Vyrinterra. I still cringe at the memory of being on duty when they needed it lowered to the sea—even with a team helping hold the lines, it was heavy as stone.

The teams of today don't have to keep their jaws on the lines as long as I had to. Each day, the sea creeps closer. What used to be hundreds of feet of open air between the Heliana and the water is slowly disappearing.

The aeroplanes—as Noam told us they were called—came back last night and earlier this morning, but they kept a wider berth, shooting bullets into the open air. I wish I could say that made me feel better, but it just told me they were gathering information about us. That kind of reconnaissance meant something greater was on the way.

Usually, the Heliana swarmed with citizens flying here and

there, and warriors training in the skies, especially in the summer when Vyrinterra's bounties were plentiful and the afternoons long. But these days had been long for the worst of reasons. The exhaustion chipped away at me like a sculptor chipped at stone—only *I* was being broken apart. I couldn't stop. I had to press on.

When the morning's seventh bell tolls, Lyreina and I fly back to the Glass Tower for a council meeting. The place feels less hallowed with each day, as if the mirrors and polished decorations have lost their shine.

The king takes his seat without any of the usual formalities. The Chief Healer and Chief Scholar had been invited, joining us sentinels alongside the king. Both take their places on the opposite side of the table. Despite her station, the Chief Healer wears the same working uniform of the healers downstairs. Her long gray hair is tied back, though long strands have fallen free. Like me, I don't think she's slept much in days.

"Thank you all, again, for coming," says the king. "Sentinel Carrick, how go the repairs?"

My colleague bows his head in respect. "All the buildings damaged by the machines' attacks have been examined. A few will need extensive work, but most could be restored within a week, when it is safe to do so."

"And the defenses?" the king asks.

"We have teams of warriors ferrying stones from Vyrinterra as we speak," he says. "The sentinels are in agreement with the generals that we need as offensive a strategy as possible. With the citizens in the Keep or in rooms in their homes, warriors and warriors-elect will take the lead."

The king puts a hand to his brow. "And there has been no word from Balmora."

Who the king is addressing doesn't matter. It is a statement and not a question. None of the warriors we sent have returned from Balmora yet. Why would they? We sent them far and with the belief that they had more time.

"Not yet, Your Grace," I answer finally. Someone has to. "By our count, the warriors should be reaching the human capital today or early tomorrow."

"Thank you, Lady Shirene." The king turns to the Chief Healer. "How many are in your care now?"

The woman bows her head low. "Twenty-nine sick, and seven have died."

"All children?"

"Yes, my king." She raises her voice. "I beg the sentinels to do more about the citizens. To tell them what is going on. They already know that children are dying. Even those without young kids will not sit long in the Keep without getting restless."

"We are all upset at the children's sickness," I say. "But we are doing all we can. Families with young children are already sheltering in their homes and not the Keep. Healers are checking on their condition several times each day. The teams have been sent. We must wait and have faith they will return."

"Save your words, Sentinel Shirene" is her response. "You have said the same script to the citizens."

My stomach tightens like a knot pulled on either side. She is right. Last night, we'd updated the city on the situation—how we wanted the older, vulnerable citizens to make their way to the Keep, while others were instructed to shelter in the most secluded parts of their homes away from windows. The sentinels had prepared my speech together, but I had to deliver it. Someday, I'll forget the desperate cries, the demands to know more. But we kept the message as steady as the sun's path in the sky: help is on the way; we just have to be patient.

"And what of the city falling?" Lyreina asks, shifting attention to the Chief Scholar. An elderly man thrice my age, his eyesight is beginning to fail him, but his wits remain sharp as arrows. So much of our history is carried in his heart and mind. "Is there nothing we can do?"

"My lady, the city falls as the prince gets worse," the Chief Scholar replies. "Apologies, my king, for being so blunt."

The king waves him off wearily.

Lyreina presses further. "Do you think it will fall entirely?"

"Skies keep us, no," says the Chief Scholar. "If the warriors return with the cure in time, then the city will be restored to her normal place in the skies."

"That said," the Chief Healer cuts in, "I know no one wishes to say it, so I will. Forgive me, my king, but don't you feel we should prepare—at least in some way—for the worst?"

I exhale, my heart thumping hard in my chest. "Which is?"

"Abandoning the Heliana," she replies.

A few chairs down from me, Renna leans forward. "Chief Healer, I'm surprised. You'd abandon the city so easily? Our warriors can and should make a stand here, on streets they know."

"And what of the people who don't know how to fight, hmm?" the Chief Healer replies. "You surround yourself with warriors, but you forget that there are other citizens at play here. Other lives. If the city falls, the humans will be on us in a matter of hours. We know they can reach us by sea, and now by air. Seeking refuge on Vyrinterra is not a permanent solution, but our people would last longer in the shelter of the bearkings' fortresses than they will here. Our city is not built to be defended."

She has never needed to be, I think bitterly. The thought of retreat is painful, but I can see why her mind went there. The Heliana would not become a second Garradin. If retreat is needed, we'll retreat. Though I can only imagine the colorful language that Princess Freanna would unleash if thousands of Leonodai started landing on Vyrinterra's shores, headed for their carefully guarded lands.

The king clears his throat. "Thank you for your words, Chief Healer. I know we would all like to believe that's impossible, but without word that the cure has been found . . . I agree it must be considered."

Renna opens her mouth to retort. Beside her, Hammond puts a steady hand on her arm.

"Your Grace," says Hammond. "If the city is to be abandoned, then we must preserve every part of Leonodai tradition that we can and take it with us to Vyrinterra."

"There is still time," Renna interjects, but the king silences her with a wave of his hand.

"Tell the scholars and trainees to begin gathering our oldest and most vital texts," he says. "I detest the possibility more than anyone in this room, but we must be ready to react as needed."

"It will be done, Your Grace," the Chief Scholar replies.

I sway with the pain of our reality. Gathering texts. Sending scared citizens fleeing to Vyrinterra. And no word from the east.

I close my eyes—it is all too much. What I wouldn't give to have Seth hold me in his arms, to whisper to me that we're going to be all right. I need him for moments like this.

"And what of the prince?" Hammond asks quietly, each word heavy as a river stone. "They will start putting the truth together for themselves soon enough. Should we tell them of his condition?"

His words snap me back to the present. Tell the citizens? It is the fair thing to do, but skies, at what cost? They would do as the Chief Healer predicts: they'd get angry, and more afraid than they already are. It would breed further chaos.

After a long pause, the king looks eastward toward Balmora. "My son has time. I will not inflict a panic on the citizens by revealing his condition now. Let us wait, and let us pray to the skies that the teams return swiftly."

The council breaks up with a scraping of chairs against the

floor and restless murmurs. Every setback of the past days has finally tipped the scale in my chest, and the guilt of it roots me to the spot. We humbled ourselves to Noam much too late. We'd sent the warriors too late, built our defenses too late. Was it arrogance that kept us from ever wondering if the Heliana would fall?

"Lady Shirene," says a voice, one that has become familiar. Lord Rhys and Lady Alys stand before me. With the Sea Queen in agreement with King Kharo's plans, I hadn't expected them to feel compelled to attend this meeting. Frankly, I hadn't noticed they had joined.

"Are you all right?" Lady Alys asks. "You look ill."

I grit my teeth. "Lost in thought," I reply, getting out of my chair. "Is there something you need?"

Rhys points across the room at the Chief Scholar. "We wanted to ask you about him."

"What of him?"

"It is strange to us," he says. "You trust him completely."

I frown. "The scholars are keepers of our history. They have a sacred duty to the Heliana, and we reward that duty with trust."

"Oh, we don't think he is lying," Lady Alys says, her tone ever a ringing chime. "Only that truth changes. You may not see it, in one lifetime. For our people, truth is like water—it will never rest, never cease folding and unfolding upon itself."

"What is your point?" I ask.

"No point," she replies. "Only a recommendation, from two lives who have seen more death and more life than most of your people. In tying yourself to the words of your histories, you are ignoring what is before you."

I frown. "And what is that?"

"Change."

The two bow their heads, and I let them leave without another word. If I open my mouth, it will not be diplomacy that comes out. My body radiates with anger. How insulting of them . . . but is my fury coming from somewhere else? We Leonodai pride ourselves on knowing our place in the world and among one another. The order our ancestors established holds up through today. There is no need to change it. There is no need to question it.

Or is there?

Lady Alys and Lord Rhys are right, I realize, the pit in my stomach growing. What we always called *order* is turning out to be stagnancy—and our people are dying because of it.

25

ROWAN

"The cure," I say. "It's here."

Excitement sends me practically flying to the cabinets to double-check them for more.

Now all we have to do is get back to the Heliana. Everything's going to be fine—the prince will live, and all the children will be safe. I'll be safe, too, though in a different way. Like Callen said, helping bring back the cure will have to absolve me.

But my search inside turns up empty. I curse. "I'll start looking outside."

"Take something warm," Seth replies. "Ox, check the other rooms."

I follow Ox to a tidy bedroom. "This your size?" he says, holding up an obviously too-large coat.

"However did you know?" I reply. He hands it to me, stepping closer as he does.

"Rowan," he says. "What are you not telling me?"

"What do you mean?"

"You went outside when Sethran told you not to, and you took Callen with you," Ox says, an edge in his tone. "You bring up the urgency of this mission a least half a dozen times a day even though we all know what's at stake. What's going on?"

"Callen followed me," I say. I lower my voice. "And I just don't want to get off course. I can't get off course."

"Kind of feels like you are already," he says.

"Ox, wait." He lingers in the door. "This will all make sense soon," I say. "I promise. Just trust me."

There's more I should say. My heart feels split in two parts, as opposite as night and day—and it's not my heart I'm supposed to be caring about.

He nods. "I trust you."

"Thank you," I say, and we walk back to the main room as if nothing happened. Pulling the human's coat tightly around my shoulders, I head out the door.

❦

Sinking to my knees, I push my hands into the muddy dirt, ready to scream. Nothing. We've looked for hours now under a pale gray sky, and we haven't seen any more of it. Seth salvaged the one flower we did find and pressed it into a pocket of his satchel.

"Its powers may already be spent," he had said sullenly. "We have to keep looking."

Back in the present, I take in the silhouettes of Ox, Callen, and Seth searching in their own sections a few hundred feet from me. We divided the area around the house into four, and I'm in the most inland section near the cypress trees.

The human had a horse. That expands the area we should be searching tenfold. What's more, he could have bought it in Ramsgate and we are wasting time out here.

At least the rain has let up. The sky is now a patchy gray and blue, which makes spending all this time searching a little more bearable.

Then the earth beneath me begins to tremble. I scan the horizon, my fellow fighters doing the same. Swearing under my breath, I get up from my exposed position on the ground and dart for the nearest patch of cypress trees, keeping low. Their gentle scent engulfs me, and I turn, waving for the others to join me.

Seth is shouting, but I can't make out the words. He draws his longsword just as a group of six riders rises from the sloped beach, their mounts headed for Seth, Ox, and Callen. Even from here, I can make out a black and silver insignia on their clothes.

Their regalia and sleek-coated horses tell me whoever they serve is no beggar.

Responding to commands, Ox and Callen turn their backs to me, and the three of them form a circle. Very quickly, I realize what's happening. The humans have spotted them, but they haven't seen me.

My heart drops as I realize what is about to unfold. If I run to them, I will only give myself away. A desperate, frustrated groan fights its way out of my throat. If Seth were beside me, he would tell me to stay, to hide and give myself the chance to escape while the others fought—but it still feels so wrong.

In the distance, the three of them raise their weapons.

26

CALLEN

"To me, now!" Sethran bellows.

I ready my axe, its grip as familiar to me as my wings are to my lion form. There's a resounding snap as Ox notches an arrow.

"Fire the moment they are in range," Sethran says, lifting his shield. "We won't get a second chance at this."

"What about Rowan?" I ask.

"If she has any sense, she'll run." He turns. "We fight."

Battle-born excitement floods my veins. Heart quick, muscles ready. The humans ride closer. Ox sends his blue-fletched arrows flying, quick as lightning striking the ground. The humans break their formation. Two of them change course abruptly to ride northwest . . . straight for the cypress trees.

"Ro," I gasp, but then the thunder of hooves is at my side, and I raise my shield high as a bullet skims off its thick metal.

Sethran lets out a war cry, his sword colliding with the flank of the horse closest to us. Hot blood sprays across my legs as the animal falls. Its rider dismounts and lunges toward me with murder in his eyes. I dodge the first slash of his sword and bring my axe swinging down. His own shield meets it, but just barely. The human is twice my weight, but untrained. Meanwhile, I've lived for this, waited for this.

I throw myself into the battle.

27

ROWAN

"No, no, no." My heart plummets in a free fall through my body, into the ground and into whatever lies below. We have to live. We have to live to save the prince, to save the city. I want so badly to help, but—

"Surviving is something," I whisper under my breath.

Pivoting, I run in the opposite direction. I don't have to look behind me to recognize the sharp clash of metal against metal, the high-pitched whinny of a horse. It's only when a pointed thunder of hooves starts to get louder that I spare a frantic look over my shoulder.

Two riders race toward me. Suddenly, one of the horses swings sideways, legs flailing. Its rider falls to the side, trampled underfoot with their hands caught in the reins. As the human's body hangs limply to the side, I spot a pair of arrows sticking out neatly from the human's back. *Thanks, Ox.*

I pump my legs and arms as hard as I can, ducking under weighty branches. Sharp cracks fill the air as I crush fallen sheets of bark under my feet. *Skies,* I pray. *Skies keep them. Keep me, keep me, keep me . . .*

My fingertips scrape against the trunk of a tree as I swing myself around it and into a shadowed thicket—but I misjudge, and just beyond the undergrowth, the ground drops off into open air. Gasping, I stumble back, now gripping the tree trunk more tightly. Far below the cliff is a wide, rocky beach dotted with debris. I push back from my vantage point as the sandy soil slides away under my feet.

The human shouts something, and I turn. Taking two knives in my hand, I crouch low until I see the human in question. He makes a rude gesture that doesn't need to be translated. My heart pounds as more dirt and earth and sand loosen. The sturdy tree I am hidden behind begins to move.

Skies. I leap from the edge of the cliff to a new spot by a neighboring tree, drawing the human's gaze to me. As he opens his mouth for what I imagine would be another threat against my body, I loose two knives and grin as one sinks itself surely in the hand that gestured, and the other in his leg. The human howls in pain just as his horse rears, but I realize quickly that the animal isn't reacting to his rider's sudden movement . . . but to the edge of the cliff surrendering to gravity.

Roots pop and snap as they're torn from the ground. As the tree tumbles, it smashes into others. I blink furiously as a blast of dust and pollen billows around me. The human grabs his gun from his side and points the barrel at me. I dive as the bullet embeds itself in the branches just above my head.

Desperately, I climb up and onto the thickest of the trees that I can reach. Finding a branch, I grab onto it. It snaps immediately, and instead, I reach for the knot of wood where it stuck out from, the best I have as I fall and slide toward the beach below us.

The human fires again, just as the ground gives.

I wing a prayer skyward, hoping once and for all that the Endless Skies will still take a deserter like me. Sandy earth, splintering branches, and the heavy *thud* of trees colliding with one another swallow me in their jaws.

Rowan An'Talla, they'll say. *She left and died on Balmora, without her friends. Without honor.*

I close my eyes and scream.

28

CALLEN

Wiping the sweat and dirt at my brow, I whip around toward the cypress trees. One of the riders is out of sight. The other's horse paws idly at the ground, a body swinging from its side.

She got away. She must have. But that scream . . .

"Callen, behind!" Ox shouts.

I duck just as another rider comes up behind me, his sword meeting the empty air where my heart would have been. I duck around his right side, swinging my shield behind me so that it collides with the human's knee. He howls in pain as his horse carries him in a wide arc away from me.

One rider shouts above the others, and the remaining humans retreat, forming a line out of range of Ox's reach. Sethran spits on the ground, blood coming with it.

"You okay?" I ask.

"Human got me with a punch," is his reply. "He could have shot me."

"Are you sure?"

"That weapon is fire and lightning—yes, he had the shot," my commander says. "But he didn't take it."

I step back, panting heavily. "Which means they don't want us dead."

Ox takes Sethran's other side, eyes fixed on the remaining humans.

"Stay on guard," says Sethran. He adjusts the grip on his sword. Ox whispers something, but I can't make it out. The last rider, the one that followed Rowan to the trees, comes around be-hind us. I swivel, trying to read his gaze, but his face is masked in pain and his hand bathed in blood. One of the humans moves his horse forward slowly, hands raised and away from his weapons.

"Peace," the human says.

For a moment, I think Seth or Ox must have whispered it. But then the human says the word again, and I can feel the shock set in like a bitter frost. He's speaking Leonodai.

"We would like to speak," the human goes on. His pronunci-ation is childish, but I understand him. I understand a *human*.

"This doesn't make sense." The humans can't possibly speak our language. I try to think of a logical answer and come up empty. It's like a nightmare, only we're not waking from it.

I take a slow breath. We need to live. But how do we get out of this? I don't know. And when a warrior is in a situation where they do not know what to do, there is only one option.

"Commander?" I mutter so only he can hear. Sethran's calm expression fails him. He's as out of his element as any of us. Every muscle in my body is ready to follow whatever his next words are.

"Speak," Sethran says.

"You are Leonodai," the human replies. I hate the way our name sounds on his tongue. "Why are you here?"

The rest of the humans around us wear grim expressions. They're wary of us. We're their stories, and they're ours. They've heard rumors of us, and now here we are.

"We are looking for medicine," Sethran says. "We mean no harm. We are trying to help the sick."

The first human translates for the others, and recognition seems to dawn on them. *How?* I want to scream. *How do you know our language?* "Why do you have swords?" asks the leader.

"We will still defend ourselves," Sethran says plainly.

Without warning, the leader draws his weapon and fires a

bullet at the ground in front of Sethran. It could have hit him. It should have hit him.

He makes a movement like *drop*. "No weapons."

Seth's shoulders slacken as he lowers his sword. "Stand down. We need to stay alive. For the prince."

Ocean mist settles onto my skin, a cold veil that keeps my senses sharp.

Warriors aren't meant to feel in battle. They are meant to obey. I drop my axe as the humans close in around us, their guns pointed at our hearts.

29

ROWAN

I drift between death and dreams. I see my mother as I've often imagined her—happy, dancing with my father long after Shirene and I had gone to bed. I see Callen as a boy climbing trees, waiting for me to catch up and offering his hand.

I see one of the Storm's End girls, though I can't place which one. Her large eyes look at me sideways as if trying to see the ground as I'm seeing it.

The taste of dirt and the ocean's roar bring me back to my senses. I assess my body, wiggling my toes and fingers first before daring to sit up. Every part of me aches. The tree I clung to rests inches from where it should have crushed my skull. I remember hitting the ground, my grip slipping. I must have fallen off at the last moment.

I cough grossly, spitting metallic blood, and fragments of my tooth come with it. Instinctively, I reach for the place where it should be, now soft and unnatural, shock coursing through me. It must have fallen out when I hit the ground and my jaw slammed against itself. My left eye is swollen to the point that I can't open it, and my head throbs as if someone were using it as a drum, but I'm alive.

For a moment, I forget my body's pain and turn my head to look up the cliff where I'd fallen.

"Ox," I say, voice barely a croak. With great effort, I turn my head, looking for any sign of the others. "Callen?"

Collapsing, I start to shiver. It's then that I notice something by my hand. Sitting back up, I examine the small drawstring bag. I hold the side down with my thumb to keep the wind from stealing it. The bag is kept closed by a faded blue thread, and there's something familiar about it. I undo the tie.

The sight that greets me makes me laugh from sheer surprise and relief. Pain ripples through me, but I can't stop. A pair of wilted red flowers. The cure.

I don't ask how. I don't think to wonder where they came from.

"Prince Tabrol," I whisper, somehow cognizant that this amount will save him. Closing my fingers around the delicate blossoms, I tug on a few of the precious petals and bring them to my lips.

Instantly, the dormant heat in my chest flares to life, the sensation not unlike what I feel when calling to birds. Magic recognizing magic.

As relief sweeps over my limbs, I clutch the remainder of the cure to my heart. Death hasn't come for me yet. I still have time, in every sense of the word.

30

CALLEN

They force us to trail behind the horses, walking in their stench and filth. Sethran tried to talk to us at first, but the leader of the humans shouted at him when he did. The second time he tried, a human punched him across the jaw. The metal studs on his glove left brutal cuts across our commander's cheek.

As if on cue, Seth spits onto the ground, his saliva still coming up crimson. Our commander got a few words out, though. "If you see a chance to free yourself, take it."

There is so much to think about, and yet my mind can't focus. Failing our people. Captured by humans like fish snared in an osprey's talon.

And Rowan. The human she fought with cradles his hand against his chest—if he is wounded, that tells me they at least fought. If they fought, she could have gotten away. But my fears sing to me, giving life to only the worst possible scenarios.

Without warning, tears well up in my eyes, and when I blink, they slide down my face like rain. I swallow back my pain as much as I can, but it's *Rowan*.

Ramsgate's city walls are made of a dark gray stone with an unfamiliar sheen. The streets are made of broken-up stones, so unlike the Heliana's welcoming, paved paths. As we're led beneath the city gates, townsfolk stop their conversations to gawk.

A soldier in the same attire as the others kicks his horse and brings himself over to us. He says something to the humans leading us, and the latter gestures angrily as they respond. After some discussion, the city soldier grabs the end of the rope from his compatriot, and we're yanked toward a stately building with tall, thin windows.

In one of them, I spot the silhouette of a man watching us. A spark catches by his face, followed by a wash of gray smoke. Smoke pours from his nostrils as he exhales with a smile of a hunter who's found his next kill.

The doors of the building open directly to a descending staircase. A thick, heady smell pours out, and I gag. Closed, with no room to breathe or move. Just what every Leonodai dreams of.

With one last determined look at the sky, I send my heart and hope up and into the clouds. If I am to die in this wretched place, I hope the skies saw fit to let Rowan live.

31

ROWAN

When I wake, I take a few breaths to brace myself before I sit up. The movement should hurt—but it doesn't. Nothing does. Heart quickening, I check my body for bruises, cuts. Anything. I touch the pads of my fingertips to my eye. Even that swelling has gone down. The only thing the cure didn't fix was my missing tooth.

"This is impossible." Getting to my feet, I take the bag and run the string between my thumb and index finger.

I know this string. It's handmade by warriors-elect early into training. The multi-step process is a lesson in cooperation with your fellow first-years. My own fingers were stained by the dye for days, despite my best efforts to scrub it off with Vera's most expensive soap.

"Where did you come from?" I ask it. I bring the bag close to my nose. A sweet floral scent shines through the salt of the ocean air, smelling of earth and berries.

I'm transfixed, so much so that I miss the figure approaching from the bluff. An unsteady footstep gives the human away.

On the ridge above me, a little girl stares down at me. She's maybe eight or nine years old, by the looks of her, and bundled in a knitted hat and cloak. Rogue strands of blond hair stray from the braid down her back. Her fists are pulled up and clasped against her chest like she's shielding something.

Meanwhile, I am ragged, hair matted and dotted with blood, and in a tattered coat that doesn't belong to me. I haven't washed my face in days and am covered in sweat and dirt, but the girl does not look afraid like she should be.

She says something in the humans' tongue as I rack my brain for what to do. She's seen me, so I know what my training would say. But she's just a girl, and the humans already know we're here. My first kill wasn't about to be a little girl, human or not.

I could take this portion of the cure and run as if I'd never seen her. But how would I ever make it? Even without humans to watch out for, it would take too long to get back in my sorry state. And if I managed to make it back, there were the other sick children to think about. How could I live with myself if I returned without enough to save them, too?

My thoughts churn faster, but everything goes quiet when the girl says one word—*safe*.

I look up.

"Safe," the girl says again. "My mother sent me to look for you. She is like you." She straightens up. "Loyalty above all."

I say the three words back before I have the mind to think any further. This girl's mother—maybe she knew a warrior. Maybe she is one. I don't have a wealth of options or time to think. I raise the bag and point to it, trying to pick simple words.

"Flower. Plant." I indicate toward my eye, which I can now open fully. "More. Will you help me?"

The girl exhales and nods. She motions to herself. "Isla."

"Rowan," I reply, returning the gesture.

She waits while I gather my strength and join her. If the girl were any bigger, I'd resent that she doesn't help me, but her petite frame seems to barely withstand the wind. She tugs at the hood of her cloak and stares at the sea with longing.

No, not the sea. The skies.

I must be delusional. Looping the cobalt string around my finger, I search Isla's eyes for traces of gold—and find them. She is Leonodai.

The revelation is marred by a dark reality. Of course children like her could exist. The scholars were not shy in our lessons when describing some of the horrors Leonodai women have suffered when captured by the humans. But to see Isla in front of me, living and breathing and looking more Leonodai with every gesture, I don't know how to feel. All my life, my mother has taught and cared for girls like her. But human blood runs in her veins, too.

Isla stays quiet as she leads me inland and into a stretch of forest. Gray trees twist up and around each other, and sheets of peeled cypress bark litter the ground. A large stone house with a battered rooftop comes into view. The dirty windows and disrepair give it a forgotten air, but the smoke from the chimney says otherwise. Patches of weeds grow unmanaged around most of the square garden plots, but two burst with verdant plants and vegetables. When we reach the doorstep, there are humans' words above the entryway and a strange symbol. The girl sees me pause. Her mouth tries to form words, probably to translate for me, but she ultimately frowns.

"This is my home," she says.

Doubt seizes me. This could very well be a human's trap— but Isla had to have come from somewhere. Cold, hungry, and battered in both mind and soul, I don't have many options other than to trust. The girl knocks a rhythmic pattern, then opens the door. My knees shake at the warmth that sweeps out, wrapping around my body like a hug from a friend.

Inside, a woman tends the fire, but she straightens up as we enter, her jaw slack with what I can't decide is relief or surprise. Gold flecks the hazel of her eyes, catching in the light of the fire burning in the hearth behind her.

"Come in, warrior," the woman says in our mother tongue. "Come in."

Warrior Ellian sits me down in front of the fireplace, hands lifting my limbs as she examines my wounds.

"You were smart to eat the flower," she says. "But you took way too much too fast. It's no surprise that your mind is a bit foggy. It'll take a few hours before you feel like yourself again. What is your name?"

"Rowan," I manage.

"Well, warrior Rowan," she says. "Welcome. You're safe here."

Ellian cooks up some hot oats, the savory smell nearly knocking me out. She feeds them to me, mouthful by mouthful. All I can do is nod and smile in response. Isla watches with curious eyes, but she doesn't come close. The girl asks a question in a mix of our languages, but I understand the words *golden city*.

Her mother nods. "Yes."

After helping me out of my armor, Ellian washes my limp limbs with cloths soaked in hot water, doing her best while my body is overwhelmed by the panacea. Did I really take that much? I can't remember how much there was. That seems like long ago. Everything does.

I fall asleep, and it's glorious. When I wake up, it's late afternoon, and my mind is clearer than before. Ellian lifts her eyes from her book when she sees me sit up.

"How are you feeling?" she says, reaching to the table next to her where a hot cup of tea waits. She hands it to me.

"Better. Thank you," I say, adjusting the blanket around my legs. "Ellian, your name sounded so familiar to me, but I couldn't remember for certain until now. You're Bel's aunt, aren't you? He's my friend, and he's in my cohort. He's talked about you."

Her eyes look out at the distance, like she is looking for something she hasn't needed in years. "Sweet Bel. All of that feels like another life. I arrived in Balmora ten years ago now, on a mission." *Ten years,* I think, remembering my father flying away to join the battle.

Ellian goes on. "King Kharo was younger then and still getting used to his power. He didn't know the costs of sending warriors so deep into the humans' lands. While the others fought at the Cliffs, we were sent to the mountains and ordered to keep clear of the fighting. We were to find the humans' king and kill them at any costs. King Kharo thought that would weaken them to the point of submission, despite the scholars believing the humans had no king."

"Do they?" I ask.

She shakes her head. "Not exactly. Each human casts a vote, and the one with the most votes is declared the victor." She sighs. "We made it this far, my fellow warriors and me. I was confident in my command, perhaps too much. We infiltrated Ramsgate at night. There were a dozen of us, and we must have killed so many. But there were always more humans, and when they sounded the alarm bells, we were trapped. Their reinforcements arrived and overtook us."

"How did you survive?" I ask.

"Luck." She sees my look and shakes her head, but good-naturedly. "I know. Leonodai don't much like to put weight in luck. But in our retreat, another warrior and I found ourselves in a church—special buildings sacred to the humans. There were women there who took pity on us. They follow the teachings of an ancient earth goddess who says no being is greater than another, and no being should harm another." I tell from her words this is something she's been told many times since being on Balmora. I want to ask her how she really feels about such things, but I don't interrupt.

"They hid us within their ranks. They gave my teammate medicine, but her wounds were too great. She died, and then the storm season came. Humans swarmed the city then, seeking shelter. The heavy rains come every year. I was without my team. I'd failed as their commander. I felt . . . such shame. So when the women offered me a room, I took it. When they gave me food, I ate. And when they offered me clothes like theirs, I wore them."

"How?" I blurt before I have the sense to consider it rude. "How could you stay away?"

"It was her," she says. "My child. Don't worry, she is probably listening." Ellian adds the last with a smile, glancing at an adjacent room that I guessed was Isla's. "I was already carrying Isla when I left the Heliana, but I did not know it yet," Ellian says. "As I was sheltered here on Balmora, the women taking care of me began to first realize it. Their behavior changed. They told me that women who dressed like them did not have children and that I'd be found out soon. I needed to be with a partner."

"There was a man I'd seen around the church," she goes on. "He helped tend the garden and do repair work for the women. They gave the man and me a new dwelling—this one. It used to be a place of retreat and meditation, but no one comes here anymore. Most of the humans in the city have forgotten it exists. Those who know about it don't come here because it belongs to the church women."

"Why didn't you run?" I ask.

"I did," she says, the fire back in her tone for the first time. "Once. I thought that if I could make it back to the Heliana before my pregnancy progressed, I'd be all right. But the women at the church had few supplies, and a storm forced me back. I wanted to live. I wanted my child to live. So I came back."

"And the man?"

"He was waiting by the door," she said. "He let me back inside, and our lives continued as if I had never left. The women would visit often, helping me get ready for Isla. The man would come here at the end of the day, wave his greeting, then go into another room. He never touched me, but he cooked and cleaned. Each time the women were here, the man would be kind to them, too. I don't know how to explain it. We spoke to each other in our own languages. I learned his words, and he learned mine. Once Isla came, he did everything so I would never have to lift a finger. The women trusted him, and I started to as well. Over time, I fell in love. I loved him."

She closes her eyes, face contorted in pain. "The rest you can imagine. My shame stayed with me, but my desire to leave dwindled. Ten years is so long, Rowan."

"That can't be true," I say. "What about after she was born? Why didn't you go back? How . . . how can you live here? So far from the Heliana? I don't understand."

The older warrior looks away from me. "You are asking all the questions I've been asking myself for years. Having Isla so far from my mother and sisters . . . I started to lose the will to live. Thank the skies Isla turned out healthy. After she was born, I got an infection and nearly died. The first three months of my baby's life, I could barely lift my arms enough to hold her."

I grip my tea tighter. "Oh."

"I've been telling myself I will go back," Ellian goes on. "Someday. But being a mother has changed me. My courage isn't gone. It's different. What if I tried to leave and we were caught? They'd take me from her—or worse. Isla would be all alone. One good look into her eyes would reveal what she is."

I fight the lump in my throat. Looking around the cabin, I look for signs of another person and come up empty. "Where is the man now?"

She pauses. "He died in an boating accident a few years ago."

"I'm sorry," I say, because that's what I would normally say to someone sharing a painful memory—though it is strange to say it of a human.

"Anyway," she says. "I never expected to hear rumors of Leonodai moving inland, but it's all that Ramsgate has been talking about for the past days. That's why I had Isla go look for you. I could barely keep her from going, anyway. She's always running around exploring the woods here. When she was little, I'd bring her into the garden and tell her to stay put while

I worked. I'd turn for one second, and off she'd go." Ellian sighs. "Now I don't fight it. It's safer for her to be running around the trees than wanting to venture into town."

I look away from Ellian and try to place myself in her shoes. Surely, it's worth the risk for her and Isla to return home. If I had to make a choice that put the girls at Storm's End or my mother in such danger, would I be able to do it? I think I would, but part of me protests. Staying put is safety. For Ellian, that has become enough.

This is something Shirene would be able to understand. Like water, she fit into wherever she needed to be and excelled there. But staying still doesn't sit well with me. I need more than that.

"Rowan," Ellian asks, bringing me back. "Why are you here?"

For a moment, I doubt whether I should tell her what's happened. She's been here too long, said she loved a human. But . . . Ellian is Leonodai. Like Noam, the heart that beats in her chest pumps blood laced with the magic of our people. She taught her daughter our steady oath. There is a part of her that is sun and skies, same as me, and no amount of time can shake that.

So I tell her everything I know.

Her jaw drops as I recount the children getting sick. Ellian's gaze goes to Isla's room, then back to me as she listens. I tell her about the teams leaving, the sentinels' lies, and about Noam. Then I mention Prince Tabrol.

"We don't have much time," I say. "That's why I need more of the cure. To save him, and everyone else."

"Skies," she says, then another curse in a thicker Leonodai tone. The sound makes me smile, despite everything. "There isn't much of the plant left. The holy women have told me that the cure was bought and sold too much for too many years. The plants dwindled, and merchants destroyed competitors' supply so they could raise their own prices. Now only one mother plant remains, and it's closely protected by the holy women and soldiers. The women tend to it and sell its flowers carefully it as a means of making money for their charity work."

I lean forward. "How much is there?"

"I don't know for sure. But I think there is enough." She closes her eyes. "They have been so kind to me to the point where sometimes I think their goddess is speaking to me, too. Now we must pray we haven't exhausted their generosity."

My skin crawls at the thought of praying to a human god, but I keep my resistance to myself. "What of the other warriors I traveled with?" I fight it, but my voice wavers anyway. "Will they have been killed?"

Ellian touches her hand to my shoulder. "Perhaps not. There is a chance."

I sit up. "What do you mean?"

"There is a new leader in Ramsgate," says Ellian carefully. "A general."

A bell rings in my mind, and I shift eagerly in my seat. "Noam told me of him. General Marchess."

She nods. "He was a foot soldier and fought at the Cliffs for years, then returned here to further his military knowledge. He has great power and greater wealth. He is known for having a fervent hatred of our kind, but also a curiosity about us."

Hope can be kind and cruel all at once. "And?"

"If the humans who took your companions bring them to this general, he will question them first, not kill them. I don't think he'd miss a chance to speak to Leonodai directly."

I try to shake off my fears in favor of hope. "How can we know?"

Ellian looks at the window and at the dying light. "It's too late to go now, and you still need to rest." She gets up to tend to the fire. "We can leave for town at first light."

"I feel fine." I stand up to prove it. Almost instantly, my vision spins, the world shifting beneath my feet like I'm back on the train. Ellian eases me down.

"The flower is very, very strong. That's why I don't keep a lot of it on hand—you never need much. I'm lucky to have any. Let it do its work. In the morning, we will go into town and speak to the women."

My head feels heavy, but I manage a nod of understanding. "Will they share the cure with us?"

She nods. "The goddess they serve would allow it. To save children, most of all."

"Okay. Ellian . . . thank you." Settling into the makeshift bed Ellian has made for me, I fight to stay alert enough to make sure I understand all I've heard. I roll the fabric of the blanket between my fingers to ground myself in something physical.

If all works as Ellian says it will, getting the cure will be easy enough. From there, I should race home to the Heliana's light, as urgently as if I'm answering the bells. My heart tears in two. The moment I have the cure, I will go, and I will go alone. Which means I'll have to leave three of the most important people in my life behind, and I will never see any of them again.

32

CALLEN

A clang of metal shocks me out of a shallow sleep. A soldier sets down three bowls of steaming stew between the bars of the cell. Hunks of bread are precariously dipped in each.

"Eat," the human says.

It takes me a moment for it to hit me that I understand him— yet another human who knows our words. How many more are there?

"Someone's betrayed us," I whisper once the soldier has left. "There is no other way a human could learn our language to that extent."

"Let's . . . think," my commander replies. "And eat. If we get the chance to escape, we'll need the energy to do it."

The food is so hot it nearly burns my tongue, but I'm so desperate for food and the small comfort of a meal that I shovel it all down, anyway. The meat of the stew is tender and richly flavored, while the grains below it provide more than enough bulk to keep me satiated. It's delicious, and I'm scraping my bowl within minutes. Reaching for the jug of water that was left in the cell, I take a deep drink. I focus on the water. I focus on feeling refreshed for the first time in days.

I'll focus on anything so long as it isn't her.

Across from me, Ox sets his bowl down half-eaten. The skin at his wrists is broken and bright red from pulling at our bonds on the way to Ramsgate, but his hands have stopped trembling. He has to be thinking of a way out, as I am now.

"The humans who found us weren't entirely afraid of us, and they didn't hurt us," I say, leaning my head back against the unforgiving stone of the cell. "And now they are giving us food."

"They want us alive, and healthy," says Sethran.

"Somehow that's worse than wanting us dead," I reply.

"We have to consider all options," Ox mutters. "They may be listening now. We can't take chances. Just act."

Footsteps sound from the door that leads to the street. We get to our feet as it opens. A group of soldiers trudges down. One of them unlocks the cell door and comes over to me while the other points a gun at my head. I bare my teeth and spit on the human's cheek as he pulls me forward by the iron chains binding my wrist.

"If you find a way out, do not come back for us," Sethran says. "You find the cure, and go straight home."

"Yes, sir."

Two of the soldiers keep their hands on my shoulders as the third leads the way back onto the street. We cross the same courtyard we came in through. A few kids playing with wooden swords stop to gape at me. I lock eyes with one and stare until my head is shoved forward. If that boy only sees one Leonodai in his lifetime, I want him to remember it.

Past the courtyard, we cut through a wide walkway lined with soldiers and townsfolk. A long-legged dog trots lazily through the crowd. A couple tending to their horses waves off a merchant trying to sell them wares. Above us on the balconies, women hang clothes on lines. I linger on the sight for a moment.

The scholars say that humans don't treat their women like Leonodai do. Their women tend to children and the house only. Sethran once told me of a skirmish he and a few other warriors had a few months back. A human actually soiled himself at the sight of warrior Io as she towered over him, twin swords gleaming. I bet he thought that a woman didn't have the guts to kill.

She did.

As I'm dragged along, I spot what looks like a market on the adjacent street. Long lines of people wait at every stall, money clutched nervously in their hands. Even from a distance, I can tell the vendors don't have enough for everyone.

I'm directed to a sturdy house of wood and stone guarded by one of the humans in silver and black. The door shuts behind us, cutting out the street noise like a blade cuts through thread. The hands on my shoulders are tighter now.

The staircase beneath my feet squeaks as I'm led up. The air is warm, and as we get to the second story, I see why. An enormous fireplace takes up nearly a third of the wall. The windows are tinted an eerie amber and the light they let in just as strange. The rest of the room is lined with books, diagrams, insects with their wings pinned down in shallow boxes, and a myriad of other things I don't understand. I'm nudged into a chair, and one of the soldiers keeps the barrel of his gun on my neck until the other human has finished tying my arms and legs to the chair.

The crackle and snap of the fire is all that fills the room as the soldiers and I wait. Over on my left, three swords hang above the doorframe. My stomach clenches. The fine blades, the inlaid decorations in the traditional pattern of warriors. Those are Leonodai made. On the desk to my left a pair of human skulls stares back at me.

One of the bookcases swings outward. A tall man, dressed in a black shirt, vest, and trousers, steps forth. A silver bird is embroidered on his velvet vest. His expression is drawn back in a permanent state of anger and distrust. I know that look well—it's the same one my father has worn since his command was taken from him. It's the look of a man who would not wait to get what he wanted. At a moment's notice, without a thought for consequences, he would grasp for it.

The man crosses the room slowly as if trying to read me. He pours a bit of golden liquid into a wide, clear glass, then comes over to me.

"I am General Marchess," he says.

I bite down hard on my tongue and concentrate on all the ways I could possibly kill him. He repeats his name to make sure I get it.

"I am a soldier like you. Now I am leader of this town. I take care of my people. Do you understand?"

His Leonodai is boorish and simple, but I do understand him. I keep my gaze set straight ahead. "What is your name?"

I think about the swords on the wall.

"You can tell me," he says.

The curved shortsword. That would look best cutting through this human's neck.

When I don't answer, General Marchess sighs dramatically. "I am not like a lot of people. The humans who brought you here have heard stories of Leonodai snatching children from their beds at night since they were children themselves. But I know you are not like that. You are worse." Then he lunges forward, his fist catching me square in the jaw. Lights dance in my eyes as I choke back a staggering cough. "The Leonodai are liars. Do you see these?" He motions to the skulls. "One is human, one is Leonodai. Can you see the difference?"

When I don't look at the skulls, he grabs a fistful of my hair and makes me. But I already knew the answer. Our bones look the same. I knew it was true, but my magic screams in protest.

"We are different," I say finally. "We would not have let children die." Too late, I remember what Rowan said about the peace offers we'd turned down.

"Oh, but you already have," he replies. "You deny my people

enough food to support themselves. Deny us peace. Now your king comes with an offer of his own, begging us for help. Well, the time for kindness has passed. I have only done what he himself did before. I stood my ground." He puffs his chest. "If I am to have the magic isle, I will have it all. That is what I've promised the starving faces that come to me each day."

I keep my mouth shut. My mind flashes to Rowan's face as we stood in the rain when she told me of the sentinels' lies, and the tired pain in her eyes. She said the sentinels lied to all of us, for years. What did we have to lose from ceasing the endless battles on the seas and at the Cliffs? It didn't make sense, unless I accepted that both sides were too selfish, too proud. . . .

General Marchess pulls a map from a drawer and lays it on the desk. Even from my vantage point, I recognize the curve of the Cliffs and the Heliana's diamond points, but the Vyrinterra they've drawn isn't quite the right shape. *Because they haven't been there yet.*

"We have spent the years learning about you from pieces the war left behind," says Marchess. "We know that you bleed and feel pain just like we do. We know you get sick like we do. And now we have built aeroplanes that fly, so we can meet you in the skies. I have waited years to bring you down," he says. "I have thought of all the ways to break you."

Meet us in the skies? "No Leonodai will break," I fire back. "A Leonodai child is born braver and stronger than any human could hope to be in a lifetime."

"I expected you not to yield. Yet." He sips his drink. "But I think I can fix that." He splashes the rest of his drink onto my face. The liquid burns my nose and eyes, and I shout in rage, but the bonds keeping me to the chair hold fast.

"Be grateful, you animal," he says. "We will give you food and water. Anything you please. Because tomorrow, I will break you, warrior strength and all. Tomorrow, we'll show this city who the superior beings are, before I launch my aeroplanes and decimate the magical races. Magic or no magic. You are no match for *progress*."

I shake off the sting of the drink. "Death fighting you would be an honor."

He smiles. "Then death it is."

33

Rowan

A warm hand on my wrist jolts me awake.

I sit up with a start, but Isla's hand tightens, and she holds up a finger to her mouth, like *shh*.

"Are you okay?" I whisper, unsure how much she understands.

"Come with me," she says. Then, another word that I think was an attempt at *surprise*.

Isla waits as I lace up my boots, but she indicates that I should try to dress warm. Keeping the blanket around my upper body like a cloak, I follow her to the door. The girl's eyes dart excitedly from me to the room where her mother is still asleep. She puts a finger to her lips again, and I nod. I'll keep quiet. If my visits to Storm's End have taught me anything, it's to trust a young girl when she has that determined kind of look in her eye.

We slip out into the night. My eyes adjust slowly, welcoming the moonlit scenery around us. A damp coolness hangs in the air, and wet earth muffles our steps. Ahead of me, Isla moves with fearless, confident steps. She knows this forest like I know the skies. I grin and quicken my pace to keep up.

After a while, she bends down to duck under the rotted, hollow core of a tree that has long since fallen. Other younger trees have surrounded it, one growing directly through where the other one split. I kneel to duck under the branches, but Isla's smaller frame is better suited to crawling around here.

"Wait," I say, shedding the blanket. Isla turns, smiling wide.

"Sorry," she replies. "I, uh . . ." She motions to her head. "Didn't think."

"It's okay," I assure her, then motion forward. "Where are we going?"

"I found this," she says. "I want to help."

I crawl through the narrow space, trying to ignore the mud that's seeped through my pant legs. Isla leads me further, but she walks more slowly now and makes sure I'm keeping close. Healthy green stalks of grasses peek between the otherwise dark earth. Suddenly, Isla turns and points to the ground just beyond another secluded thicket.

"I heard you asking about the flower," Isla says. "Is this enough?"

I look where she's pointing and gasp.

The red blooms are wet with dew and rain, and they are everywhere. Clusters of the cure burst from nestled alcoves between the cypress roots, between rounded rocks, and below the grasses.

"Yes," I whisper, tears coming to my eyes. "Yes, this is enough."

We retrieve the blanket and repurpose it into a kind of bag, then carefully collect as much of the cure as I dare take from this sacred, hidden source. Murmuring Noam's memory device to myself, I pick enough petals and stems to heal a hundred children. The sheer, unrelenting relief of holding so much of the cure in my hands is a feeling beyond words.

"How?" I ask Isla as we gently fold up the blanket. I gesture to the cure we're leaving behind.

She shrugs, completely unaware of the gravity of her gift to me. She picks at a handful of the cure, tying one of the stems around the others until it's a tiny bouquet. "I like the trees."

She's always running around exploring the woods here. That's what Ellian had said. Isla spent her whole days—no, her whole life—exploring what little of the world was safe for her to. The fact that she could find what no one else could was a matter of the world having given up on looking, and Isla not knowing that she shouldn't.

I put a hand on her shoulder. "Thank you, Isla." She leans forward suddenly, wrapping my arm in a tight squeeze.

"Thank you, too," she says.

"For what?"

"For finding us."

We walk the short distance back to the cottage. Ellian stands in the doorway, looking more curious than cross. She's woken up to a missing daughter before.

I wait while Isla excitedly reports to her mother where the plant came from. For a moment, Ellian looks frustrated, but it melts into confusion more than anything else.

"She never told me," Ellian says, switching to our shared language. "If I'd known, I would have sent you there."

"That's okay," I say, laying the blanket out on the ground. Isla, reading my thoughts, excitedly fetches my bag from where I'd left it near my bed.

Ellian crouches down, taking one of the delicate flowers between her fingertips. "This will save the prince," she says reverently.

"It could save a hundred princes," I reply, trying to focus on that joyful fact and not the growing pit of dread in my stomach. "It will save the city. I just have to make it back in time." My hair falls in my face, and I brush it back, annoyed, as I look at the growing light coming in from outside. "Tabrol has at least day and a half left, maybe even two. If I leave right now and don't stop, I can make it. I can find the train again and—"

Ellian frowns. "What of your companions?"

I freeze, my heart pounding as I draw out the words. "I'll go on without them. I have to."

"Will you be able to make it all the way back on your own, though?" she asks. "It's a long way from here back to the Cliffs."

My heart thuds. "The prince does not have time for me to take detours."

"It's not a detour," Ellian replies quickly. "If we go into Ramsgate, I could help you get passage on a riverboat. Barges travel back and forth, bringing materials from the mines and mountains to Ramsgate. I can walk you to the city, and we'll see if we hear of your companions. If not, you can take a barge."

I open my mouth to protest again, but Ellian's face has lit up more in the past minute than I've seen since we met. If she believes in this plan, I will, too. "It's no train," she adds. "But every hour you save is important, isn't it?"

I know from Renna's anger and Noam's surprise that the disease is unpredictable. If I shave off even an hour's time from my journey, that will be worth it.

"But what about my eyes?" I ask. "One good look at my face would give me away."

She thinks. "I have a wide hat you can borrow, and I'll give you a dress to hide your uniform. So long as you act shy, no one will think twice. If you're willing to part with those earrings, I'm sure we could fetch enough that a river trader won't ask questions."

I touch the pearl first, as if the blue stone in my other ear wasn't there at all. The pearl I could part with. I don't know about the other one. *This is not about you,* I remind myself. *Tabrol needs to live.* The sentimental value of one earring couldn't outweigh the future of our people.

"Okay," I reply. "Let's go to Ramsgate."

Ellian insists on getting some food in my stomach for the journey. "I'll hurry," she says, seeing my look. We'd just agreed how urgent my mission was. My stomach, however, agreed with Ellian.

Minutes later, she and Isla have finished prepping a small plate of vegetables and eggs mixed together. The flavors are strange but wonderful, and though my mother would wish me to be more polite in a moment like this, I eat more than my fair share of the bread. I'll need every ounce of energy to get back to the Heliana.

"Do you like it?" Isla asks.

The steady, deliberate cadence of her words makes me smile. "Yes, thank you."

Isla giggles and wipes her mouth on the sleeve of her dress. "Do you live on a floating island?"

"Yes," I reply, matching her words so she'll understand. "I do live on a floating island."

"She's been waiting for someone new to practice on," Ellian cuts in. There's a look in her eye I don't quite understand. Pride? Regret? "Evidently, I'm a boring practice partner."

"My name is Isla," Isla says. She says each word with the solemnity of a scholar. "I am Leonodai."

Yes you are, I think. Whatever the human who Ellian loved was to Isla, for the short time they shared, I can see her mother's influence more clearly. Dress her in human clothes and teach her the human words, but Isla has magic.

When we're done eating, Ellian hurries to ready my disguise. Isla watches from the doorway of her mother's room. She says something in the humans' tongue—a question, by her tone.

Turns out *no* sounds the same in the human tongue as it does in Leonodai. The girl stomps her foot and disappears into her own room.

"Did she ask to come with us?" I ask Ellian when the other woman comes back, bearing a dress and hat as promised.

"Yes," she replies. "Someday she'll know why she couldn't. Here."

I take the clothes with a sigh. It's much safer if Isla stays here. She'd slow us down with her smaller strides, and if things go wrong in Ramsgate, she'd only be in the way. Still, I feel a pang of pity of her. For me to arrive and leave without her learning much, if anything, about her heritage must be hard.

I put on my damp uniform first, much cleaner thanks to Ellian's washing, then slip on the dress. While the long sleeves will cover the vambrace, I'll have to leave my breastplate behind. My shortsword and knives fit under the dress, although the former pokes uncomfortably into my lower ribs.

"I'll wait outside," I say. "There's something I want to do first."

I head into the garden as Ellian puts on her own hat and says some things to Isla that sound like stern instructions.

Taking a deep breath, I use my free hand to pull my long hair forward. At least one of the humans who ambushed us knows what I look like, and I'm not taking chances. Before I can second-guess myself, I take one of my knives and press it into my hair, hacking away until everything below my shoulders is gone. When it's done, I run my fingers through my uneven locks and laugh.

Ellian joins me, and I give Isla a hug goodbye. She presses something into my hand. It's a bundle of paper folded upon itself a few times and wrapped around something soft.

"No," she says when I go to open it. She says something to her mother in the human tongue.

"She says to give it to the prince," Ellian explains. "As a gift from one Leonodai to another."

"Thank you," I tell Isla in Leonodai. Isla believes I'll get home in time to save Tabrol. I have to believe that, too. I tuck the precious package into my underclothes beneath all my armor, and with her mystery gift next to my heart, Ellian and I set off.

The rain from the night means mud sticks to our boots with every step, but I don't slow. In the patchy sunlight, the land looks less foreboding than it did the day before. I squint as I take in the sea behind us and the rolling hills ahead that lead to Ramsgate.

"How often do you go to town?" I ask.

"Only when I need to," she says. "I prefer to visit traders at the outpost where the train stops, but sometimes we need things that are only found in the city."

"Does Isla come with you?"

"Not often." The rest of her words string themselves between us—*it is safer for her to stay because the city is a danger.* "I wish it were different. She should be around children her own age."

A light wind carries over the landscape as we walk together, eventually finding a road that cuts toward the city. The trees lining the forest whisper and sigh to one another as they're rocked by the wind. It's a strange sound, both new and comforting at once. The sky above us is a subdued gray blue. Ellian sees me looking up and then does the same.

"I miss it," she says. "All these years, I thought I might forget what it's like to go up there. To be free."

"Do you ever get lonely?" I ask.

"Yes" is her reply. "But less often now. I've come to terms with my life. The followers of the goddess are kind and visit when they can. Isla keeps me so busy, sometimes it feels like a whole day has passed before I get a chance to sit down. And, of course, for years, I wasn't alone."

I fall quiet again, focusing hard on the road at our feet. I'm not ready to hear about her love for the human man. I still don't want to believe it is possible. Then again, there is so much I've learned in the past days that I barely believe the sky is blue anymore. I know as well as anyone that you can't fight where your heart wanders. First, mine went to Callen. Then, years later, it fell for Ox.

Both are one year older than me, and while I'd known Callen for years, I met Ox on the training grounds our cohorts shared. I was so proud of Callen when he was chosen to help mentor the trainees specializing in axe fighting, and Ox, too, returned to train the archers.

Six months ago, there was a dance to celebrate High Winter. As with High Summer, many Leonodai try to stay up the entire night. Vera and I had napped most of the afternoon for that exact purpose. The dance was lively, with pairs of dancers entwining themselves in each other's arms and exchanging glances that were hot with longing. Vera was whisked away by a handsome partner, and I excused myself to find some water. As I poured a glass, Ox came up beside me. He wore a long-sleeved blue tunic with a darker vest over it. I remember because I'd never seen him in something so formal before.

"Hey," he said. "Happy High Winter."

"Hi, Ox. Thanks. You too," I had replied, trying to catch my breath. The music reached a crescendo as the song neared its end. "Are you having fun?"

"Yeah," he said. "I'm not usually a High Winter celebration kind of guy."

I cocked my head to the side. "No?"

"I love getting a good night's sleep," he said. "But I'm glad I made an exception tonight."

I smile. "Why's that?"

"So I could ask if you want to dance."

"Right now?"

"Right now." He motioned to the glass of water in my hand. "Unless that cup is your dance partner. In which case, I'll back off."

I can only imagine my confused look—I wasn't used to Ox's humor yet. "Somehow I think he'll manage," I replied, setting the cup down and following Ox to the dance floor.

I wish I remembered the next minutes better: Ox's first gentle touch on the small of my back, the flushed expression on his face as the dance went on and we both were out of breath.

When the music died down, Ox returned to his friends and I to mine. When dawn broke across the horizon and cheers erupted from across the city, I flew back to my room without remembering to say good night to Vera. I was dizzy from the dancing and breathless because I couldn't get Ox out of my mind. I couldn't think of sleep, either. I was too busy trying to remember if any of the other girls ever talked about him when we gossiped together, or if I'd seen him ask anyone else to dance.

"No," I whispered into the dark. He had sat the rest out.

From then on, we flirted secretly, as if the challenge was to not let anyone know what was going on. He'd steal kisses on the back of my neck under the guise of a hug. We made bets on who could fly faster than the other, and raced until we were even, pretending to lament that we'd have to try again the next day. A few times, I was late to my drills just as I had been as a first-year trainee. But it was fun—it *is* fun—to have someone like that.

So what about Callen, who's been my anchor all these years? I feel horrible now, knowing how he felt all those months. Those times I was with Ox, and he was still swept up in his own feelings that he failed to notice what was happening. Just as I failed to notice that he was in love with me. I didn't want to hurt either of them or lose one for the other. It is all maddening, girly silliness that Vera would have reveled in were I able to share all this with her.

But she's at home, probably alongside the rest of our cohort, gathering resources from Vyrinterra and bolstering our defenses. Maybe she's taking commands from my sister and the other sentinels, trying to keep ahead of the humans' next attack.

Both of them are where I should be. There is no way I wouldn't have been noticed missing now. News of my desertion would ripple from the Underbelly to the Glass Tower. I cringe at the thought of someone telling Shirene. On top of everything, she'll have to deal with the shame of having a deserter for a sister.

My hands go to my bag's strap lying securely across my chest.

I have the cure, and I am headed back. I have to believe that it will be enough for the king to pardon me.

A moment later, just as a wind picks up from the north, Ellian and I crest a hill, and I know the time for selfish thought has ended. The enemy's capital city lies in wait before me, and I am headed into its heart.

34

CALLEN

In the morning, more food is brought to us. Last night, I recounted what General Marchess told me, from the flying machines to the supposed famine, to giving us anything we wanted. It was the last of these that forced Sethran, Ox, and me to come to the same conclusion: Marchess wanted us at our best so that when he broke us, he'd get the most satisfaction.

"Who do you think we'll be against?" I ask Sethran.

"Some of their soldiers, probably. Even if we win, we don't have the cure. We don't have time." He puts his fist to the wall, pushing against it as if he could break it. "We will fight as long and as hard as we can. That's our role now."

"Not to them," Ox says. "To them, we're entertainment."

I close my eyes, letting that sink in. Warriors are trained to never give up. In reassessing our mission, Sethran isn't giving in. He's embracing the reality that our path ends here, in the jaws of our enemy.

So when the soldiers come to get us, we go. When I'm pulled forward for walking too slowly, I quicken my step and focus every breath on whatever we are about to face. I am ready. This far from the prince, and without Rowan, I have nothing left to lose.

One of the soldiers in front of us grunts as he adjusts the large bundle carried in his arms. As he stops to shift the weight, I see a flash of a Leonodai sword hilt reflecting in the light. At least the humans had the decency to give us our own weapons back.

We round a corner, and it all makes sense. I don't know whether I should be excited to see something so familiar in such a strange place or if I should be afraid. But an arena is an arena, and I know it well.

We're shoved, chains and all, into a holding cell. After locking the cell behind us, one of the humans motions for us to put our hands through. I do as I'm told, my eyes tracking the human with our swords. The chains clang to the ground, their sound muffled by the increasingly loud cheers from the crowd that's gathering in the stands above.

Guns pointed, the soldiers motion for us to back up, and Sethran mutters for us to do as they say. Once our backs are to the far side of the cell, the humans toss our weapons and shields haphazardly onto the ground. I hand Ox his bow, and he trades it for my axe.

"We can fight for her," he says. "Both of us."

I touch his shoulder in respect, and he returns the gesture.

The humans guarding us snap to attention as General Marchess approaches. Like yesterday, he wears black from head to toe, only this time, he also wears a bright purple cape. The colors scream against the grayness of the city around us. It is meant to show his wealth. To give his people someone to put their hope in.

If they are truly starving, I think, *why wouldn't they put their faith in a man like this?*

"Leonodai," General Marchess says, "I will enjoy watching you die."

Sethran spits on the ground at General Marchess's feet, catching the human's immaculately clean boot. Our commander straightens up, raising his sword into a fighting position. "You are confident we will," Sethran fires back. "Do not underestimate us."

Marchess turns away just as foot soldier runs up, breathless. I don't catch all he says, just part of the humans' language that sounds like a Leonodai name, Ellia or Ellian.

"Whatever happens, fight like hell," Sethran says, drawing

my attention back. "My order stands. If you see a way out—any way that might help us find the cure—take it."

The heavy thud of boots on the arena stairs above us creates a rhythm like the beat of a musician's drum, and I fall into it. The only exits will be out through one of these passageways or straight up. I wonder if Marchess purposely designed this arena thinking we'd be here someday. I wonder if he knew how cruel it'd be to put us under the open skies we can't fly home to.

I don't have much fight left in me, but I've got some. Tightening and untightening the grip on my axe, I try to focus on what's forward, not behind. The gate in front of us rattles as it's pulled up.

The crowd roars, eager for us to die.

35

ROWAN

Minutes after getting into town, and I'm already very much over that I have to bunch up my dress to keep the hem out of the muck on the street. Skies alive, I miss being in clothing that's meant for agility. Ellian sets the pace next to me, one hand on her basket and one on her own skirts.

"There's a market just ahead," she whispers. "It's always my first stop. The people there see and hear everything."

I avoid the gazes of the humans lining the streets, especially the soldiers. Even after all these years, Ellian seems only slightly more at ease than I am. She's evaded their detection for so long. My being here could ruin it for her for good. Lowering my head submissively as she suggested, I follow where she leads.

In the humans' city, there is no music, just the steady sound of humans conversing with one another, and the clicking of gear on their horses' saddles. Women in dresses like my own walk in pairs or beside their men, their arms linked. At any moment, I expect to hear the shout of someone sounding an alarm, but the townsfolk are wrapped up in their own business, and no one pays us any mind.

It's a relief when Ellian finally turns and we enter a tiny market. Here and there, a rooster crows madly, and dogs bark as they dart between the legs of vendors and customers alike. The sight of the latter makes me tense—but these are not hunting dogs. From the looks of the ribs showing through their fur, I could outrun them even in my human form, bunched dress and all.

After talking to a shopkeeper and purchasing a pair of woolen socks, Ellian takes my arm, pulling me aside.

"That man saw them bringing three strange men in yesterday morning. They were placed in the custody of General Marchess."

I swallow. "Do you think they're alive?"

"Yes."

I want to grab Ellian by the shoulders and hug her. "Where?"

"Somewhere in the fort," she replies. She swallows. "But . . ."

A cheer rises up from the distance, followed by the low groan of the humans booing.

"What's that?" I ask.

"What I feared," she says. "It sounds like it came from the arena, which means he's fighting them." My heart lifts—Leonodai can handle battle—but Ellian shakes her head. "It's not like that, Rowan. The general only sends men to the arena when he is done with them. He'll be the victor once the others are dead."

"Let's go," I say, but Ellian hesitates. *Isla.* She's risked so much for me already. I know where Ox and the others are. I can take it from here.

Around us, humans are hurrying toward the arena. Another mix of cheers and roars flares up from the distance. *Roars? How is that possible?* I focus on my magic and try to call it—but of course it doesn't work. But I know the sounds of lions fighting as surely as my own voice. What in the skies is going on?

"Ellian, you should stay," I tell her, pulling her off to the side of the road. "Think of Isla. The war with the humans denied me a father. I won't let my fight deny Isla her mother."

She starts to cry. "Rowan, I don't deserve your kindness."

"Yes, you do."

"No, I do not."

Then she looks away from me. Takes a step back. I hear the movement behind me a moment too late.

An unforgiving hand grasps me from behind and forces my

arms down. Reflexively, I reach for a knife, and curse when I remember I can't reach them under the dress. The strap of my bag is drawn taut across my neck as someone pulls it from my person without any care for my ability to breathe. The feeling awakens something in me, and I start to scream and scream and scream.

"No!" I shout as the bag is pulled free, taking all of my hope with it.

"I'm sorry!" It's Ellian's voice. I'm whipped around until I'm staring at her again, my blood boiling as desperate tears well up in my eyes. Cold metal snaps down on my wrists. There must be a dozen soldiers surrounding us, each twice my size and fully armored. The black-and-silver insignia I'd seen on the soldiers who ambushed our team yesterday is on their uniforms, too.

"How could you?" I shriek at Ellian. "You are one of us."

She shakes her head. "That was so long ago, Rowan. I loved a human, that was true. But the rest . . . I lied, Rowan. They know about Isla. They have always known."

I try to twist away from my captor and only succeed in falling to my knees. Beneath my dress, the hilt of my sword jabs into my side. "What?"

"After I gave birth to her, they poisoned me for weeks. They said it was medicine at first, and I didn't realize what was happening until it was too late. They said they'd do the same to her unless I taught them everything I knew."

The soldiers drag me out of the main street and closer to the sounds of the arena. I twist and kick my legs out, but the small satisfaction of meeting what I hope is some human's rib cage is quickly doused by the panic of someone tightening their grip around my neck. I swivel around as best I can, trying to find which of the humans took the cure. Instead, I see it lying in the street, forgotten.

Ellian's desperate voice sounds from my right. "Rowan, I couldn't . . . I can't lose her. I was nearly dead. So I agreed. They showed pictures, and I told them the words. I have for years now.

I was so afraid they'd kill her. I couldn't stop. Once, I tried to run, and when they caught us, they took Isla from me for days. Gave her back to me starving. It was the most horrible . . . my poor Islaine. I vowed to never, ever do anything to put her in danger again."

Islaine. In hearing the name, my mind is whisked back to the Heroes' Path, the statue of Scholar Islaine and her golden hand before me. A child named for a scholar who ensured the longevity of our culture. It's all so backward, and my body reacts on instinct—kicking and screaming, howling curses at the humans until all eyes are on me and my struggle.

One of the soldiers pushes Ellian back, but her words keep spilling from her in a rushed avalanche of pain. "The humans heard of the attack at the coast. They sent lookouts everywhere. I promised long ago to turn in any Leonodai I met. Isla—she didn't know that I was going to turn you in. She doesn't know what the humans did to me when she was born. I'm sorry. I am so sorry."

A rough cloth bag is shoved over my head, and I'm carried away as Ellian continues to beg for my forgiveness. Then her voice is gone.

I can't stop the tears from forming at my eyes and streaming down my cheeks. Ellian lied to me. She betrayed her fellow warriors, her own race, for the life of one. Is that selfishness? Is that weakness?

It's human, I think bitterly.

The human holding me tightens his grip as we go, and when I protest, he feels me up, roughly, hands lingering in places where only a lover's should go. Fear slices through me. I know what humans do to Leonodai women. I have heard the stories.

But in irons, and trapped in a city I don't know, I have no idea how to get out of this. I can't think of any options, any observations that would save me. There is a clang of metal, and I flinch. My mother's earring catches on the rough cloth of the bag as it bunches at my neck. Something triggers at the back of my mind.

I'm scared.

I'm scared, and I want Callen.

I want him here with me, comforting me as he has for years. Between the bad sparring matches and the lost competitions, from my father's death to having my dream of being a warrior put on hold—it was always Callen. He was there at my side because he cared. Because he loves me.

And skies be damned. I love him, too.

As the hood is pulled back from my head, I find myself face-to-face with a human standing prouder than the rest. Tall with dark hair and a beard that's meticulously cut, his whole demeanor screams wealth, and the silver bird emblazoned on his chest tells me this is exactly the human Noam first warned me about. The people's king, the leader they chose: General Marchess.

"The last one. And a woman," he says, slowly and in our language. Every syllable hurts more than the next.

He motions to one of his men, and they undo the bonds at my wrists. Marchess inclines his head to the arena behind him, where the cheers rain down like thunder and the sound of shouts has become too familiar, too close to my heart. "Perhaps you are as weak as Ellian. My predecessors were right to keep her here. What could I make you do after a few weeks of poison, hmm?"

I have had enough of the humans, enough of their city and their cruelty. Enough of their lies and their noise and the way they poison the sky with smoke and fire. So I choose my first words to this human carefully.

"I will fight you," I say. "I will fight you until I die."

The human shakes his head. "A stubborn breed. Very well. You'll get the same fate as the others." In one smooth movement, he punches me right in the stomach. The move catches me off guard, and I double over, gasping for air, as the soldiers roll me into a holding cell. I get up and onto my knees just as the gate goes down, closing off my only chance at escape. My chest heaves as I try not to vomit or cry. I only succeed at the first.

Tears flood my vision as I stare at my hands on the packed earth of the holding cell. The heavy footfalls of the crowd above send dust into my hair, and refuse from prior occupants of the cell clogs my senses. Yet none of that is as horrible as the absence of my bag with the cure and my people's future inside.

I failed.

We all have—but worse yet is that I had held the flower in my hand. I had felt the earth where it grew. I had enough of it to save the prince and every single sick child, but I came here instead. No wonder Ellian pushed for me to go through Ramsgate. I was stupid to trust her and to let my heart convince me it was worth it to try and find the others.

Without the cure, I have nothing. But I still have to fight.

I pull up the dress Ellian loaned me and lift it over my head then toss it to the ground in rage. I've never been prouder to be back in my ivory and blue. I touch each of my remaining knives to ground myself, and then unsheathe my sword.

The gate lifts. With a shout, I run toward my fate.

36

CALLEN

In the stands above us, General Marchess must be laughing. He knew exactly what he was doing when he chose our opponents.

The stallion was first, released kicking and bucking with all his strength. They'd fitted him with a crude armor, which was more of a shock than anything else. After a few charges, Ox got the noble beast in the eye. Next, they loosed a pair of black bears—starved by the looks of them and wearing poorly fitted helmets as well. Sethran and I charged them together as Ox took a defensive position.

With a battle cry, I'd run forward, looking for a sign, any sign, of Knowledge, but the glassy black that met me was the only confirmation I needed. The bear turned enough that my swing to its paw met its mark. Ox took his shot and made it. Without hesitation, we turned. The other bear charged, too quickly for us to attack. I slid my axe to the side and rolled out of the way, finding my axe once more. Dust rose in the air. The bear turned for Sethran alone, but our commander was ready. When the animal swung, he flattened himself against the ground, then twisted to get the bear from below.

As the animal fell, I felt a pang of hope mixed with dread. Without an ocean to have us fight in, I knew what was next.

The lioness is hardy and huge. Unlike the bears, she has been properly fed, and she fights. Her armor is the best of them all. Still not perfect, but the plates interlock correctly, and her helm is secure. General Marchess said he studied us. Somehow he found a lioness without Knowledge, in lands beyond where Leonodai have ever been.

Dents in the metal mark where our aim was true, but not enough to puncture it. The lioness's wild eyes thrash from side to side. There is no soul there. Nothing. It's as crazed as the humans around us, and just as lost.

Still, something in me hesitates. We continue to dodge as best we can, to the enormous entertainment of the humans who throw rotted food and horse dung down onto us. *I am better than this. We are better.* I find myself wishing for more aid, but when the gate clangs open and I see what the humans have sent forth, I curse the skies, wishing anew that I'd asked for anything else.

Rowan's hair has been cut to her shoulders, but I'd know my girl anywhere. Her head is raised and proud, the gold in her eyes catching in the light as she takes in the crowd above us.

Then she looks at me. She turns, taking in our enemy on the other side of the arena. Ox and Sethran both call to her to warn her of the danger, but her name falls from my lips as a strangled cry. Eyes on the lioness as it circles the arena, I run over to Rowan. She meets me halfway, curling into my embrace like she needs it as much as I do.

The feeling of her hugging me back is a stronger magic than anything I've found since the Heliana.

"How the skies did you survive that landslide?" I ask.

"Luck," she says, pushing me back to keep her attention on the lioness.

"Leonodai don't believe in luck."

"This one is starting to," she counters. "Skies, is that . . . armor?"

"Supposed to be."

The lioness is dazed for a moment, taking in a new contender. Then it charges. Ox throws himself forward, shield raised, as a distraction to throw the lioness off. Rowan, fresh in the fight, lets out a battle cry as she makes a large arc on the opposite side, adding to the chaos. While the animal roars at Ox's charge, she lands a hit across its nose, blood spraying in the gash's wake.

The lioness charges again, growing and shrieking unnaturally, and I ready my axe for another go. Rowan throws a knife, but it bounces off the armor. The lioness backs up and for a moment is distracted by the other felled animals.

We take the moment to regroup. Ox reaches for Rowan, and she squeezes his hand in return, but she addresses Sethran. "Commander. What's the plan?"

Sethran shakes his head. "We have to survive, even if that means killing her."

Rowan stares hard at the lioness. "I know, but we could do it in an honorable way."

The three of us turn to her. Our commander shifts on his feet. "What do you mean?"

"A fast death. One with dignity," Rowan replies. "And then, we stop fighting ourselves. Seth, there isn't a way out of this."

Ox shakes his head in disbelief. "You're giving up?"

"I'm accepting the truth. We can't last forever."

Hearing the truth from Rowan hits harder than it did when I was saying the same to myself. We tried. We made it this far. But she is right. We can fight our best for hours, but eventually, we'll fall.

"Think of how you want to go to the Endless Skies," she says, voice trembling. "I want to go on my own terms. What say you?"

It's a moment I wouldn't have the words to fully capture, even if I had all the time in the world. And time is something we don't have. The crowd grows ever more restless around us.

"Let's do what we must," says Sethran.

"Yes, sir," we reply together.

The lioness waits on the far right of the arena, sides heaving as foam and saliva drip from her jaws. One of the soldiers guarding the arena's edge reaches down with a pole with a flame burning on the end of it. He shoves the fire into the lioness's hide, and she roars in pain. The sound slices into my chest.

As the lioness starts to charge, Rowan and Sethran run to the right together, coming up on her blind spot, where blood seeps from the wound on her nose, but the animal aims at me. I count down the seconds, waiting for the precise moment to dodge . . .

Swinging my axe to the side, I let the momentum carry me out of the animal's path just as she stops short, pivoting to face Rowan and Sethran. In a flash, Ox appears on the opposite side and sinks an arrow behind the lioness's right foreleg. The animal collapses with a thunderous sound. She kicks out feebly, blood trickling from the wound. Rowan wordlessly tosses one of her knives to Sethran, who catches it by the handle. In a swift, smooth motion, he kneels beside the dying beast and takes the killing blow at her throat.

We've won, but it doesn't feel like it. Rowan drifts toward the lioness, kneeling beside Sethran. She cradles the animal's enormous, proud head in her arms. As Rowan presses her face into the animal's fur, our commander puts his hand on her shoulder. Above us, the crowd's mood has turned like a tide going out. They've never seen anything like this. They're curious, shouting to one another and trying to understand.

I take a place on Rowan's other side, while Ox bows his head. My chest tightens at the sound of Ro's crying. When I look to Sethran for answers, I find a shine in his eyes, too.

We did our best. It just wasn't enough.

"Stand," our commander says quietly.

The four of us get up together. Taking a step back, Sethran drives his sword into the ground, and I follow suit to drop my axe. Then he raises his gaze as the clouds above us shift, covering the arena in patchy light. We are Leonodai, not humans. We are different, and we'll make sure they remember us.

Rowan's hand searches for mine, and I take it.

The crowd's din fades from my ears. I look up and realize it's not my imagination. The humans' eyes are on us, quieted by confusion and unexpectedness. Some boo at the stillness.

Seconds pass like seasons.

Then a horn sounds, and a gate rises on the opposite side of the carnage.

General Marchess stalks toward us, clapping slowly. The spectators immediately start to cheer, their eagerness for spectacle seeming to draw the very air from the arena. *This man has promised them so much*, I think. He's their hope, not completely unlike how Tabrol is ours.

"Well," says General Marchess. "You surprise me. But you haven't proved anything except that you don't like to kill your own."

He raises a hand, and a dozen soldiers swarm the lowest level of the stands, brandishing guns that are different from those I've seen before. The townsfolk cry out in surprise, their shouts rippling from one end of the arena to the next. The guns the soldiers carry are longer, but the humans hold them to their eyes for aim like Leonodai archers do with their bows. *Excellent,* I think bleakly. A longer range.

Marchess raises and lowers his hand. A gunshot fires in response, and I flinch, reaching for Rowan, but none of us fall to our deaths. At our feet, the lioness's body shakes as it takes the bullet. Rowan lets out a horrified gasp and, in the next breath, draws one of her knives and throws it. Marchess screams.

"Bitch," he spits, drawing the knife out of the same hand that gave the order to shoot the lioness. "Even death is too good for your kind."

Rowan looks at me.

"I love you," I whisper.

We wait for the shots.

Instead, there's a loud grunt from above. One of the soldiers falls into the arena like a discarded doll. Two more collapse in quick succession as Marchess's head swivels in confusion, and the crowd screams as they dive for cover. The other soldiers look around in bewilderment as another pair of arrows find their marks. I'd know the blue of the fletching anywhere.

A Leonodai shout cuts through the air as a pair of warriors bursts from one of the arena's stairwells. The archer moves with unmatched speed, taking out the soldiers beyond a sword's reach while the other shoves past fleeing spectators to the front of the stands. The figure leaps down into the arena, throwing back the hood of her cloak as she does.

"Io!" Sethran cries in a mixture of relief and amazement. "Skies alive."

Warrior Io smiles and cocks her head toward the holding cell that we came from. "Let's save the talk for after we save your skins, yeah?"

A bullet cuts the air between us, and Io ducks. "This way!" she yells. I lurch forward, grabbing my axe as the others retrieve their own weapons. Marchess barks orders, clutching his bleeding hand to his chest, but his words are lost as the fleeing crowds jostle frantically past the soldiers.

Io runs straight for an iron gate and its teeth lift out of the ground as we get closer. She slides beneath the creaking metal. As the rest of us follow, she looses two knives toward the arena in quick succession. The soldiers who meant to attack us from behind don't even have the chance to aim, let alone fire. Their bodies slump to the ground.

Now on the other side of the gate, I see another warrior at the winch that powers the gate. Once we're through, he lets it go, and it falls with a resounding thud.

"Jai!" I call, my blood pounding with adrenaline and relief.

"Nice to see you, Callen," he replies, picking up his pace to match the rest of us as we blindly follow Io forward. In the moment, I can't recall who else was on his team, but he must not have been their only archer. *Sentinel Renna gave different kinds of teams to different commanders*, I realize. All the better the odds that at least one team would succeed.

I don't know much about Io, other than that she terrifies most first-years and revels in her reputation. "Please tell me Io knows where she's going," I say between breaths.

"We got into the city, didn't we?" he replies. "Same way back out."

We follow Io's lead as she makes a break for an open street ahead. Flashes of light reflect off a river on the other side of the city wall. Rowan looks over her shoulder at me. There's relief in her eyes, but pain, too. I know why she is hurting.

Despite our new numbers, we are running scared. The prince's death is days away, and we still don't have the cure. If we escape, the best we'd have to hope for is a chance to defend our city as she fell. We've faced death once today, and something tells me that from here on out, death is never going to be far from us.

37

ROWAN

Io turns down an empty alleyway with a dead end. The sound of water calls from the other side of the city wall. In the ground, a square metal drainage hole reveals the steady rush of the river below us. Jai and Io lift the grate up, with Seth adding his strength once he puts together what's going on.

"What about the rest of your team?" Seth asks.

"They have orders to run in the opposite direction from here as a distraction," Io says. "This river stretches to the north until it turns some half mile beyond. The current is against us, but we'll have to make do. Now let's move."

Sethran ushers me forward, and before I lose my nerve, I leap into the waters.

My boot catches on the slick rock and mildew beyond the grate, and the motion tilts me off-balance. I smack into the river shoulder-first. The cold envelops me, slamming my body sideways and forward into the dark. My head goes all the way under, but I right myself enough to feel river stones beneath me. Then the ground drops out from under me, and I'm falling into the deceptively strong current as it tries to pull me the opposite way.

All Leonodai are used to swimming in the rivers back home, but swimming for fun meant I'd only wear the lightest of clothes. I know the very first thing I should do is kick off my boots, but we have days of travel until we reach the Heliana—but I can't drown before then.

Feebly, I start to take them off when an arm loops around

me and someone's cheek presses awkwardly into mine as they pull me with them.

"Hang on, this way," Callen says. He alternates kicking and treading water with practiced strokes, but the current is strong and he's weighed down by armor.

"Callen—" I start, shifting so I can use my own free arm to keep us upright. Callen maneuvers me around in such a way that I'm behind him, one arm around his shoulders, but it makes things worse. I kick free, trying to keep close.

"Shoes," I gasp desperately, but like me, Callen seems to know we'd need them.

His hand finds mine, and pulls me to our right. "No. Almost there."

Blessedly, the current slows as the river curves away from the city. Callen and I swim toward the shore where Io is already climbing out of the water. She looks back, walking over to help Ox, Seth, and Jai from the river.

We reach the muddy riverbank. I gasp for air as Callen crawls to his knees next to me. His chest rises and falls with labored breaths. I run my hand through the unfamiliar length of my hair, grateful to be alive.

"Everyone all right?" Io asks, eliciting weak nods from the others.

I look back at Ramsgate, trying to imagine how long it would take to get back to Ellian's cottage. The city would be on high alert for us. Ellian may be on her way back already, and she would keep Isla from guiding me back to where the panacea grows. Feebly, I look up and down the river. Not a single boat travels these waters. Another lie.

"What do we do now?" Callen asks.

The two commanders share a glance. "We haven't seen any of the cure," Io says, bunching up the front of her uniform to squeeze out some water. "Have you?"

Seth shakes his head. "We were searching the area to the

southwest of the city before we were captured," he replies. "We only found one, and the human had already used it. No idea where he got it from."

"Then we keep looking," Io says.

"The humans will be all over here in minutes," Seth counters. "We should look, but we need to hide first."

I close my eyes, wishing I could drown out the sound of their voices. The truth catches in my throat like cloth on a dagger. Tearing. Dragging.

I could lie, but I shouldn't. What's more is that I don't want to. I'll think more clearly having been honest, and the Heliana needs all her fighters thinking clearly. . . .

Everything from my undergarments to the leather bindings of my vambrace is saturated with water, and we don't exactly have the luxury of being able to lay out to dry. I reach down to wring out my own clothes, buying myself time, when there's an itch at my chest. I scratch at it, not thinking, until it continues to bother me. My fingers pull at my underthings, and then I remember— Isla's present.

Red seeps through the paper like ink. I barely hear the others asking what I am holding as I shakily peel back the wet parchment. "Skies alive," I say. "She's saved us."

"Who?" Io asks just as Seth does.

I lower my hand, and they all see it plain as day—the cure, wilted and wet but intact. Gingerly, I separate a few of the tightly pressed petals, counting them in my head. For a moment, none of us speak. The relief floods me again like a dam broken anew.

"How?" Callen asks.

I close my hand around the precious cure. "I'll explain on the way. Hand that to me," I say, reaching for his waterskin. I quickly dump out the dregs before gently funneling the flowers inside. "'A petal a year, a stem a season.' This is more than enough for the prince and all the other kids."

"The prince?" Io frowns, her dark brows drawing in as her

gaze demands answers from me. My jaw goes slack. Skies, I never wanted to give this news once, let alone twice.

Seth steps up, placing his hand on Io's shoulder in respect. "That, *I* will explain on the way. Let's go."

Minutes later, Io is cursing up a storm. "We have to get back before it's too late."

We trudge through the hilly terrain, using the river as our guide. I walk beside Callen and Seth, the latter even more pensive than usual. Io takes the lead while Jai and Ox hold the rear.

Ramsgate looks smaller as we leave it. The river and the distraction at the city gave us a lead, but the humans will take to their horses and have the dogs sniff us out soon. Hopefully, the river gave us some cover, but we can't rely on it.

We need faster transportation, but without wings, we're stuck going at what feels like a snail's pace. It feels good to be among faces I know, but the physical toll of staying so active is already hitting me. The only good thing Ellian did was give me breakfast. I keep a hand on the waterskin with the cure, as if letting go would make it disappear.

Once we have put some distance between us and the city, Io asks for a full explanation. I recount all of it the best I can, from Ellian's story to the secret patch of the cure that Isla showed me. I leave out the joy in her eyes when she practiced her Leonodai with me. There is a part of Isla—a large part—that needs more than Ellian is ever going to be able to offer.

"Isla knows she's Leonodai," I say. "And eventually, she'll be found out by more humans than just Marchess. I wish I could have taken her with us."

"You didn't know what Ellian would do," Ox offers kindly. "She'll find her way home someday."

"I hope so." Isla deserves to know the history of her namesake and of all her people. Maybe someday, I will meet her again.

The day stretches on and on. We have enough water from the river, but food is scarce. Jai shares the rest of his rations, and I hold the tiny pieces of dried berries on my tongue as long as I can. I keep pace near Callen, not wanting to be far from him ever again. Is it possible for love to be realized in a single, horrible moment? Is it real?

I glance at my best friend, and I know. *Yes, yes, it is.*

When we next speak alone, I want it to be right. And Ox . . . I didn't imagine those feelings. I don't know how I'm going to say what I have to. Something about the past days has made it all clear, and when it came down to it—my being scared, alone, and captured by the humans—it wasn't Ox's arms I wanted around me. It was Callen's.

Still, this isn't the time for painfully honest conversations, however necessary. Nothing is as important as getting to Prince Tabrol.

Afternoon sets in, and I realize that Seth hasn't spoken a word to me all day. I would have expected him to check in as he usually would. When Io finally calls for a short rest at long after dusk, he keeps close to her and Jai. The former is in his cohort, sure, but something is off.

We climb higher up a mountain ridge than my exhausted body would like—but I see why Io picks this spot. The bluff is backed by a sheer rock face to one side, while thick foliage and trees enclose us on the left. If we are found, Ox and Jai would still be able to attack with whatever arrows they have left, and the rest of us could retreat into the trees.

After some deliberation, Io gives the okay to get a fire going, but only a small one and as hidden as we can get it. The six of us huddle close to the flames, desperate for warmth. Ox finds a place across from the fire, and I'm grateful for the distance between us.

Jai and Ox leave for a while to hunt, returning with some berries, foraged roots, and a plump quail. It's not much, but it's something. The ache disappears from my stomach as I eat while Io and Seth debate how long to rest. The fire snaps and cracks as it burns, and I focus on its light.

I can't help but think of the last fire I saw, the one I set at Storm's End. How was my mother doing? I hope Shirene had visited. Vera would, too, once she realized I had truly left.

"So, how did you find us back there?" Seth asks Io, breaking my reverie.

"We got to the city this morning and were holed up in some neglectful gardener's plot." she replies, running a cloth up and down her curved shortsword. The metal gleams in the firelight. "When we ventured out, the streets were mostly empty. We followed the sounds to the arena. Once I saw you fighting in there, I gave the orders that would get you out." Io waves her hand idly. "You know the rest. Rescue, running. River."

"Thank the skies for you," Seth says. "I owe you a drink once we're home."

"I'll remind you of it," she replies, but her cheer fades quickly. "I was afraid no one else survived the attack at the Cliffs. The humans have gotten smarter."

"We avoided the worst by diving into the trees early." He fills her in on the rest of their journey and how they met up with me. He tells her about Exin, about his and Ox and Callen's capture. "The train was a lucky break."

"We should look for it again," Io muses. "A train is our best hope, now that Tabrol is sick." She sighs. "I can't believe Ellian betrayed her own people."

"I don't understand, either, Commander," I say. I fiddle with the end of my short hair and gaze into the fire. "I don't know which parts of her story were true. All of it could have been a lie."

I want to believe that parts of Ellian's story were sincere, but the only part I feel sure of is that she loves Isla. Is it right of her to keep her daughter away from the Heliana? I picture Bel welcoming his little cousin to a new home, taking pride in teaching her everything she should have been learning her whole life.

"Speaking of not being honest," Seth says. "Rowan, how did you know that phrase you said on the riverbank?"

A lump grows in my throat. "What?"

"The one about the cure. 'A petal a year, a stem a season.' The sentinels told that to the warrior teams right before we were sent out. They didn't say it when warriors-elect were also in the Tower. You said the warriors-elect were sent to tell the existing teams about Tabrol. The sentinels wouldn't have needed to share the saying with you to do that."

Five pairs of eyes swivel to me. "I . . ."

"Warrior-Elect," says Seth slowly. "How did you know that saying?"

My title. He used my title. It's the same nonsense Shirene pulled—using my rank against me. Hadn't I just fought with them? Walked all day with tired legs and tired limbs—

I am exhausted. And I am done. If I am going to start being honest with everyone in my life, I might as well start now.

I raise my head to hide my fear. "The sentinels are lying about where their information is from. They've lied from the start. The scholars didn't know anything about the cure, but the sentinels knew of someone who did—the deserter, Noam. He's the one who has been helping us. Without him, we'd know nothing."

"That's absurd," Seth replies flatly. "How would you know if the sentinels were lying?"

"Because Sentinel Shirene told me," I fire back, making damn sure to emphasize her name. "It was an accident, but she's the one who let it slip. Once I realized what was going on, I went and found Noam on my own. He told me about the cure and how it works. The sentinels lied when they said they didn't know where he was. And they had to keep up their lie when they explained how they found out about the cure."

I let the words pour out of me. If I stop, someone will start to chastise me, and I am done with people thinking they know more than I do because I am younger, or because I haven't taken the oath. As if that makes a difference with who I am and what I stand for.

"Noam is staying in the palace. He has been since the sentinels realized they needed his help," I continue. "I talked with him myself. Since he deserted, he's lived peacefully with the humans. That's what they've wanted all along. Did you know the humans offered peace before? I didn't. And that's because the king and sentinels turned them down."

With the weight of both commanders' judgment bearing down on me, I barely keep the courage to keep my head up. "Seth," I say. "Please say something."

He looks away. "I don't know what to say. You deserted."

"I didn't desert," I protest. "Not really. I had to go. I was the only one who knew everything." The firelight casts desperate shadows on the rocks around us. "You know me. You know I would only do what was right."

"What would have been right," he says, standing up, "was for you to never have left the Heliana and to have trusted that the sentinels know what they're doing. The sentinels and scholars are one voice, and that keeps the city safe. Children are dying as we speak. If what you say is true, and Noam helping us after all, what good would it have been to remind the people of his disloyalty?"

I don't know. But I stand up, too, meeting Sethran face-to-face. "I wanted to make a difference, Commander. And I did. I survived long enough to find Isla and the cure. Without me, you'd be empty-handed, and Tabrol would be dead long before you decided to call off the mission. I am not afraid of the consequences at home. Not anymore. I can defend my actions. Loyalty above all. *Sir*."

"Enough," says Io. "Sit down, both of you. Orders or no orders, we're no good to the prince or any of the other sick kids if we bicker ourselves to death out here." The bite fades from her tone. "For now, we rest. That's an order. Especially for you, Warrior-Elect."

"Yes, ma'am." But I don't sit back down. Instead, I walk determinedly away from the rest of them and take a spot alone in the shadows of the nearby trees. Leaning against a sturdy redwood, I bring my hands to my face and breathe. In, out. In, out. *Don't let any of them hear your crying.*

Deserter. The word rings in my mind like a bell. Sethran's disappointment is palpable, but I didn't desert. It wasn't like that, not entirely.

But if Sethran isn't able to see past my actions to my intentions, what hope do I have that the king will? *You'll save his son,* I think, gripping the waterskin at my hip. *You'll have saved the city.*

It will be enough. It has to be.

38

CALLEN

I volunteer for first watch. Looking at Rowan alone by the trees, I know I wouldn't be able to sleep, anyway. We keep the fire going, but only just, as the night insects chirp louder and the stars take hold in the sky.

"Don't get cocky, Callen," says Io as she turns away. "The moment your wits start to leave you, tag in someone else. We can't take any chances."

"Yes, Commander."

No way in the skies are my wits going to leave me right now. I'm tired, but Rowan is hurting. I want to be there for her, if she wants me there. Io, Jai, and Sethran go to sleep right away, but Ox stays up. He and Jai had split the remaining Leonodai arrows. He runs his fingers idly against the fletching.

"Did you know she left without orders?" he asks quietly.

He doesn't say *deserted*. I nod.

"When did she tell you?"

"Does it matter?" I reply. "She did what she felt was right. What *was* right."

Ox sets the quiver aside. "Callen, how many times do you think we've sparred?"

"What?" I ask.

"Over the years of training. How many times?"

"What does that matter?" We trained together for four years. The number would be in the hundreds.

"I remember us being pretty evenly matched." Ox inclines

his head in the direction of the trees. "Just funny that I'd lose when it mattered most. I had a feeling she'd choose you."

What? Heat rises to my face. "I don't think she has."

"Then your observation skills need some work" is his reply. "She went to you in the arena like no one else was there. When she did that, I knew. Once you know who you want to die next to, you know who you want to live for." He shakes his head. "And it isn't me."

Io rolls over with a groan, a scowl on her face. "I thought I gave an order to rest."

Ox exhales a small laugh. When Io turns back, he inclines his head to the trees again and mouths the word *go*.

When I'm confident everyone save Ox is asleep, I walk over to Rowan, keeping my movements as controlled and as quiet as possible. Is Ox right? He and I had been competing for her heart long before I realized it. I want to hope. I want him to be right.

She turns when a twig snaps under my foot. I put a finger to my lips and point farther into the forest.

We walk just far enough away from the group that they won't hear us if we whisper.

"Are you okay?" I ask.

Rowan tilts her head up. We're so close that I feel her breath on my cheek. "It doesn't matter. We have to save the prince. That's it."

"They would have found out eventually."

"I know," she says. "That's why it doesn't matter." She gives me a weak smile. "I could use a hug, though."

I put my arms around her in an instant. I bury my face in her neck, and she does the same in mine. *Am I making things up, or did her lips brush my skin?* I move to let go. She doesn't.

"I know this still isn't about us," she says into my ear, her voice tiny. "But I want to say I'm sorry. When the humans captured me, I thought for sure that was the end." Rowan pauses a moment. "But I wanted you there. I wanted you there with me, for better or worse." She loosens her arms from the hug, but keeps them around me. Her fingertips come to a rest at my neck. "I love you."

I don't have to think. "I love you, too."

She pulls me in, and I swear by the skies the magic inside my heart flares up to meet the magic in hers.

I kiss her hard, trying to put into one kiss a lifetime of loving her and being her friend, trying to put into one kiss how sorry I am that we got separated at all. How glad I am that she is alive, and here.

All at once, my mind clears completely. It's just me and Ro, Ro and me.

I wrap my arms around her waist and up her back, pressing her tightly against me. I can't get enough of her body against mine. I'd never felt it like this, pushing up against me with an energy that was equal parts surprise and disbelief, eagerness and inevitability. We part to catch our breath, but one look at the wild glint in Rowan's eyes draws me right back in. I throw myself into the longing, the ache of having loved her for so long.

And it's not just me. The longer I hold her, the more Rowan leans up to meet my lips, her hands running through my hair.

When she pulls back, she's breathing hard. "Wow."

"Wow," I echo. I put my forehead to hers. "Ro, what changed?"

She sighs. "I think . . . I think that I knew, but a part of me wasn't ready. And I only listened to that part." Rowan pulls back. "I have to apologize to Ox."

Oh. I swallow. "How you feel isn't really your fault."

"This was," she replies, pushing against me again. The sensation sends me reeling. "Will you still want me if they don't let me become a warrior?"

"Of course," I say. "No matter what happens, I want to be at your side. For as long as you'll have me."

"Okay," she says. I take her hand, and we walk back to the camp. Together.

39

SHIRENE

Sleep is a blessing.

With the other sentinels on watch tonight and the remaining warriors ready to defend against the next attack, I had been sent away for rest. I didn't fight it. I barely have the foresight to pull the pins from my hair before collapsing onto my bed.

I wake in fits and bursts, my heart racing as my mind tricks me into hearing sounds that aren't there. Each time, I lie there, totally still, waiting for the droning to return and the roars of our defenses to sound in response.

But the only sound that greets me is that of the ocean below us, growing louder with each hour as the prince's health slips away as quickly as a falling star. Last I saw the curly-haired boy, he was barely able to open his eyes, and coughing so much . . .

The memory erases any hopes of further sleep. When the bells toll, I count the hours—at least I got a full night's rest.

I bathe quickly and redress in a new set of robes. I keep my hair back the way Rowan likes to have hers: a tight braid tied off at my shoulders, though it doesn't have the same effect with my hair's shorter length.

I head outside to survey the city and check for fresh damage. The sun rises early and fast, reminding me of the season. Is it really still summer? It feels like months have passed in the span of days. The citizens should still be recounting their festival memories, not hiding in boarded-up homes and trying to keep themselves and their children calm. At this hour, the only sounds are those of the forges. I fly there, landing in the street adjacent to the city's most prominent weaponsmith.

I call out a greeting. The owner, a larger Leonodai with a grizzled beard and face smeared with sweat and soot, responds when he sees me. "Greetings, Sentinel."

"Good morning," I respond. "How goes the progress?"

"Good, my lady." He wipes his hands on a nearby rag that was already so dirt-covered, it may have made his hands worse. "The bearking's materials arrived by boat last night. The bearking's princess herself delivered them." He inclines to the far end of the forge, where a pair of figures in the moss-green colors of the bearkings are instructing two other smiths. "Two of their smiths came as well. Some of the work they insist on doing themselves, but it's no matter. The shields they are making are unmatched, my lady."

I try to hide my look of surprise. Freanna must have been swayed by her wiser kin. I send a silent thank-you to whoever of the bearkings got through her thick skull.

"Thank you for all your service," I say earnestly. "It will not be forgotten."

He bows his head. "Loyalty above all."

"Loyalty above all."

Heartened by the small piece of good news, I fly for the palace. I cross over the Heroes' Path, its walkway completely deserted. We've lost a total of nine children so far. If we survive the next days, I'll find a way to add their names to the Path. Each one of them deserves to be remembered for much longer than their own lifetimes.

I find the other sentinels in one of the antechambers of the royal family's quarters. A long wooden table stretches the length of the room. Pale light from the wall-to-wall windows eliminates the need for candles, even at this time of day. There had been talk of boarding up the windows, but the king said to save the resources for the people. He and the queen slept in the shelter of their own rooms, guarded throughout the night by both warriors and sentinels.

A small breakfast has been prepared for us, and I help myself to a plate. I take a seat by the window, the smell of the salt water below no longer something I have to really search for. We are sinking fast, a visceral reminder of how close we are to the end.

Still, the prince holds on, and so will I.

The king's doors open, and immediately, we rise, though the king waves off the formality as soon as it's done. I pick at my food as Hammond fills him in on the night's news.

"No attacks at all, Your Grace," says the Second Sentinel. "Our scouts reported activity near the humans' fortress at the Cliffs, but nothing moving our way."

"Welcome news," the king replies. "With what Sentinel Renna assured me last night about our defenses, it appears we are as ready as we can be. Thank you all for your tireless work."

"It's our honor," says Hammond.

The king turns to me. "Sentinel Shirene," he says. "Would you walk with me to the nursery? The queen requested to speak with you once you returned."

"Yes, of course," I reply with only a small jolt of panic. The king may forgo the rules as he wishes, but I had only been the King's Voice a matter of days. It still feels new to walk beside him, knowing I can speak my mind freely if I choose.

It is a short distance between the living areas, but I match the king's slower pace. His dark blue robes are a stark contrast to my own white attire—a king and a ghost.

Our steps echo as we walk past an enormous stained glass window depicting the creation of the Heliana. At the bottom, the first king and queen lift their hands, casting light skyward. Toward the middle is the island herself, lifted by the selfless sacrifice of the king's ancestors. At the center is a picture of the palace at its finest—a setting sun caught in the prisms of the Glass Tower, casting fiery beams of color into the sky.

King Kharo smiles when he sees me looking at the window. "It's one of my favorites," he says.

"Mine, too, Your Grace."

We come to a stop. Am I in some kind of trouble? It's a silly thought, but here I am—alone with the king. It has never happened before.

"Sentinel," he says, "I wanted to walk with you not only because the queen wanted to see you, but for another reason as well. Late last night, as I was briefed on the plans for the city's defenses, I was told of a missing warrior-elect."

"Oh," I reply. "Missing how?"

"Apparently, she has not been seen in days and has failed to report to her station. I'm told that members of her cohort have been questioned, but by all appearances, she's gone."

I frown, the king's words not hitting home—until they do. My jaw goes slack, and the king nods.

"I will assume you have not heard anything of your sister."

"No, Your Grace," I reply. "Skies. Gone? Has Storm's End been checked?"

The king inclines his head toward the queen's rooms, and we resume walking. His gaze goes to the ground. "Yes, and Matron Talla was just as shocked as you. I have not shared this knowledge with anyone else, but you understand how serious desertion is in an hour like this."

"I do," I reply instantly, because it's true. The last time I saw Ro, we fought. But that alone wouldn't make her leave. I can't think of anything that would. She's talked for years about being a warrior. She's endured the same training as I have, broken in body and mind only to be rebuilt a stronger fighter. A stronger person.

I realize suddenly that I have been quiet for too long. "Forgive me, Your Grace, but Rowan would never desert." As I say the words, they ring truer in my heart, like the high celebration bells.

"I don't mean to burden you further," the king says. "I ordered news of her absence to be kept as quiet as possible, so you shouldn't hear of it again. Still," he says. He stops, and when I look up, I realize we've made it all the way to the Queen's Tower. "I felt you would want to know. I apologize if I misjudged."

I shake my head as I gather my thoughts. "You didn't misjudge, Your Grace, but I don't believe I have misjudged my sister, either. Whenever she is found, I know she will have a reason for her absence."

At this, the king smiles. "You are very sure of her."

"I haven't always been," I reply honestly. "But her heart is true."

"I trust your judgment, Lady Shirene. You are my voice, after all."

He knocks twice on the door before entering. The prince's room has changed a little day by day. First, a bed was brought in for Prena, then another for the queen herself, who refused to be even a room's distance from the prince. Both are there when we enter.

"How is he?" the king asks, walking directly over to his son. When Prena hesitates to answer, I know it's not good. As the healer and king talk, the queen stands and comes over to me. Like the king, she is dressed in midnight blue: a color to catch the mood of our past days.

"Did you get a good night's rest, Sentinel?" she asks.

"I did, Your Grace," I reply. "Though I am sorry to have not been around when you asked for me."

"I am glad you got some sleep" is her reply. "Skies know we need it. Follow me, please."

The queen leads me back into her chambers and toward a large chest at her bedside. Reverently, she kneels and lifts the lid with a quiet determination. Inside, a lightly tarnished set of silver armor sits nestled on heavy blankets. The queen picks up the helm, its color distinctly different from the rest. Light reflects off the rainbow patina of the metal.

"This set was gifted to me when I became queen. Skies knows how old it is, but it fits better over a gown during military ceremonies. Just for show, of course, but this helm is my own from when I was a warrior," she says. "What is your custom piece?"

"My shield," I reply. "My father was a warrior, and that was the piece made for him as well."

Queen Laianna stands, still holding the helm firmly in her grasp. "I know I cannot," she says, voice trembling with a rage I know I can't fully understand. The rage of a mother's heart. "But if I could, I would fight."

My own heart clenches. "I know you would, Your Grace."

She straightens as she looks to the windows. "You remind me of myself," she says. "I was scared to accept the king's hand, but I accepted, anyway. I've seen you grow in these past days."

"Thank you, Your Grace," I say with a nod. "It is my duty. Loyalty above all."

"Above all," she echoes. "Sentinel, I would ask something of you."

"Anything, Your Grace."

"Will you stay with me?" Her warm brown eyes meet mine. "Skies keep me, but I know my son will not see another sunrise. I just know. It will help me to have another warrior here."

I glance at the nursery. "The teams may yet return."

"I know," she replies. "And I hope they do. But if they don't, warrior Shirene, will you stay?"

I look back at my queen and bow my head low. "Yes, Your Grace. I will stay with you until the end."

40

ROWAN

Sleep never used to come easily to me, but with Callen on watch and his hand resting idly on my side, I'm out the moment my eyes close. I stir when Callen gives watch to Jai, then drift back off.

My hunger wakes me. Sitting up, I count our numbers—Io is gone. She must be on watch somewhere out of sight. Since Callen's now holds the cure, I borrow Sethran's waterskin and take a hearty drink. At the horizon, the midnight blue mantle of night has turned the faintest bit lighter. It is probably two hours until dawn. The forest rustles with early signs of life as mist curls around the base of the trees.

I walk the circle around where we've sheltered and head back for the trees, stretching my legs. My stomach growls again, and I reach into my pocket for the last of my share of our scrounged meal from last night. Warriors are trained for hunger during the second year of training. Our instructors kept food back, giving us nothing but water while keeping drills the same. At the end of the day, we all got a half of a dry loaf of bread. As the trainers feasted on seasoned fish and all sorts of rich fare, we were given the choice to eat the whole thing, or save parts of it. It was a lesson in discipline, and the need to think ahead. Do you eat it immediately, not knowing when your next meal will be? Or do you save it for when you're at your wits' end?

I do as I did in my training, and eat. An aching belly is an aching belly, and the way I see it, strength found right away can carry you until you find more.

"Good morning, Warrior-Elect." Io nods as she comes up to me. She motions to Sethran's waterskin, and I hand it to her. After she takes a drink, she sighs and looks out on the land. "I respect that you told us the truth," she says. "You didn't have to do that."

I stiffen. "It would have come to light, anyway, ma'am."

"Still," Io replies. "I'm not surprised. If you're anything like your sister, I know your heart was in the right place."

"I'm not like Shirene. She wouldn't have left," I reply. Quickly, I count up the years that Shirene has been a warrior. "You were in the same cohort, weren't you?"

"We shared a room first year," she replies. "You are more like your sister than you think."

"How?"

"Because you're learning," she says calmly. "There are plenty of warriors—sentinels, too—who only obey, only follow. The Heliana needs those warriors, but it also needs the ones who doubt and ask questions. If you hadn't left, we would never have known how the humans learned our language. We wouldn't have found the cure. And that ass of a human wouldn't have a knife wound in his hand."

The last of her words gets me, and I stifle a laugh. Still, I feel every ounce of shame pressing down on me like I am twenty feet below the sea's surface.

"If obedience was the only thing that mattered, you might never become the best warrior. Not second best or anywhere near the top," Io says. "But what makes you a great warrior is knowing where to draw your lines and how you act on them." She puts her hand on my shoulder in respect. "When it comes time to defend your choice to the king, you can count on my help. And it's not just because you're Shirene's little sister."

"Thank you," I reply. "That means a lot to me."

She trudges back over to the others, rousing them with not-so-gentle shoves with her foot. She gives the order, and we move out.

❦

Every ridge we climb over seems higher. Every hillside steeper. The terrain goes from grassy to muddy to thick with trees. Overhead, an overcast sky makes it nearly impossible to judge the angle of the sun.

Up ahead, Io holds up her arm, and we come to a tense stop. Jai swears under his breath, and when I catch his eye, he shakes his head with a smile. *I'm tired,* he mouths to me, and I nod in agreement. But with Prince Tabrol's life in our hands, we have to push harder than we ever have before.

We are shadows against a bleak horizon, and we are running out of time.

We hear the first hoofbeats about an hour after sunrise. When we come to a moment's rest at the top of a large hill, Jai pulls his quiver forward, taking stock of the arrows he has left.

"Commander," he says, addressing Io. "Permission to stay behind."

Her large eyes take in his determined gaze and the bow in his hands. Without a word, we all understand what he's decided— he'll stay back and buy us valuable time.

Io gives him a firm nod. "Loyalty above all."

"Loyalty above all."

I don't know Jai well enough to give him more than a thank-you and a quick hug, but the other warriors share a longer goodbye. Rivers build canyons, and being of the same cohort is a bond that runs just as deep. If this were Vera or one of my friends, I'm not sure I'd ever be able to let go.

We press forward. Jai watches us go, surveying the nearby trees for a vantage point. My last look at the warrior is him scaling a pine that's thick with needles. Leaving yet another one of her own seems to light a fire in Io, and the sparks carry to the rest of us. Jai is willing to die for this cause—surely I can run a little longer.

Mist swirls between the hills and valleys. Clouds heavy with rain move in from the north. Io pauses to look at them, her breath labored.

"Just one day left," she says. "With that storm and no food."

My shoulders drop. We won't make it.

Droplets of rain pelt a collection of boulders nearby. The water rolls over us, making tiny sounds as it hits our armor. On any other day, I probably would have cried seeing and feeling the weather snuff out whatever hope we have left, but I'm empty and exhausted. We all are.

A sound cuts through the rain. A sound that, as of a few days ago, I know well.

"The train," Seth says. He jogs in the direction it's coming from. A minute later, he returns, waving his hand like, *Come on.* "There are tracks close by. There's an outpost a half-mile away. The train will stop as it passes."

Io shakes her head slowly, cursing under her breath. "Skies keep us. We take the damned train."

Our commanders go first, staying low as the forest starts to thin. Io gives a *hold* signal, and I crouch, the ferns brushing against my cheeks as the smell of mud and half-rotted plants meets my nose. Ox kneels down, too, close enough that I reach out and put a hand on his arm. He gives me a smile, but it doesn't reach his eyes. "I can't believe you kept that from me," he says quietly. "That you deserted."

"If I'd told you, then you'd be complicit in the secret," I whisper back.

"You told Callen."

"It just slipped out," I say. "I promise."

"We're moving." He puts some distance between us, and I don't try to close it.

Focus, I remind myself. There will be plenty of time to try to make it right with Ox later.

Up ahead, I see a straight line of earth that's been tilled and made into a road. Near it, a human settlement bustles with activity, illuminated by lanterns hanging on either side of the doors. Shadows move from inside, and when the door swings open, the sound of laughter carries from within.

I look out onto the plains. The inky black of the rails spills into the distance, cutting a straighter path than I remember seeing last time. This isn't the same train, but it is headed the right way. Next to the outpost is another building left open to the air. I breathe in deeply, and recognize the smell. Hay and dust. Another barn, but this one is massive. We must be on the edge of a farmer's property, one with animals to till the land.

The whistle of the approaching train sounds again, much louder this time. A group of humans exits the outpost and shouts at one another, rallying one another. A line of donkeys bray and protest as they're pulled from the shelter of the barn.

The train comes into view. Smoke screams out from the front as the machine resists breaking, squeaking and wheezing with effort. Finally, the machine stops, and the humans on board hop off, greeting the others. Unlike the first train, the metal of this one still shines. It's either new or at least better maintained than the other. One of the humans steps into the light, and I see the same silver sigil that General Marchess wore back in Ramsgate. It seems all the humans on this train are under his spell, or at least under his coin. This train is his, which tells me that wherever it's headed must be part of his strategy.

The train cars open, and the line of animals is moved forward.

"We move when the last of the animals is loaded on," Io says. "Stay low, and don't take any chances."

When the line of donkeys dwindles and fresh smoke starts billowing from the front of the train, Io signals us to move. I follow the others, and we run as quietly as we can down the rocky bluff, the sound of stones tumbling masked by the sound of the train whistle.

Sethran lifts Io onto a short platform jutting out on the car behind the one the donkeys were loaded into. The animals' smell permeates the air, earthy and thick. I start at the sound of Io jamming her sword hilt into the door of the car, the Leonodai metal scraping against the lock. After a couple of pushes comes a resounding clang of the lock breaking.

"Got it," she says. Sethran steps back and motions with his hand for us to get on.

Being back on the train is surreal. This car is filled to the brim with supplies—crates of grain, bolts of cloth, rope, and boxes upon boxes of metal nails line the walls. The five of us squeeze together. Seth closes the door behind us, pushing a crate up against the door to keep it from rattling open again.

Soldiers walk along the side of the train. Latches click shut. The whistle blows. From ahead of us, the donkeys shift and snort, unused to such cramped quarters.

Finally, the train lurches forward. I focus hard on the sound of it—*thud, thud, thud*. Like the ringing of bells, it gives me something to put my mind on that isn't the danger of us being back on this thing or that I need to apologize to Ox. Across the train car, Callen smiles meekly at me. Ignoring the quickness of my heart, I pull the cure to my chest and keep it there.

We gain speed quickly, the track below us clicking in a steadier rhythm than the older tracks did. My spirits lift. With this machine's faster pace, we could make it home before sundown.

Skies keep us. Everything was going to be all right.

The smell of smoke jolts me from a light sleep, sending my body into an automatic sense of alarm. Between the smoke is something else, too—gunpowder.

The train slows.

Io and I scramble up. She nudges the others with her foot. "Up. Now."

I take a step toward an opening in the train's side, where a knot of wood had long since fallen, leaving a hole. I lean close and am met with a blast of pine-scented air.

The unmistakable light of late afternoon catches on the trees as they disappear from my sight as quickly as they came. The sun is still to my left, but the angle is wrong. We're no longer traveling *due* west.

"The train turned," I say gravely. A moment later, I jump back, because not ten feet from my vantage point is a human watching the train arrive. "We're in the northwest, near the mountains."

Io crouches to the ground, face focused. "Everyone, pour out your waterskins," she says. "Rowan, give me yours."

Io undoes the cap of my waterskin, and my heart lurches at the sight of the precious panacea spilling onto the floor. A moment later, as she starts filling Sethran's waterskin with it, I understand. She's dividing the cure among all of us. "Only one of us has to make it to the prince. Whatever you have to do to escape, you do it," she says. When she's done, I take my share back and wrap the strap securely around my body. I think back to the maps I've seen of the humans' settlements.

"We're at the mines," I say. "We must be."

Io flinches. "The humans gave up the mines years ago. The bearkings say that happens sometimes, when the ground fails to give out any more of what they seek."

The train eases into a slower pace, and the shouts of humans rise around us. Sethran steps around me, moving me out of the way with a gentle touch of my shoulder. He looks out a moment, using his hand like a cup around the space, keeping it dark as he looks out.

The train comes to a complete stop. A tremendous *snap* and *clack* echo from the car in front of us. Hooves scuff against the splintering wooden planks, followed by brays of protest and strain. It's only a matter of moments before the humans come for the food and supplies in this car.

"My orders hold," Io says, straightening up. "Get to the prince. At any cost."

41

CALLEN

Sweat beads at my brow. At any moment, the humans will open the doors. The small fraction of seconds we'll have to escape undetected will come and go like the beat of a wing.

"How far from here to the Cliffs?" Rowan whispers.

"Minutes," Sethran replies. "Ten, maybe fifteen."

"Skies keep us," she says. We shouldn't have blindly trusted the train, but of course we're too late now—and it got us this close. To go west, we'll have to go directly over the mines, or through them.

I look out of the car again, carefully. The train has stopped in a U-shaped settlement teeming with workers, miners, and Marchess's soldiers. The miners carry themselves with a heavier stride, pickaxes in hand as they trudge toward the tunnels. The soldiers are more subdued, more confident.

"Why are they all here?" I whisper. Something must have drawn them in like ants to honey. I consider what Io said about the bearkings and say, "They must have found something else worth taking from the earth."

"What about those flying machines you mentioned?" says Ox, addressing Callen. "They'd need some kind of power, like the train burning fuel at the front. Maybe it's here."

A pair of voices cuts our wondering short. Ox, closest to the door, tenses up. Axe in hand, I step up behind him with a quick touch of respect on his shoulder. I know he won't forget Rowan quickly, but we are both warriors of the same cohort. We should have an effortlessly trusting relationship like Io and Sethran's.

There's the metal clunk of a latch coming undone, followed by the strain of the sliding wooden door opening.

Ox lunges out, his sword flashing. He cuts the first human across the chest. The second starts to shout, but a swing of my axe cuts him short. The two fall, their deaths swift. Ox ducks around the back of the car while the others climb out. To our right, more humans have come looking for the first two, and they start shouting when they see us.

"Go, go!" Io says. "Get to the Cliffs. Get to the prince!"

I break into a sprint. The human dies with surprise on his face without having put up a fight. Scanning for the black-clad uniforms of General Marchess's soldiers, I follow Io, who's taken the lead, as she dodges around the far side of the mines, retreating slightly back down in the direction of the train tracks. I follow up the side of a pile of broken rubble, my feet sliding on the loose stones.

Then, finding purchase, I leap up and onto the natural curve of the land above the mined area when the first bullet whizzes past my head. I duck, crouching before jumping up and diving behind a thicket. More shots ring out, but not just at me. Taking the chance, I lunge toward better cover behind a discarded pallet of crates.

The pop of the gunfire continues. Looking up and around the crates, my heart seizes as I catch a glimpse of Rowan and Ox, cornered between what looks like a common area for the workers and the entrance to the mines.

Snapping forward, I catch my breath and try to decide what to do next. Ahead of me, Io and Sethran are also biding their time, trying to judge their best move. *Just one of us needs to make it.* The thought comes to me unbidden, but it's true.

If I can cause enough of a distraction, it will buy everyone time.

Sweat trickles down my forehead as I turn and take in the crates I'm sheltering behind. The ground beneath me is still loose.

Without time to think of anything better, I shove the top crate with both hands. To my surprise, it still is full of something, because it's heavier than I expect, but it topples to the ground, sliding on the stones until it's in a free fall down to the opening of the mines below. I do the same for the other boxes, shouts of humans and the crashing cacophony of the splintering wood following behind it.

Then I run farther up to the top of the mines, away from Io and Sethran. Praying my armor is strong enough, I tuck onto my back as best I can and slide down the opposite side, leaving clouds of dust in my wake. When my momentum stops, I look up and behind me to see if any humans have followed.

Standing on shaky legs, I check my body. Blood trails down my upper arm and the side of my leg where the armor doesn't cover it, but otherwise, I'm all right.

Ahead of me lies nothing but open land. My spirit rises, only to be snapped back down as if shot with a human's bullet. Rowan.

She and Ox were out of the path of the falling crates—weren't they? They must have been. But even with the humans distracted, she and Ox wouldn't have had time to escape the way Io, Sethran, and I did. Trapped on three sides, only one would have remained open.

They went into the mines.

42

~

Rowan

The mines push inward and downward, and in the span of moments, I feel like I'm suffocating. With both arms out, my fingertips brush either side of the walls. Small lamps line the mineshaft, cutting my vision with bursts of light and harsh shadow. With every step, I think, *This is what it felt like at Garradin. They couldn't get out. They ran out of air. . . .*

Ox runs ahead of me. When the crates began to fall, they pulled earth with them, creating a rockslide. The humans were trapped and crushed under the weight of the dirt, and that's the moment Ox grabbed me and pulled me into the westernmost tunnel of the mines.

We can't be more than a few feet into the earth, but already, it feels like too much, like there's no air to breathe. I catch a glimpse of Ox's face in the lamplight. His eyes are wide, face flushed with sweat and fear. Nothing I'm thinking is unique to me.

"Ox," I say. "How are we going to get out?"

"There have to be air vents," he says. "Same way there are vents in the tunnels below the palace. The humans need to breathe, too. Come on."

I trust him, my own mind struggling to keep up with the twists of the tunnel. Ox is continually choosing left and avoiding the veins that go deeper into the ground. Shouts from behind us tell me we're so close to being caught. My heart thrums in my chest, my breath coming in weaker and weaker gasps. Suddenly, we round a corner and see light.

Not six feet off the ground is a vent—a small one, but one is all we need.

"Hurry," says Ox, and he ushers me forward. He kneels and lets me use his cupped hand as a step, then boosts me up. Rocks cut into my skin as I crawl through the square passageway, maybe a foot and a half thick. Ox shouts at me from behind, and before I can say anything back, he pushes me out and into the dirt. I fall hands first onto the outside of the mine and get up, reaching back for Ox.

He takes a short running start before making the jump, catching the edge of the air vent. Then, with a groan, he reaches up and clasps my forearm. I pull him through. Or at least, I try to.

"No," I whisper, trying in vain to pull him again. Ox must find footing in the wall because his weight lifts more easily, but it's not enough. The vent itself is too small. Ox adjusts, then discards his bow and tries again, but broad shouldered and nearly a head taller than I am, there's no way he's going to get through.

"Skies," I say. "Come. On."

Ox lets go of my hand, and for a moment, I think the humans have got him. Instead, he pushes his waterskin toward me. Pulling it forward, I throw it to the side, reaching for his hand again.

"Ox, you have to find another way out," I say. "Go. Please. Find another way out."

He has an expression on his face that's beyond description—fear and peace at once. "Rowan, you have to go."

"I won't leave you."

"You have to. Take the cure. Go to the city."

I don't move. I absolutely cannot, will not leave. I start digging at the sides of the vent, only succeeding in moving pebbles and dust. There is the sound of a sword unsheathing as Ox abandons his bow.

"I'll hold them off," he says. "Get going, Rowan An'Talla. You have a city to save."

Then he moves back into the darkness, and I know I will never see him again. I want to shriek into the tunnels and have the sound of my heartbreak echo around the mine—but to make a sound would give me away.

Grabbing both of our shares of the cure, I stand up on unsteady legs and half run, half stumble down the side of the mines. Collapsing against the trunk of a sturdy pine tree, I press the waterskins to my chest and scream silently, rocking myself back and forth.

"Just get to the city. Just get home," I tell to myself. Sunlight breaks through the trees, and I'm pulled toward it like the sun is pulled toward the horizon—steady and true. Something starts to awaken in my bones. Magic.

Warrior or not, I am Leonodai. And I'm going to save the city Ox loves.

Loved.

I wipe fresh tears with the back of my hand, my anger adding new weight to everything I am trying to process and understand.

I run, wild and untethered, toward the west.

43

SHIRENE

The bells sound—raucous and ready. Beside me, the queen jumps at the sound. She holds the prince close to her chest, rocking him back and forth. Prena, skies keep her, passed out from exhaustion not long ago. Her eyes flutter open.

"Aeroplanes?" she asks.

"No," I reply, counting the bells' tolls. "The humans have launched their ships." I get up, but remembering my promise from before, I give the queen a reassuring look. "I am not going far."

I run through the queen's rooms and out onto the adjacent balcony of the Queen's Tower. It faces south, but if I stand at the end, I can make out the wall of black masts of the ships leaving Balmora's coast. I envision them streaming out of the protected cove at the Cliffs. Their numbers seem only slightly greater than usual, and my hope rises. The underwater attacks from the sea-folk are bound to hold them.

From the northern side of the city, the first wave of our defense flies forward. Teams of four carry nets full of stones to drop on the unsuspecting ships. But the ships are approaching fast, skimming over the waves. Is this their latest strategy? Move quickly enough that we can't take them all out in time—

BOOM!

A tremendous explosion slams the ground from below. I thought I'd be ready for the impact. I am not.

The Heliana has fallen.

The city bobs like a toy boat on a rippling pond, lurching my body upward, only to suck it back down as I hold fast to the balcony's railing. Leaping up, I take my lioness form, beating my wings to stay steady in the air as crashes continue to sound from the city below. Buildings topple as if they are made of sand. Above me comes a horrible snap as gilded arches fragment like broken bones. A strange, shrill chiming saturates the air, and it takes me a fraction of a second to put it together—glass.

Adjusting my wings, I dive back into the palace as a million shards of glass rain down from the remains of the Glass Tower. I retake my human form, sprinting back the way I'd come. The palace has come to a rest at a slight angle, with toppled chairs and finery settling into bunches against the far wall as I burst back into the queen's room and the nursery. "Queen Laianna!"

The prince's bed moved with the impact, but it's not overturned. Prena kneels beside the queen, who is no longer rocking Prince Tabrol but shaking with her whole being as if her heart is being ripped from her chest.

She screams, and that's when I know. The crown prince, the lifeblood of the Heliana and the future of the Leonodai people, is dead.

Somehow, the queen finds the strength to lift her head. Her red eyes find mine. Not with kindness this time but with blazing pain and anger.

"Go fight," the queen says. "Take my armor. It'll fit you. Go fight for us, warrior Shirene."

44

CALLEN

I catch the sound of someone running in the forest behind me. Dogs bark in the distance, eager to hunt us down. I hesitate, torn between needing to hurry and hoping . . .

Relief sweeps over me as Rowan emerges from the brush. She sees me and lets out a small sob.

"Callen," she gasps. Not too far in the distance, the sound of humans shouting carries over the mine. She pushes me back, as if remembering something horrible.

"Rowan—"

"We have to go."

We run. My body protests every move, desperate for rest and food, but the sunlight filtering through the trees spurs me on, as does the blind determination in Rowan's eyes.

I don't have to ask her where Ox is. She has two bags of the panacea looped around her chest, and tears have cleaned her cheeks on an otherwise dirt-smeared face. Racing through the trees with a wounded body and grieving mind, she is just as much a warrior as everyone else who's taken the oath. I don't know how far we run, or for how long, but when I spare a look over my shoulder and see the first flash of a dog's teeth, I know we're nearly out of time.

"Rowan, the dogs!" I yell just as she yells, "Sethran!"

We burst from the trees. Skies alive, we've made it to the Cliffs—and we're not alone. Sethran and Io fight a few dozen feet from us, each with three humans lunging at them with swords. Two already lie dead on the ground, their skills no match for the pair of warriors.

I look past them to the sea. My limbs shudder with an unholy mix of the pure relief and the pure terror as the Golden City comes into view.

"No," I gasp.

The Heliana has fallen completely. She floats—an uneven island, but an island nonetheless. General Marchess's ships bear toward her. Smoke rises from some of them as Leonodai and sea-folk fight back.

Rowan lets out a war cry as she unsheathes her shortsword, and my attention is pulled back. The first human to spot us has some weight on me, but I am stronger and fueled by something beyond their reason. Rage. Anguish. With every swing of my axe, I can feel my limbs loosening, heart lifting, and lightness returning to me as I revel in the golden glow of the sun cresting over the trees.

Io and Sethran fight like one soul—Io charges, bashes an attacker with stone from the ground as Sethran follows right behind her, sword drawn, to catch the human as he scrambles to get up.

Then the dogs are on us.

Rowan's scream cuts the air. I whirl around, bringing my sword down against the flank of the animal that's sunk its teeth deep into her leg. The dog refuses to let up. Then, with a vicious yell, Rowan finds her shortsword that had fallen behind her and brings it down. Crouching beside her, I pry the animal's jaws from her calf. Blood pours hot and fast between my fingertips.

"Callen," she starts.

"You're gonna be fine," I say, putting pressure on the wound, "We have the cure—"

"Callen, stop." I look at her as her body trembles. The clash of swords quiets from behind us as Io lets out a victorious yell, but Rowan isn't looking at them. She is looking at the Heliana. "Do you feel it?"

"What?"

"Our magic."

I look to the west. I draw a breath, hoping to shift into my lion form, but I'm not close enough.

But she's right. Something is happening underneath my skin, like embers given fresh fuel. I set the cure on the ground, wiping my bloodied hands on my pant legs before pulling some out for Rowan, but she waves it off. "The kids are going to need it."

"And you won't be able to to give it to them without taking some." Forcing the bruised flower back into her hand, I keep my eyes on hers until she relents and puts a single petal in her mouth. I press more of it into her hand with a frown, but she stuffs it into one of the empty pockets of her throwing knives' sheath.

"I'll take more if I need more," she says stubbornly. "I promise."

Io's and Sethran's shadows meet us just as Io says, "You two all right?"

"One of the dogs got to Rowan," I reply.

"I'm fine," Rowan protests, but Io inclines her hand like, *Stay down*. "Our magic is coming back."

"We're close enough to the Heliana," Io says, nodding. "But not close enough to be able to fly."

"How long does it take?" Rowan asks, looking from the sea to Io and back.

"I don't know. We have been away for a while."

The unmistakable sound of horse hooves thunders behind us. The humans' reinforcements will be here in a matter of moments.

"Skies keep us." Io unclips the bag of the panacea from around her waist and makes a break toward a pair of boulders nearby. She kneels, pressing the waterskin into the shadows be-tween the stones. "All of you. Hide your share."

I do as I'm told. If we die, the humans might forget about the cure—but there are always Leonodai patrolling the coast. When they find what's left of us, they'll find the cure, too.

Sethran comes over and takes Rowan's share of the cure, tucking those two bags in another spot away from where Io and I put ours. Rowan gets to her feet, leaning all her weight on her good leg. Sethran and Io take up either side of us. It seems like a moment for goodbyes, but it doesn't take any words.

"We fight to the end," says Io.

I look at Rowan, hoping to kiss her one last time, but her gaze is on the west. Her new, short hair dances around her neck.

"Callen," she says. "Do you remember how when we were kids, we'd test our magic by jumping between the rooftops?"

I nod. "Yeah."

"What if it works the same here? What if our magic is asking us to trust it?"

It all clicks, what she's thinking. "Rowan, no. If you're wrong, you'll die."

She reaches around my neck and kisses my cheek. "And if I'm right, we live."

Before I recover from the kiss, she's off and running, limping on her bad leg. Sethran calls her name, but she doesn't turn.

"Come back!" he yells. "Rowan, stop!"

I send a prayer skyward as she leaps off the edge and into the open air.

45

Rowan

I regret it the moment I jump.

The empty air brings nothing but panic as I call on my magic time and time again as the sea rushes up, eager to be my last sight.

And then—I feel it.

The moment is like the mirrors in the Glass Tower, casting light and memories into a thousand images and feelings that flash in my mind faster than I am falling.

I see my whole life on the Heliana, from my mother leading classes to the last time I hugged my father when I was seven. I hear the music of the High Summer festival. I feel the pride and awe from the first time I saw Shirene in her sentinel robes.

Salty air whizzes by me, bringing more memories. Feeling exhausted in the early days of training. Vera and I staying up past curfew back when we shared a room in the Warriors' Hall, laughing and daydreaming. I see Ox in that first moment he asked me to dance, so sure of himself and confident in my answer before I knew it myself.

And Callen. I thought he was an anchor bringing me down, but just because he is steady doesn't make him deadweight. He stayed my friend after my father died and the other kids didn't know how to act around me. He encouraged my becoming a warrior, sparring with me before I was even old enough to formally train. He's seen me scream and lash out. He's seen me cry and be vulnerable. There isn't a single corner of my memories that Callen isn't in, and every one of them shines.

I've been unsure of myself for so long, but it's like Io said—I am learning. I am learning, and I am at peace with that. In this impossible prism of a moment, alone and plummeting toward death, I accept it.

The spark of magic in me explodes.

I let out a roar as I shift into my lioness form and swoop up, climbing higher and higher. My wings catch the air as they push me back up the way I'd come and beyond the cliff.

The humans scatter when they see me. Their fear permeates the air. My leg, still throbbing in pain, is manageable now that I don't have any weight on it. One of the humans fires at me, but it the bullet flies harmlessly through the long edge feathers of my wing. Diving, I sink my claws into the soldier Callen has been holding back. The human flies like a toy in the opposite direction, and I catch Callen's grin before he, too, steps back and over the edge of the Cliffs.

A heartbeat later, another roar joins mine. The humans stare in awe—but only for a moment. One of them takes aim at me and I duck, shifting back into my human form for a moment to make myself a smaller target. Immediately, I regain my lion form with a rush of life-giving magic. When I look back, the human is aiming at me again, hand on the trigger—

A flurry of arrows rains down from above. Looking skyward, I make out the shapes of a dozen or more Leonodai warriors, bearing down fast.

The skies have never given me a finer gift.

46

ROWAN

Pivoting, I beat my wings and swoop toward the trees, searching desperately for the bags containing the cure. I seize the leather strap of my bag in my jaws. Io dives into the underbrush beside me, and I toss her the second bag.

"I'll go to the Keep," Io says. "You fly for the Queen's Tower."

"Yes, Commander."

Arcing upward through the forest, I break out above the tree line, opening my wings as wide as they can go. Golden sun blesses the feathers, filling my blood with heat and hope. As I make a break across the water, I hear Callen following below me. Sethran follows, too, but he won the race on High Summer for a reason and is beside me in no time.

"Queen's Tower!" I roar. "Io went to the Keep."

Ahead of us, winged black machines swirl in uneven arcs around the city and over the open waters to protect the humans' ships below. Somehow that enrages me more. The skies are our haven, our home. I refuse to let them take that, too.

The Heliana grows larger and larger. Groups of warriors fly out from between the city's rooftops. Each team carries a net full broken rocks, the ropes grasped in their jaws as their wings strain with effort. A commander nearby roars orders overhead as we fly above the stone-carrying teams. They'll rain the stones down, I realize. Birds and Leonodai alike needed balance to fly. One stone could break the wing of a machine, or at least throw it off course.

My spirit soars. We've learned how to fight back and stay safe at the same time. Even with our city drifting in the water, our people haven't given up. I glance back at Callen, who, true to his word, is flying right at my side.

We will fight, I think. *We'll fight until the very end.*

———

Callen, Sethran, and I land on the warm white stone of the balcony of the Queen's Tower, treading carefully to avoid the fragments of broken glass. I take my human form, clutching the cure to my heart as sweat pours down my forehead and chest. Sethran breathes heavily beside me, the determination sharp in his eyes.

"Shirene!" he calls.

The Ninth Sentinel emerges from behind the curtain, her head low. At first, I don't recognize her—her armor is different. Leonodai-made, sure, but that wasn't what she used to fight in. Shirene's cheeks are flushed, tears streaming freely down her proud face.

"Seth," she says. "It's too late. The prince is dead."

"What? No," I gasp. *This can't be real.* "But we have it. We have the cure."

"It does not matter. He died minutes ago."

Minutes. Minutes too late, and how many did we lose? Jai. Exin. Ox.

And probably more names I don't know yet. No, not names. Beating wings, beating hearts. To have failed and lost them. It's too much.

I make a sound halfway between a scream and battle cry. "No. It can't be. Please. We came so far."

Sethran takes a step forward to comfort Shirene, then hesitates. Even now, he's better at remembering rank than I am. "Where are the other children?"

"Most of the sick are here in the palace, others are sheltering at home," she says. "We put our older and most vulnerable citizens in the Keep. The warriors-elect are standing guard, but it's only a matter of time until the king surrenders." Her eyes flicker to the sky as one of the flying machines falls in a wide arc, angry smoke billowing from its tail end as a flurry of gold wings and roars send it down. "It's over."

"No, it's not," I fire back. I can't keep it in. If what Shirene says is true, then nothing I worried about since leaving the Heliana matters. I want to fight, even to the death. "Seth is right. There are still children we can save. And those children *matter*. Listen to that!" I say, pointing angrily toward the city. "Our people are fighting. Our friends are fighting."

Shirene flinches. "Rowan, the heir is dead. You know as well as I that the Heliana relies on the prince's magic. And now there is none. There is no hope."

"Maybe not for the prince," I fire back. "But I felt my magic come back to me once we hit the Cliffs, even after the city was in the water. I refuse to give up. Not after everything we've lost."

Taking my share of the cure, I shove it into Sethran's chest. "Here," I say. "Take this to the other children. Or have someone else do it. I'm going to fight."

Before any of them can say anything different, I grab Callen's hand and pull him with me. He follows, and the two of us leap from the Queen's Tower in our human forms. For just a moment, we're falling. For just a moment, we grab onto each other, his lips meeting mine.

In the next, we've both taken our lion forms. Sweeping low along the rooftops, we fly toward the fight.

⁓

Screams and roars echo at us from all sides, peppered with the sound of gunfire as we land two streets back from the front lines. My blood pounds wildly in my veins.

Someone from his cohort must recognize Callen and calls out his name. He responds, following the voice into a building that is usually a school for dancers. We take our human forms as we duck inside. The wide wooden floor is littered with dust and blood, but in the midst of it is Callen's father.

General An'Kivva looks up when he sees his son, his mouth gaping for just a moment. A look of relief crosses over his face, before quickly returning to his usual, serious expression. The advisors at his side call his attention back, but the look is enough for Callen.

"They gave him a command," Callen says in disbelief. A small smile crosses his face.

"I bet everyone is being called on to help," I reply.

He nods. "I'll find out where he wants us."

Callen's just stepped away when out of nowhere, arms wrap around my shoulders. I push at my attacker instinctively, until I recognize the smell of the perfume on her skin. Vera always buys the expensive stuff.

"You!" she says. She releases me from her grasp, and I turn around, only to wrap her in a hug. "You are so stupid. How could you?"

"I know."

"What were you thinking?"

"I know," I say. "I couldn't tell you I was leaving. I wasn't going to make you lie to our superiors."

Her eyes well with uncharacteristic tears. "No, dummy. I meant cutting your hair like this. I barely recognized you."

I stifle a laugh, tears matching hers. "I'll check with you next time I decide to disobey the king and leave the Heliana. And give myself a haircut."

"Yes, please do." Vera leans in close. "Please tell me you found it and didn't leave me for no reason."

My heart thuds. "Yes."

Vera lights up, then comes crashing down. "But the city still—"

"Still fell, I know. We were too late. Don't tell a soul," I beg, inclining my head to the northwestern part of the city. "We have to fight. As if there is still hope."

Vera takes the news with a deep breath. "There is," she says. "You brought it. You came back."

I touch her right shoulder with my hand. "Why are you here at the front? Shirene said warriors-elect were guarding the citizens."

"We were. Just a while ago, sentinels came down and told everyone to fly for Vyrinterra." She pauses. "Now I know why. It was pure chaos, Ro. But at least people will be safe."

"Only if we can stop the humans here," I reply.

Callen comes back over. "Oh, skies," Vera says, and she gives him a hug, too. "Thank you for not letting her die out there."

"Never. Now c'mon." He hustles toward the door and inclines for us to follow. "The humans landed one of their ships near the Northern Gate. Their supplies are on it."

"So?"

"Guns run out of bullets," he says. "If we can dislodge the ship from the Heliana, they'll be trapped here."

I nod. "Let's go. V?"

She grins. "I'm with you two heroes."

I know she means it—heroes to the other children—but as we make a run for the Northern Gate, her words sting. We still didn't save the prince, but I'd rather die trying to stave off the humans' assault than give in to Marchess and his greed.

Callen takes his lion form, and Vera and I follow suit—just at the right moment. As we rush around a corner, a human in a black uniform charges from the other side. I tuck my back legs up, guarding the vulnerable part of my underbelly. As I arc upward, Vera lunges forward from behind me, her claws extended. We leave the human's strangled cry in our wake. Callen glides from rooftop to rooftop, keeping low as we get closer.

Carefully, I lower my wings and step around Callen for a better look. The ship comes into sight. The humans beached the craft just beside the Northern Gate. Holes in the underbelly tell me that the sea-folk tried to sink it but didn't make it in time.

"I'll distract the soldiers," Callen growls. "You two push the ship from the front left side. The way it's tilted, it should fall to the right more easily."

"Be careful," I say, batting my wing to his. "Keep your helm down." With the right angling, a Leonodai in lion form would be mostly protected by their breastplate and front-facing armor. Mostly. "Fly fast."

He nudges my forehead. "Always."

Tiles come loose from the rooftop as Callen leaps toward the ship. Shouts sound from below, but Callen's roar is quickly joined by another as a nearby warrior comes to his aid.

"Now!" Vera and I jump together, swooping low. The humans' gunfire peppers the air. Behind me, Vera lets out a low snarl, followed swiftly by "Armor! Skimmed armor, keep going!"

Jumping over the fallen stones of the Northern Gate, Vera and I reach the ship's hull. The craft reeks of metal and blood and human, and my stomach roils. But my mind clears as Vera catches my look. We'll ram it.

I fold my wings back and down. We move as one, backing up to ram our armored shoulders against the wood. The ship groans as our combined weight slams into it, but after the third try, I check the evidence in the dirt on the ground—we've barely moved it an inch.

"Up," I tell Vera. "Let's push it from the deck."

Taking to the sky, we start to dive wordlessly when a third shadow crosses overhead. I look up as a resounding roar rips through the air.

The Ninth Sentinel has joined the fight.

"On three!" Shirene yells. Vera and I obey her command. Summer wind whips by me as all three of us fold back our wings and dive, free falling, toward the railing on the edge of the ship. The impact sends me spinning up and off to the side as my ribs rattle in my chest. The frigid plunge of ocean water follows right after.

Instinctively, I flare my wings in the water, pushing against the pressure without much success. My claws scrape idly against nothing as I swing myself upright. Taking my human form, I kick toward the surface when from the corner of my eye comes a flash of vibrant white and pale blue.

I break the surface for a gasp of air, then look into the water again.

One of the sea-folk watches me. Human from the waist up with a long fish's tail the color of moonlight, she wears armor on her wrists and chest—Leonodai-made, but marked with a different crest. Her large eyes drink me in, and the placid expression on my face jogs my memory. *The ambassador for the Sea Queen.*

She rushes toward me, closing the space between us with a flick of her tail. Icy hands clamp down around my wrist as she drags me down.

Skies. She's going to drown me.

Kicking, I try to pull my arm back, but it's like fighting a winter storm, her grip is so tight. She pulls me sideways, and my lungs begin to squeeze when she suddenly surges upward, letting go as she tosses me to the surface. A rounding boom explodes from behind me as the humans' ship crashes down off the Heliana. The ground gave way, just like it did back on Balmora. The ambassador pulled me away from it just in time.

I turn, trying to find her shape in the water as I tread above it. I give her a nod, hoping she sees it. The Heliana's shadow passes over me, and I nearly forget to swim. The ship didn't just dislodge. It *fell*.

I don't know how. Skies alive, I don't know how it's possible. The city is rising.

47

CALLEN

I extract my sword from the human's side and kick him down. Blood drips from my blade, and my chest heaves. The ground below my feet pushes against me, and it doesn't take long for me to realize we're climbing in altitude.

A *boom* sounds from behind me, and a rain of seawater follows after. The frigid droplets send shivers across my skin as I search for Rowan among the Leonodai flying skyward after ramming the boat. Shirene ducks and dives with an agility to rival falling stars, roaring orders to a team of warriors who've just crested the buildings beyond. Like the ones we saw when approaching the city, the teams carry nets laden with stones from the riverbeds. My gaze follows as the team swings outward, dodging the lingering gunfire and letting the heavy rocks fall. The stones crash onto a building that usually houses a lively sweets shop, collapsing the roof. Screams from the human soldiers sound from the rubble. We can repair later. We can rebuild.

Right now, we are still in the fight.

I finally spot Rowan soaring skyward, her wings flinging seawater with every beat. She flies over to me, shifting into her human form as she lands.

"The Heliana is rising," she gasps. "Look."

"I know," I reply. "But the prince is dead."

"Exactly. I don't understand." The sounds of battle carry from the street beyond. "But we can figure that out later."

She runs toward the fight, and I follow right on her heels.

Blood pulses in my veins in time with my footsteps as we meet a trio of humans brandishing swords. None of them have guns. They were so confident in their weapons that they failed to bring enough supplies for this attack. They are down to iron and bronze, same as we are.

Ro and I fight together, our limbs falling into the dance of warfare in a way they never did in sparring. Rowan ducks low and lashes out with her blade, causing the human she's engaged with to jump back in defense—straight into my own sword. She pivots, leaping with her right leg while she stabs backward with her sword, meeting an oncoming human's shoulder blade.

A call comes from above us as two arrows fall in quick succession. The soldier falls dead. Rowan wheels around, looking for more enemies. Her bad leg trembles, but her grip on her sword never falters. The moment of relief stretches, and stretches again like a welcome horizon.

Roars carry in the air—they are not cries of pain or war but of victory. It's only after I catch my breath that I dare to hope.

We've won. Blinking sweat from my eyes, I squint into the sun to see who aided us, but Rowan recognizes him first.

"Ox!" she screams, sheathing her sword as she runs for him. The two embrace, but for once, my heart doesn't sing in jealousy. "How did you escape?" she asks.

His hair and skin are smeared with soot and dirt. "Oh, you know, I talked my way out of it. They were quite reasonable."

"Ox."

"Fine, fine," he says, relenting. "The first ones to find me were unarmed. I fought them off best I could, then snuffed out the lights and waited. When it was quiet enough, I dug my way out of the vent." Ox looks around the remains of the battle. "Skies, we did it."

Rowan makes a sound like, *Oh,* and I leave her to break the news about Tabrol. Summer wind wraps my bones in a familiar grace as I jog over to the remains of the Northern Gate and look over the edge. The teal of the sea winks back, not far below us, but still below.

Rowan, Ox, and Vera come join me. "The scholars have always said that the city would fall if the royal line fails," Rowan says. "But it has failed, and we're still here."

"The king still lives. That was enough for all the years without an heir," I say, but I'm trying to make sense of it all, too. That's what we've always been taught, what we've always believed.

It's as if all goes quiet except for one simple truth: the scholars were wrong.

Rowan looks to the palace. "Do you think it was another lie?"

"That's too big of a thing to lie about," Ox says.

I put my hand on Rowan's shoulder. "Maybe they were just . . . wrong."

"Let's find the others," she says.

We follow the sounds of roars and conversation to an open plaza on the edge of the market district, not far from Storm's End. I catch Rowan looking in the direction of the school, her body visibly relaxing at the lack of smoke plumes from that direction.

The bells sound. Rowan and I are both greeted by name. Vera hugs Rowan from behind, her tears creating river patterns down her cheeks as they wash away the splattered blood.

Sentinel Renna emerges from the crowd of fighters and gives a respectful touch on my shoulder. Even her renowned scowl breaks as she smiles at me. "Good to see you, warrior Callen. Did all your team return?"

Exin. His memory is distant, yet bright as a new burn. I shake my head, and Renna bows hers. "Skies keep them, and us."

The bells continue calling throughout the air, only to be interrupted by a series of cheers as Shirene, resplendent in her new armor, appears in her lioness form on an adjacent rooftop. A voice calls her name so earnestly and desperately that it can only belong to Sethran. The cheers get louder as she dives in her lion form and then retakes her human one only to run straight into his arms.

Rowan calls out to her sister.

Shirene glances up, stepping back from Seth to look at us.

And that's when a bullet pierces her armor, ripping directly through her chest.

48

ROWAN

"No!" I shriek, my hand whipping back to grab at my last knife. The warriors around me scatter as I scan every doorframe, every window. *No. No. No.*

Another gunshot sounds, and I duck instinctively. A shadow slumps from behind the door in the clothing shop past where Sethran is now crouched, screaming and holding my sister. I sprint toward it, the joyous call of the bells clashing with the horror of his sobs. I hear the word *healer*, and several Leonodai take to the skies at once. Others go for the rest of the street, checking for other human stragglers.

Callen is right behind me as I get to the doorframe. Dark blood seeps out from below it. The realization dawns on me, and when I push the door open, the human soldier's body falls with the thud. His head is totally gone, replaced by gray spatters and blood.

The sight makes my stomach turn, but I can't help but stare at the vile, vile sight. Callen grips my shoulders.

"He took his own life," he mutters, but I barely register his words. A mad hope seizes me, and I dash back outside. Two healers land beside Sethran, taking their human forms instantly. Their hands go to their supplies—salves and rolls of white bandages. Seth sobs as he holds Shirene close. Trembling. Whispering.

I dive beside them, desperately shoving my way between the two healers. "Move!"

I plunge my hand into my knives' sheath, where I put the rest of the cure Callen had tried to give me. Seth understands what

I'm doing and gently opens Shirene's mouth while screaming for water.

"Please," I beg. "Please work."

We press the cure between my sister's lips as someone hands me a waterskin. We try to get Shirene to drink. We try. I touch my fingers to my sister's neck and feel her pulse beat once, twice . . .

But there is so much blood, and it doesn't stop. The red stains my filthy warrior-elect uniform and Shirene's beautiful sentinel attire. Her eyes flicker for just a moment, her gaze landing on Seth before her head falls heavy in his hands.

All around us, the bells sing, triumphant.

EPILOGUE

ROWAN

I have been in what remains of the Glass Tower many times now, but never with the entire city's eyes on me.

For the first time in our history, warriors-elect are to be sworn in on a day that isn't during High Summer. Then again, the city has already seen its fair share of firsts in the past six weeks. The first funeral for a golden prince, then one for a sentinel. The first time a warrior-elect—me—stood in front of Vyrinterra's ambassadors and sentinels to challenge the decisions they'd made. The first time a deserter had been formally invited back home to speak their piece, in hopes of creating a lasting change.

The proof is all around us. The Heliana floats above the sea once more, despite what the scholars always taught us. Even after the devastation of Tabrol's death and the battle that followed, the Leonodai people stand as one. The city has come together in so many ways that at times I feel like we are stronger than ever before. The Heliana's people hold her magic, not just the royal line. The scholars can do with that what they wish.

Today, the Tower is packed, with many citizens lining the back walls, where stands have been erected to fit in as much of the public as possible. Late summer air carries from one window to the next, the first hints of the changing season. The area to the right of the king, the reserved place for warriors, is just as crowded. I find Ox's face in the crowd, and he smiles that roguish smile of his. Names of friends are called, and I cheer them with everything I have. Vera, then Bel. So many of them survived

the Fall of the Heliana, as the city is beginning to know it. We
have lived to see her in the skies once more.

The king calls my name, and I step forward.

My feet are bare as a sign of humility. My hair, which Vera
insisted on doing for me, is full of her expensive oils and glossier
than it ever has been. With the sentinels' permission, I bear a
white ribbon on my upper arm, in memory of my sister.

My past and present are with me. Before me, my future.

I kneel before the king. He seems to have aged far beyond the
time since that fateful day. The proud, noble gaze I've always
imagined myself seeing when I took the oath has been replaced
with a disquieting pain. I know that pain. It binds us together,
the way only grief could.

"Rowan An'Talla," the king says once more. "Do you swear,
from this day forth, to serve the Golden City, the Citadel of the
West, the Heliana, and all of her people?"

"I do swear," I answer.

"Do you swear to put loyalty above all, to answer the bells
whether they call at first light or the last?"

"I do swear."

The king accepts a new warrior's uniform from Sentinel Renna.
The latter meets my eyes, her gaze going to the ribbon on my
arm. As the King's Voice, Shirene would have been the one to
hand me my robes. I accept the uniform, keeping my eyes low as
they well up with tears.

"Rise, warrior," says the king.

And I rise.

Ox and I skip the celebrations. We're at our usual place on the
rooftop, no longer lying together but content in each other's com-
pany. Ox had smuggled up a small picnic of celebratory treats,
which we munch on idly. My appreciation for food has doubled
since our return. Below us, the Hall is lit from Underbelly to

ceiling with congratulatory calls. The city beyond us, though still under repair, is lit with lanterns and the smaller celebrations between family members.

It's strange to look down at my own body and see cobalt blue. The fabric of the robes is finer than my old one and ten times as soft. The king's pardon is no small gift, and I carry it in my mind always.

As I have for many nights now, I look to the east.

"You know where Callen is," says Ox. "Why not just go?"

"I'm not going to test the king's mercy twice," I retort. "Callen wouldn't have known the ceremony was changed to today."

Ox pours another half glass of wine and hands it to me. "Nothing's going to stop him from flying straight back once he hears. This is your moment, warrior Rowan."

"Thank you, Ox," I reply, holding his gaze. "For everything."

In the days after we returned to the Heliana, finding time to make things right with Ox had been a challenge. I could barely stand to leave Storm's End, and when I found the strength, I had to be there for my mother. It was not enough for the sentinels to sing Shirene's praises to the citizens once everyone was safely returned to their homes. It wasn't even enough for the king to send us a signed letter. My mother threw it in her desk drawer without even opening it.

When Ox and I finally found a moment to meet, he was way ahead of me. "I already know, Rowan. And it's okay."

"I'm sorry," I told him. "I know it sounds like a lie, but I didn't know how he felt, or how I felt, until High Summer. Everything that happened with us was real. It's just this other feeling was real, too."

He'd pulled me in for a hug and kissed the top of my head gruffly. "If he hurts you, you know who to call to help set his stuff on fire."

"Ox."

"Okay, fine. We'll throw it in a river."

Callen had already been gone for a week at that point. As our city grappled with the loss of the prince, the destruction of so many buildings, and the recovery of the sick children, Noam was busy advocating for the Leonodai to make a show of peace.

Shortly after our return, Noam's mountain village had been peacefully taken over by another of the human kingdoms. Turns out that General Marchess wasn't just at war with us, but with other humans as well. Noam's new rulers had swept in to Marchess's land through the mountains, claiming victory after victory. The threat of General Marchess wasn't gone, but at least we had help keeping it at bay.

At the same time, the sentinels held public meetings where the citizens could come and listen to Noam and ask questions of the once-deserter. Callen went to every one. I went with him, but preferred to cling to the seats in the back.

"I've consulted the leaders of the village," Noam had told the crowd. "And they want to strengthen our bonds of peace. I've asked the king to send warriors back with me. Citizens, too, if they are willing. There is much that Leonodai can learn from humans, and vice versa."

When the call for volunteers was sent out, Sethran unexpectedly answered. Callen did, too.

"Are you sure?" I asked when he told me. We were in the grotto, faces flushed from kisses that never felt like enough to make up for lost time. It was strange to be crossing the line of friendship like this, and a part of me was still hesitant. But Callen was a light in my grief, and I held fast to it.

He nodded, fingers stroking the bare skin at my shoulder. "General Marchess said his people were hungry. That's why they had tried for peace before and why he went mad trying to capture Vyrinterra."

"We offered them trade," I countered. "If they wanted food, they could have had it."

"But after years of us denying it to them, it's hard to discount their anger." He sighed. "If there was any truth to what he said, then I want to know it for myself. Maybe we can learn the land better and start to heal it. But if you don't want me to go, I'll stay."

I did want him to stay. Everything was still so overwhelming—my own grief, my mother's. The city's. But if he wanted to go, I respected that. He could stay close to Seth, and his volunteering would look great in the eyes of the sentinels.

"Go," I had told him. "I'll miss you. But you should go."

Back in the present, Ox escorts me back to Storm's End, taking the long way over the still-broken Northern Gate and down through the outskirts of the city. In the water, I spot the flick of watchful sea-folk's fins. Even though the Heliana has regained her place above the sea, she sits much lower than before.

I can only imagine how baffled the scholars must be to not come up with answers. But in my opinion, it is high time we start seeing things as they are and not as we always believed they were.

With a quick hug goodbye, Ox takes off for the Warriors' Hall. I peek into my mother's room to check on her. She's already asleep though it isn't past tenth bell. I know it was a lot for her to come to the ceremony today.

Closing the door quietly behind me, I tiptoe to her office. The murmur of chirping birds outside is the only sound as I light some candles to illuminate the dark. Sitting down at her desk, I run my hand across the steady, familiar surface. I don't remember the last time I was in this room alone. I must have been Isla's age.

Isla. I think of her more often than I admit out loud. One day, if the peace Noam seeks and Callen is helping build becomes real, I'll go back for her. It isn't right that she is living without knowing her full self. Part of me expects the girl to show up on the Cliffs at any moment, having made the trip herself. I would gladly teach her to fly.

Curiosity bests me, and I open the drawers to look for the king's letter. I find it, but before I open it, another folded parchment catches my eye, as does the sight of my name written on it. I unfold the letter, looking first at who sent it. My heart jumps.

There is no stopping the tears as I read Callen's words, scrawled writing and all. His words burn into my mind as I ask myself the question of *What if . . . ?* What if he'd died out there. What if he'd left me only this, his words, his heart, in a plain parchment without so much as a seal. What if he'd gone to the Endless Skies before I could know for sure.

The sound of the birds cuts off, replaced by a rush of golden wings.

Standing, I walk as fast as I dare to the balcony. With a trembling hand, I open the doors. The smell of smoke and pine trees clings to Callen's clothes, and he must not be eating well because he'd lost some of his bulk. His gentle eyes, humbled by the time and distance, find mine. "Hi, R—"

I throw my arms around him, stifling whatever his next words will be. One of his hands wraps around my waist while the other cradles the back of my head.

"I came as fast as I could," he says. "The messenger was there when I returned from helping build up a dam. The moment she said the ceremony had happened, I started flying." His arms slacken. "Skies, I must smell terrible."

"I'll get over it," I say, and he leans in to meet my kiss.

This, I realize. This was missing. Not only Callen himself but a feeling of peace. Callen brings a lifetime of shared memories with him. Shirene is gone, and we've lost so many friends. But this? This I refuse to lose.

I deserve to wear my warrior blues after everything I've been through. I am still my own person, still Rowan An'Talla, still my father's daughter. But Callen is like a sunrise—his light makes every part of my life warmer, brighter. Better.

"Stay here tonight," I say.

His breath catches. "Already bolder than usual, warrior."

"Skies. You know what I mean."

He laughs. "I do, and I'll stay."

The study door opens, and I jump, heat rising to my cheeks as my mother enters. She looks from Callen to me, then gives us a knowing smile.

"Welcome home," she says.

And we are home—the both of us.

ACKNOWLEDGMENTS

The Endless Skies first came to me in a dream: the image of a winged lion in a secluded grotto, a lion that dream-me knew to be a prince. Though the plot changed ten times over, the messages of loyalty and love never wavered. This is my oldest story, and my most dear. To hold this book in my hands as an actual, finished creation is a feeling beyond words. And I definitely did not get here alone.

A huge debt of gratitude to Diana Gill, who saw everything this story could be and who gave me time to perfect it. To my kick-ass editor Rachel Bass, who is as much of a fan of this adventure as I am: thank you for the wise (and often hilarious) notes, and for keeping me sane as we revised during a global crisis. To everyone at Tor Teen who made this book a reality: Anneliese Merz, Laura Etzkorn, Saraciea Fennell, Andrew King, Heather Saunders, Kristin Temple, and every one of the book-making champions I have yet to know by name. You are my heroes.

A standing ovation to cover artist Larry Rostant, cover designer Lesley Worrell, model Carrie Kseniia, and make-up artist Rebecca Clare for bringing my girl Rowan to life. You created the exact kind of cover that I have dreamed of having since I was a kid. It's perfect, and I am so grateful.

None of this would be possible without my agent-extraordinaire, Elana Roth Parker, who puts up with my panicked, late-night emails and never complains. Thank you for taking a chance on me, all those emails ago. Much love to #TeamElana, who have rooted for me from the start. Cheers to us and our matching team mugs! A special shout-out to Lily Meade, who made me so many gorgeous promo graphics; and to Anna Bright, for being the tulle-skirt-wearing book cheerleader that everyone deserves.

Thank you to the many friends who I have been lucky to make over the course of this book's journey, including Grace Li, Rachel Griffin, Kristin Dwyer, Adrienne Young, and every wonderful person who I am accidentally forgetting. Thank you to the inaugural cohort of Writing with the Soul. I am so humbled by your talent and perseverance.

To all who blurbed this book, though I won't know who you are until after I send in these acknowledgments: thank you for your time, support, and immeasurable kindness. I promise to pay it forward wherever I can.

Huge thanks to all the readers, bloggers, booksellers, librarians, and educators who fell in love with this book and shared it with friends. I get to have my dream job because of you—and I'm so grateful.

Endless love to Joss Diaz and Kalyn Josephson, my virtual writing date buddies, who endured a draft of this that included the sentence "the warm was warm" and somehow still want to hang out with me. I'll see you on Sunday . . . but give me two minutes to make my coffee.

I could never forget the 5quad: thank you for being the kind of friends who not only send me encouraging IG messages and are flexible around my deadlines, but who also sit me down to have a lengthy talk on happiness and career when I really need one. I love and appreciate all of you so much.

Thank you always to my family, whose support for my books gives my heart purpose. To my mama, who never sent me home with anything less than five frozen meals so I'd have more time to write. To my dad, whose excitement over each and every publishing milestone makes them all the more meaningful. To my sister, for reading a very ugly version of this and giving me line edits when I didn't ask for (but very much needed) them.

Special shout-out to the Moos, who are never more than a text and a virtual cheers away; and to Richard, for always asking me how writing is going and being genuinely interested to hear the answer.

Finally, to Gaston, who not only deserves the dedication, but also a space here. I legitimately don't know how we did puppyhood, pandemic, and book deadlines all in the same few months, but we did. You are the reason I didn't give up on myself. I love you. You are everything.

ABOUT THE AUTHOR

SHANNON PRICE believes in good bread, good wine, and good books. She lives in California, where she dreams of one day living in a house by the sea.

spricewrites.com
Twitter: @spricewrites
Instagram: spricewrites